CHAOS LUCK WRATH

Alliances are broken and hearts stolen.

BROKEN ALLIANCES SERIES
BOOK 4

SADIE WINCHESTER

For all the good girls. Don't ask twice.

OFFICIAL PLAYLIST

A Grave Mistake - Ice Nine Kills

Adrenaline - Zero 9:36

Adrenalize - In This Moment

Black Hole - We Came As Romans, Caleb Shomo

Cold Blooded - Of Virtue

Come Undone - Bad Omens

Death Wish - Royale Lynn, Danny Worsnop

Fight Fire With Gasoline - Self Deception

Hallelujah - No Resolve

Hell And Back - Self Deception

Here's My Heart - SayWeCanFly

In The End Mellen Gi Remix - Tommee Profitt, Fleurie, Mellen Gi

It's Got My Name On It - Tommee Profitt, Sarah Reeves

Limits - Bad Omens

Qwerty - Mushroomhead

RATATATA - BABYMETAL, Electric Callboy

Scarlet - In This Moment

Thank You For Hating Me - Citizen Soldier
There's Fear In Letting Go - I Prevail
Throne - Bring Me The Horizon
Without You - My Darkest Days
Watch Me Burn - Michele Morrone
Wrong Side of Heaven (Acoustic) - Five Finger Death
Punch

The official playlist can be found on Spotify.

(Tap "Search" in the Spotify app, tap the camera icon, scan and go!)

What a wild ride this has been! I kicked off the Broken Alliances series with my debut novel (Stay In Your Layne) and never expected it to evolve into a four-book series. Becoming an author has been such an incredible experience that has forged amazing friendships with readers and authors alike.

To everyone who has stuck with me throughout this series, thank you so much. It means the world to me that not only have people read Layne's story, but have continued to follow it throughout four books. For something that had been just a silly little story in my brain to turn into something others can enjoy, that truly amazes me.

It is never too late to shoot for the stars and I hope that you all follow your own dreams regardless of what anyone tells you.

Much love (and smut),
Sadie

Your mental health matters.

Please visit SadieWinchester.com or email SadieWinchesterAuthor@gmail.com with any questions regarding content/trigger warnings.

CHAOS LUCK WRATH

cha·os /ˈkāˌäs/

noun, see also: Joey De Luca

1 complete disorder and confusion.

2 the inherent unpredictability in the behavior of a complex natural system (such as the atmosphere, boiling water, or the *beating heart*)

luck /lək/

noun, see also: Layne O'Reilly

1 success or failure apparently brought by chance rather than through one's own actions.

2 the events or circumstances that operate for or against an individual

wrath /ˈrath/

noun, see also: Gage De Luca

1 strong vengeful anger or indignation

2 retributory punishment for an offense or a crime : divine chastisement

Chapter One

THE AFTERMATH

Continued from Incoming Layne Shift

A hand waved in front of her face. "Miss?" The man dressed in a cheap gray suit stood in front of her. The emptiness of her emerald eyes stared ahead, not seeing the man or the hospital waiting room they were both in.

Layne sat there in her soiled wedding dress; sections of her hair had come loose from their previously pristine position in her bun, and Joey's blood stained everything, including what was left of her heart.

Chaos

This was what her life consisted of; it was how he entered her life.

Luck

Both good and bad followed her everywhere; it was how he managed to save her from herself.

Wrath

Equally, her affliction and what she planned to inflict on the world; it was what put him where he was now.

Gage returned with a bottle of water in one hand and a cup of coffee in the other. Seeing the middle-aged man in front of Layne, he immediately rushed over, setting both beverages down on the table next to the set of seats where Layne was. "Hey, hey, hey! What the fuck are you doing, man?"

The man frowned as he looked up at Gage. "Detective Adams. I need to ask Ms...." He checked a notepad in his hand. "Ms. O'Reilly, a few questions about what happened in front of St. Mary's today."

Before Gage could tell him to get lost, Layne said her first semi-coherent words since leaving the church steps, "De Luca." The tone of her voice was cold, flat, and empty, much like the rest of her felt.

"What?" The detective looked over at her, being caught off-guard by her sudden decision to speak up.

"My name. It's Layne...De Luca." Her eyes finally moved slowly through the sludge of emotions they were drowning in to settle on the man looking for answers on the day's catastrophe.

The man cleared his throat. "Oh, um, yeah, so, I'm really sorry, but it's standard protocol that we get statements from witnesses as soon as possible while everything is still fresh. The remaining witnesses have been less than cooperative. I was hoping you could provide some clarity."

Layne's voice continued to remain soft and monotone, "I didn't see anything." She had seen everything, and she continued to see it on replay inside her mind. A fresh set of tears welled up in her eyes as she squeezed them shut, expelling them onto her cheeks.

The detective frowned again. "I'm sure there must have been something that stood out—"

That's when Gage interfered, placing a hand on the detective's shoulder with a solid grip. "Now isn't a good time. She said she didn't see anything." He knew that was bullshit, they all had seen it.

He took a few steps away from Layne, guiding the detective with an arm around his shoulders as he lowered his voice. Several moments later, Detective Adams handed over a business card to Gage and went on his way. The card was immediately dropped into the trash.

Gage came back, picking up both beverages and sitting down next to Layne. "Baby, you should at least drink something. It's been hours."

When she said nothing, he leaned over to whisper in her ear, "I told you to do something; is this how you show me you're listening?" It was his last-ditch effort to get any level of reaction from her. It failed. He frowned, lowering his forehead to her shoulder while his lips kissed her arm lightly.

With her eyes still shut, flashbacks of the day were on a continuous loop in her head. The love and the pain. He told her it was okay, and yet nothing was. The second a sob started to crawl from her chest into her throat, she opened her eyes, shook her head, and stood.

Choking down the sob, she looked at Gage. "I wanted a lot of things from him, but I never wanted him to sacrifice himself for me. I'd rather give myself to all the monsters lurking under my bed at night than to have him do what he did." Truth be told, those monsters were already poisoning her thoughts and beckoning her to surrender herself to the darkness calling to her soul. Without Joey, the fire within her was slowly being snuffed out.

Looking around at the piss-poor attempt of the hospital to look warm and welcoming, all she could see was despair and pity. "I can't be here." She wasn't sure where she could go to find her escape, but sitting for hours inside this waiting room wasn't it.

Gage's hand reached out and wrapped around her wrist. "Layne..." He wasn't sure what he could say to her to make this better because he was feeling just as lost inside.

Before she could pry his grasp off of her, a doctor approached. It was a woman in her late fifties wearing dark blue scrubs that gave a boxy appearance to her body. "Mrs. De Luca?" She looked at Layne with eyes full of empathy, likely mastered from countless depressing conversations with families of patients.

Layne looked up at the doctor who was now standing in front of her. This was it. This was the moment she didn't want to be present for. She had played it out in her mind a thousand times over in the past hour alone. She could hear the words over and over that, yet again, someone was sorry for her loss. He was dead and gone with no chance of ever coming back to her. She would be told that the doctors did all they could, and it still wasn't fucking good enough.

"I'm Dr. Monroe; I am the surgeon who worked on your husband." She pulled a tablet from under her arm.

Hearing someone refer to Joey as her husband made Layne's heartache burn even deeper. Gage's arm was suddenly wrapped around her shoulders, holding her firmly as they both braced for impact.

The doctor tapped on the screen several times as she drew in a deep breath to share the news. "He is currently in our Intensive Care Unit. I was able to extract the bullet from his chest and repair the tissue." She continued to go into the finer details of what had been done during the surgery, using her tablet as a reference point, but Layne was still stuck on her first sentence.

"He's in the ICU?" She stared at Dr. Monroe and wondered if this was her mind playing games on her. Had they renamed the morgue?

Dr. Monroe nodded. "He lost a lot of blood, and he's not out of the woods yet, but he's extraordinarily lucky the bullet barely nicked his heart. If it had been only a hair to the left, it would have been fatal."

Layne's body was involuntarily shaking like a leaf, and her lungs felt like they couldn't get enough oxygen. The renewed wave of hope had come from nowhere and crashed down on her. She didn't even feel the rolling set of tears on her cheeks.

Gage hugged Layne into his side, feeling the same relief and hopefulness upon hearing the doctor's words. "When can we see him?"

Dr. Monroe tucked her tablet back under her arm. "We'd like to monitor him for a little while longer to make sure he's stable after surgery, but I will have a nurse come get you when you can go to his room."

Whatever else was said, Layne couldn't have told anyone because her mind was solely on seeing Joey for herself. What if the doctor had gotten patients mixed up? Maybe she was mistaken, and Joey was lying in a cooler with a tag on his toe.

About forty-five minutes later, a nurse came to lead Gage and her into a room located in the heart of the trauma ICU. When she entered, it smelled so sterile and not at all like the leather and sage she wanted to be greeted with. When she approached the bed, she saw him lying there unconscious and quite pale. Tubes provided him oxygen and drained excess fluids from his chest, IVs provided his body with medications, and monitors constantly checked his vitals.

Her hand covered her mouth, stifling a sob. Gage squeezed her shoulders reassuringly as his body released some of the tension it had been harboring since they had arrived at the hospital.

Layne stepped up next to the bed, carefully taking hold of his hand while her fingers trailed over the side of his face in disbelief. Touching him and feeling his warmth made it real. He was still here with her, and he hadn't left. His life hadn't been robbed of him in the name of Layne's survival.

Her words shook with the weight of her tears still on them. "You listen to me, Joey motherfucking De Luca. I swear to God, if you die on me now, after all this, I will hunt your soul down and never let you hear the end of it."

Gage joined her at Joey's bedside, lightly patting his brother's shoulder. "You've always been a stubborn son of a bitch." He tried to make the commentary light, but his own emotions were getting caught on the words.

She stood there watching every breath he took into his lungs. Each minor movement of his body had her attention. When it was clear she wasn't letting go of his hand, Gage brought a chair over to her so she could sit. Layne rested her head on his arm, both of her hands steadfastly clutching onto the familiar skull tattoo on his hand.

"Hey, Layne!" The crack echoed in the air. Joey's weight on top of her. His cocoa-colored eyes were full of physical and emotional pain.

"Hey, Layne!" Liam's voice filled with nothing but hatred.

"Hey, Layne!" All her sense of security was shattered.

"Hey—"

She startled awake, lifting her head from the edge of Joey's bed to see the nightmare wasn't entirely over. Her heart was galloping a little harder in her chest to the point she could practically feel it in the back of her throat.

"Layne," Gage's voice repeated her name for a third time. His hand lightly rubbed the exposed skin of her upper back to ease her out of her nap.

Groggily, she responded, "Yeah?" Her fingers rubbed the slumber from her eyes as she tried to erase the fog that had settled over her. Glancing up at the clock on the wall, she had only managed to snag an hour of rest.

He had a large paper bag in his hand. "Rebecca dropped off some clothes for you to change into." She hadn't been allowed beyond the nurse's station since she wasn't considered immediate family, but Rebecca had met Gage for a few minutes to get an update and to see what else she could do.

Layne shook her head. "No." Her eyes looked at the unchanged, slack expression on Joey's face. "What if he wakes up and I'm not here? What if he… and I'm not?" Her fears were getting the best of her and making her unable to say the morbid alternative.

Gage squatted down next to her, a hand soothingly rubbing over her thigh. "Baby, he's not going anywhere in the next ten minutes." He offered her the bag with her clothes in it. He had already changed out of his tux and into a set of casual jeans and a solid blue t-shirt that his buddy had dropped off while Layne had been catching some rest.

Layne stared at the bag for a minute, then sighed as she stood from the chair. She leaned over and kissed Joey's mouth softly. "I will be right back, okay?" There was no telling if he could hear her or not, but it made her feel better to think he could.

It took what little strength she had in her to release Joey's hand and grab the bag instead. Gage stood and motioned in a direction across the hall. "The nurse said there's a bathroom right over there you can use."

After Layne left the room, Gage plunked down into her chair. One elbow rested on his knee while the fingers of his other hand roughly ran through his cropped hair. "She's hurting, Joe. Hell, I'm hurting. If you check out, you'll be taking her with you. You gotta pull through this for all of us." His emotions tainted the last few words that passed through his lips.

Finding the easily marked bathroom, Layne stepped inside. She stared at herself in the mirror. The day had begun with her looking and feeling her prettiest. Now, her eyes were swollen and bloodshot from the tears, her makeup smudged into dark circles around her eyes, her hair frazzled, and the red bloodstains still marred her fair skin.

Mentally, peeling off her wedding gown had been the most painful part of the process. The weight of the fabric should have been a relief when it fell to the floor, but her body still carried an incredible emotional load. Looking in the bag of clothes, Rebecca had done her typical thing. Not only did she pack two outfits, but she had tossed some spare toiletries in there as well. After scrubbing any speck of dried blood from her body and washing her face, she brushed out her hair, putting it in a ponytail.

Layne chose a pair of black leggings, slip-on sneakers, and a lavender tank with a dark purple zip-up hoodie over-top. She shoved her dress into the bag, unable to get it to fit fully, so the skirt was cascading out the top like a fountain of tulle. Why was she even keeping it? It had to be bad luck to keep something that you wore when your husband took a bullet for you, right?

Emerging from the bathroom, she came back to Joey's room. She dropped the bag onto a small sofa that doubled as a sleeping space. As much as she hadn't wanted to leave and try to put herself together, Gage had been right to urge her to do it. It left her feeling slightly more human and briefly chased away some of the darkness consuming her thoughts.

Gage got up from the chair, his eyes red from the few minutes he had to allow the day's events to sink in. He walked over to her and wrapped his large arms around her, giving a near-crushing hug. "You look gorgeous."

Her partial laugh fell flat. "Liar." Her arms wrapped around his waist, and she let him hold her for the amount of time they both needed. "How is he?" It seemed a silly question since she hadn't been gone all that long.

He pulled back and turned to look at his brother. "Still here, just like I told you. You should go get yourself something to eat. There's a cafeteria down on the first floor."

Immediately, that was a hard pass for her, and she shook her head. "I'm not hungry." It felt like she was being chased away from Joey's side, and her defense mechanisms began to rise up in protest.

Cupping her face, he stared at her. "I need you to eat. It's not going to do anyone any good if you pass out 'cause you're too damn stubborn to take care of yourself."

Frowning, she pulled her face back from his hold. "I'll be fine."

He groaned in annoyance that this was going to be a battle. "Sitting here refusing to do anything but stare at him isn't healthy. Joey would be kicking your ass right now for forcing the question to be asked twice." The moment the words flew out of his mouth, he instantly regretted it.

Layne's hurt came bubbling back up to the surface, and she pulled back from Gage.

"I'm sorry, you know I didn't mean to…" His eyes were apologetic as he reached out for her, but she kept herself just out of the reach of his hand.

Her eyes shifted to where Joey was lying. His condition hadn't changed since they arrived in the room. It was neither better nor was it worse. "I'm going to go get some air. Call me if anything changes."

She reluctantly left the room in search of some space to clear her head. When Layne got past the sliding glass doors that led outside, she was greeted with a small breeze filled with cool air. Finding a bench to sit on, she stared up at the sky, letting the one question fill her head. Why? Why was this happening to all of them? Why did Liam have to do this? Why hadn't it been her?

There should have been unparalleled rage directed at her brother, and she was sure, at some point, it would rear its vicious head. Right now, the only thing she felt was small, lost, and shattered, all thanks to the crippling grasp of fear her brother left her with.

SPARKLESS

S hould she have walked out on Gage the way she had? No, but her mind was all over the place right now. Emotions were erratically jumping from one point to the next without any logic to guide them.

She mindlessly flipped through hundreds of messages left on her phone while sitting outside the hospital. The senior associates of her crew were looking to her for their orders, Rebecca was checking in, and some of her allies were sending their fucking useless thoughts and prayers. Layne didn't have any answers for herself, let alone anyone else. The messages went unanswered. Before she tucked her phone away, a new text popped in.

GAGE

Are you okay?

LAYNE

What do you think?

GAGE

Please, come back up here.

We're in this together, and I can't help if you won't let me.

Layne wanted to ask him why she should bother returning to that cold and depressing hospital room, but she realized that she wasn't the only person in pain. Gage found himself watching his big brother struggling to live just as much as she was.

She spent several more minutes convincing herself to go back inside. Yesterday, she would have kicked her own ass, but today? She had lost that spark that made her want to put up a fight.

"You are the spark that keeps my heart pumping blood through my veins."

Her eyes squeezed shut, expressing a few more silent tears as the pain tore into her heart a little more, and the memory of Joey's words drove into her shattered soul.

"I will love you so hard for the rest of your life that you won't ever have to worry about losing that spark."

Inhaling a shaky breath, she mentally scolded herself for perhaps loving him too fiercely. If he hadn't been so wrapped up in loving her back, maybe he wouldn't have stepped in front of her. Alternatively, she wondered if this was happening to her as punishment for having not loved him enough. Maybe getting fucked at the altar in church could have been God's tipping point, too.

Quickly, her fingertips pushed the tears off her cheeks as she readied herself to go back inside. Every muscle in her body felt triple its weight, making the process of standing more challenging than it should have been.

On her way back through the main entrance, a vaguely familiar face was just leaving and captured her attention when he spoke up. "Ms. O'Reil—I mean, Mrs. De Luca?" Detective Adams smiled apologetically.

She stopped in her tracks to look at the man, struggling to recall his name. "Hi…"

He saved her from having to fumble for his name. "Detective Adams, we spoke earlier."

Right. When she was wallowing in the thoughts of her husband's presumed death, he had been interested in getting her retelling of the tragedy.

"I'm sorry, I don't have anything that can help you." The verbal apology was the best he was going to get out of her. She simply didn't have enough energy to muster up a fake smile for the sake of appearing polite.

The detective immediately shook his head. "No, I understand. I just wanted to make sure you got my contact information in case you do have anything you'd like to share." Though he had previously given it to Gage, he had a suspicion it wouldn't get passed along. He dug into his suit jacket, pulled out his business card, and extended it toward her.

Hesitantly, Layne took the white piece of cardstock from him. She gave it a glance front and back before sliding it into the pocket of her black pants. "I already told you that I didn't see a damn thing." Irritation started to rise in her voice.

He nodded at her. "Just hold onto that in case you ever

need it." His face filled with empathy before he added, "I hope your husband makes a full recovery."

Layne muttered, "Thanks," before she turned and left him standing in the entryway as she found her way back upstairs to join both her guys waiting for her in the ICU.

When she walked into Joey's room, Gage wasn't present. The only other person in there was a nurse who was changing out one of the bags hanging from the metal stand next to Joey's bed that dripped into his IV. The young raven-haired woman was about Layne's age and gave a polite smile. "I will be out of here in just a second."

"It's fine, do what you need to." Layne went over to the empty chair at Joey's bedside, plunked down into it, and the nurse was out of the room as quickly as she had stated.

Both of Layne's hands took a tight hold of Joey's hand at his side and rested her face on it while she closed her eyes. She quietly whispered, "I feel like I've given you all the spark I have left in me, and it's still not enough."

The swell of emotions crept up on her again, and she buried her face into the cheap hospital-grade blankets as she suppressed a sob. Her shoulders shuddered as they soaked up the cries and screams she wanted to unleash.

A hand came to the back of her head reassuringly. "It'll always be enough, Layney." Joey's hoarse voice spoke through his grogginess as he opened his eyes to see her clutching onto his other hand while visibly upset.

Her body stilled, wondering if she had fallen asleep again or if she had just devolved into hearing things. When she lifted her head, she saw his heavenly brown eyes staring at her. She choked on another sob, but this time one of gleeful disbelief.

"Joey!" She released his hand and immediately stood to lean over and smother his face and mouth with her kisses of relief. The tears that were still fresh on her face fell onto him as she pressed her face up against the tattooed bird wings on the side of his neck in an attempt to latch herself onto him in a hug.

He lightly returned her kisses but struggled to hold back his winces of pain as she leaned against him. His hand rubbed her back reassuringly. "I told you it would be okay." Joey's last couple of words fought through a groan of his body's reminder that he had been shot in the goddamn chest and undergone a major surgery.

Hearing the discomfort in his voice, she eased up off of him. "I didn't hurt you, did I?"

Shaking his head in a lie, he gave her a light smile. "Never."

Using the bottom of her sleeve, she dried her face off until just the red splotches left behind from her tears remained. Her glossy hues stared at him in disbelief that he was awake and talking. Before more questions could be asked, the door opened, and Gage walked in with a handful of snacks.

Not only was Gage surprised to see Layne had returned, but Joey was awake. He juggled the food in his hands, nearly dropping an apple to the floor. "Hey, man! Fuck, you gave us a hell of a scare."

He set the food down on a small table quickly before going to the side of Joey's bed opposite Layne. Relief filled his face as he looked at his brother and bent over to give a partial hug with a gentle pat on Joey's shoulder. Joey's hand returned a tap to Gage's bicep.

Layne smiled, unable to come to terms that this was real as she looked at both Gage and Joey. Finally, she pulled herself away enough from Joey's side to ease back into her chair, her fingers lacing with Joey's. "How are you feeling?"

"Like I got shot." He smirked, seemingly, he hadn't lost his sense of humor.

She rolled her eyes and tried to suppress the smile, still tugging at the corners of her mouth. "Thanks, smartass." Layne sat there, simply staring at him, overcome with gratitude that he hadn't been eliminated from her life.

The three of them sat there talking about everything and anything except for the person responsible for the assassination attempt on Layne. She didn't dare to even think his name and instead opted to focus all her thoughts and energy on Joey's road to recovery.

"When you get back home, I'll make sure we have plenty of your favorite snacks stocked up and whatever else you need," she reassured him. He wouldn't be leaving here for a little while, but having him back home with her was something she could look forward to.

Being happy to just be on this side of the dirt, Joey grinned as he watched Layne make plans for all of them. He had a second chance at a life together with her, and hell if he was going to waste it.

Gage took a sip from his bottle of water. "I hate to bring the mood down, but before we start making too many plans, we should talk about the obvious here." His eyes looked at Joey first, looking for his agreement.

After a deep inhale, Joey winced as he sat up a little straighter in his bed, fumbling with all the fucking tubes and wires attached to him. "What do we know?"

Her eyes darkened with a glare at Gage for bringing up the topic she had been actively avoiding. "We don't need to talk about this." Layne knew she couldn't ignore this forever, but she wanted to stay in this bubble of happiness a little while longer.

Joey couldn't pretend to understand what she was going through, given her brother was responsible, but he did recognize the signs of her internally shutting down if they didn't tread carefully. "Layne, you can't ignore what he did."

Gage chimed in with his opinion, "We don't know what the hell else Liam is up to."

She lashed out with a spark of anger for the first time since the incident. "I'm not fucking ignoring it! I'm going to take care of it!" Immediately, her sharp tongue and even shorter temper had her sinking down into her guilt.

The past twenty-four hours had taken its toll on her. The sleep deprivation, the highs and lows, and all the stressors that had her running on fumes by this point. Layne put a hand to her forehead and dragged it down over her face as she squeezed her eyes shut in frustration.

"Layney…" Joey's soothing voice spoke her name, attempting to pull her back from spiraling.

She didn't make a move from her current position as her thoughts began to swallow her whole.

Standing from his seat, Gage came up behind her, rubbing his hands over her shoulders. "Look, now that Joey is awake, why don't you get some rest, and we can pick this up later, hm?" He leaned over and laid a kiss on the back of her neck directly against the curves of the shamrock inked into her skin.

Stubbornly, she shook her head. "No, I'm fine." She had been using that word a lot, and it was the furthest thing from the truth. Layne didn't want to rest knowing her idiotic brother was out there, knowing her nightmares would taint her memory of what should have been the happiest day of her life.

"Come here." Joey's hand tugged on her wrist, drawing her hand away from her face. When she opened up those beautiful green eyes, they were shaded by sheer exhaustion. He didn't have much room to shift, but he gave her enough so she could at least perch on the edge of his bed. His arm pulled her down to his side, his strong arms squeezing her tightly.

Layne lay there in his embrace, wishing she could bottle up the feeling of him for eternity. Remaining vigilant of his injury, she laid her arm across his stomach. His hold on her helped to relieve some of her tension.

Joey pressed several kisses across her temple. "Go home, let Gage take care of you, and get some rest."

"I can't," she murmured against him.

"Yes, Layne, you can. I need you to. I didn't fight like hell for you to run yourself down." His fingers lifted her face by the chin. "You're going to need the rest. When I get out of here, my cock is going to be making up for lost time." He grinned playfully before he closed the gap between their mouths. Passionately, he locked his lips onto hers like he hadn't tasted her in years.

It was enough that when she finally came up for air, she was already looking a little more amenable to listening to reason.

"I love you. We will be back as soon as we can, okay?" Layne stole one more kiss from him to hold her over until they returned.

While she pulled away to gather her things, Joey looked at Gage. "Don't—"

His little brother cut him off, "I know. I've got her."

Gage waited for Layne to collect her things before leaving the room with her.

Once the two of them left, Joey exhaled and leaned back. His brows pinched together as he winced in pain, his hand lightly resting on top of his chest. He had done his best to mask the injury's toll on him for Layne's sake, but holy fuck. This brush with death and coming to terms with his own mortality had him seeing things in a very different light than he had ever before.

Chapter Three

TROUBLES & BUBBLES

age decided to bring her back to his condo in Hudson Yards. There was too much uncertainty surrounding Liam to take the chance of going back to O'Reilly Manor. On the way, Layne texted Sammy to let him know that she needed him to get her home secured. Everything had to be checked from attic to basement, all the locks changed, and the entire residence secured better than Fort Knox. There was no telling what else Liam may have had planned.

After unlocking the door and pushing it open, Gage held a hand out to stop Layne from entering. "Wait."

She drew up a brow at his sudden change of mind. "What is it?"

He gave her his typical smile filled with boyish charm. "I know things didn't go as planned yesterday, but if you're going to have the De Luca last name, I'm going to do right by it."

Before she could ask him what the hell he was going on

about, he bent over and scooped her up into his arms. Turning sideways, he carried her into his unit over the threshold.

Layne giggled as her hands clutched onto him. "Are you really that superstitious?"

"When it comes to you, Lucky Charm, I'm not taking my chances." He grinned. Continuing to hold her in his arms, he carried her back to their bedroom and into the master bathroom before setting her down on her feet.

He twisted the faucet on the dark granite tub, filling it with steamy water. Tapping a switch on the wall, he activated the feature that kept the tub at a warm temperature.

Gage stepped over to her, his eyes melting into soft brown hues. His fingers slid the zipper of her hoodie down. "Layne, I want to take all your worries away for a little while."

As his hands pushed the sweatshirt from her upper body, she felt her breaths fill with the familiar heaviness of desire. Her body began to ease as the scent of the oils and salts in the bathwater began to fill the air with eucalyptus and mint.

He hooked his finger onto the thin gold chain of the discreet collar he had bestowed on her, pulling her closer to him. His lips drifted across the side of her face until his mouth was at her ear, whispering, "Let me."

Her hands came to the front of his chest, fingertips exploring the curve of each of his muscles underneath the cotton t-shirt. "I don't even want to remember where I am when you're done." She pleadingly gazed up at him with her eyes still reflecting the pain of tears long since dried.

"Baby, the only thing I need you to remember is how goddamn good my cock feels stuffed inside you." His finger released the thread of metal around her throat and grabbed her by the back of her neck. Gage's lips crashed against hers, kissing her hungrily.

Each of their hands worked at removing the other's clothing. Layne's hands shoved Gage's shirt up hastily until she couldn't reach up any further to get it over his head, and he assisted in yanking it the rest of the way off. He, in turn, lifted her shirt from her and relieved her of her pants and underwear in one downward motion. Layne's fingers popped the clasp of her bra, dropping it to join the pile on the floor.

Now free of all her clothes, she eagerly pulled at his belt until it gave way, and she worked his zipper down over the large size of his cock, already trying to spring free. Layne's hand slid into the front of his boxers, seeking out his stiff length. Grabbing him, she worked her hand down to the hilt of his swords and back up to the tip.

The deep groan of his voice echoed against the tile walls of the bathroom. The way her fingers curled around his thick cock, firmly working over each inch, had him spiraling into thoughts of the rest of her body squeezing around his dick.

Falling prey to her distraction, he nearly forgot his place. He smirked and grabbed her jaw. "Did I give you permission to touch my cock, baby? Are you so fuckin' needy for it that you forgot how to get on your knees and beg for me?"

Layne pouted and tried to kiss his observation of the

minor infraction away as her hand continued to stroke him. He wasn't having any of it, though. His hand took the length of her ponytail around his hand and tilted her head back before she could try to distract him any further.

Gage grinned, dropping his other hand to remove her grasp on his solid length. "It seems you need a little reminder, don't you?"

"Yes, Sir," she purred.

"Hands on that towel rack and stick your ass out for me." He took his hands off of her to motion at the stainless steel bar that currently had two white body towels folded over it.

Layne looked over at the bar affixed to the wall and smiled. Without arguing, she nodded and walked over to it, her hands yanking each towel hanging from it onto the floor. With some sass in her movements, she curved her hands around the cool metal before she bent at the waist and pushed her ass backward.

Seeing her in a position that he could easily sink himself into, he gave another groan of approval. He quickly finished the job of removing the rest of his clothes. Despite the temptation to just ram into that perfectly tight pussy of hers, he had other plans. He walked over to one of the drawers of the bathroom vanity and reached inside, retrieving one of the few gifts he kept for such an occasion.

Standing at her side, he smirked knowingly at his intentions. His hand reached behind her, dragging a cool metal object between her thighs, coating it with her arousal. "You know what happens when you don't keep your hands to yourself, baby?"

She moaned quietly, feeling the smooth object drag along her slit. Her eyes begged him for something more to sate her lustful appetite. Layne shook her head in response to his question. "No."

"I'm going to make sure you keep them busy." With the small plug now coated in the wetness from her body, he dragged it to her tight back entrance. Gage slowly pushed the acorn-shaped toy into her until it was seated deep inside of her.

Her hands tightened around the rack as she groaned out, feeling the plug gradually stretching her while it was worked inside. It took much more effort to accept Joey into her ass, but the sensation of the toy now inside of her provided an equally welcomed sensation.

"Good girl. You like taking it in your sweet ass, don't you?" His cock was throbbing as he inspected the flare of the metal base between the rounds of each cheek. He gave a hum of approval at the sight.

"Yes, it feels so good." Layne began to straighten up but was met with Gage's hand against her back.

"Oh, you're not done learning your lesson yet, Lucky Charm." His sinful desires prompted the corner of his mouth to pull up into another smirk. Backing up one slow step at a time until he was at the edge of the bath, he sat on the ledge of the rectangular inset that surrounded the infinity pool-style tub in the middle of it. His eyes never left the gorgeous sight of her partially bent over for him with her ass filled with the toy he had filled it with.

He leaned over and turned off the running water that had the tub at their disposal whenever they got around to it.

Right now, there were more pressing matters requiring his full attention.

He gave his order, "Come for me. If you want to use those hands for something, you're going to use them on that greedy cunt of yours. I want to watch as you get yourself off."

She hadn't even made a move yet, and he already had a grip on his hard cock, fisting it in long strokes.

Layne peered over her shoulder back at him. "But I'd rather have you." Her eyes lowered to the sight of his swollen dick in his hand, her body aching for it fiercely.

Sternly, he spoke to her, "Baby, I can take in this view all damn day, but you better hope you come before I do if you want any of this."

Holding her position at the towel rack, she dropped a hand between her legs and stroked her fingers over her clit, slick with her desire. Her first moan pierced the air. The tips of her fingers began to rub circles against the sensitive bundle of nerves, prompting her body to fill with pleasure. "Mmm…" Imagining Gage's rough hands coursing over her body, she got lost in the sensation of her fingers working her body over hills of pleasure.

Hearing Layne's moans of self-derived excitement, Gage took his time with himself with each stroke. His cock grew harder as he witnessed every movement she made. He couldn't wait to fuck the ever-living daylights out of her the moment she made herself come.

Layne began to ache for the sensation of her inner walls stretching around a hard cock. Her fingers slid back and pushed two deep inside of herself. She started slowly, working them in and out before picking up the pace with the climb of her needs. "Ohh, Gage," she moaned out as her body began to tremble, knowing he was watching the intimate affair she was having with her body.

He released a low growl in excitement as he watched her slim fingers push inside her tight pussy. "Fuck, baby, I wish you could see how fuckin' delicious you look right now. Your ass filled and your fingers fucking your hot little pussy."

Her hand squeezed onto the towel rack tighter, threatening its stability in the wall, while her hips engaged in a sensual dance with her fingers shifting inside the depths of her core. Having the plug buried inside of her ass while she did so made her crave release all the more.

Layne's knees began to quiver as her peak neared. Driving her fingers inside of her and curling her fingertips, she cried out as her pleasure spilled over the edge and the warmth of her orgasm covered her small digits.

Gage moaned out as his hand squeezed his dick, pumping it harder as he watched Layne make herself come. There was something about making her get herself off that filled him with a heated sense of satisfaction.

She slowly came down from the high of her release, panting as her hand fell from between her thighs. Her body remained bent over, hanging by the one hand that refused to let go of the bar it was latched onto for dear life at this point.

"What a good job you did, baby. But now," he let go of his cock and stood from the edge of the tub before quickly closing the space between them. His hands took her by her waist and pulled her upright with her back against his chest. Gage's hand slid up around her throat, squeezing around her necklace to capture her attention. He growled a whisper into her ear, "It's my turn."

Gage grabbed the hand she had just fucked herself with and sucked her flavor off of each finger. The taste of her body was considered an extra reward for himself after refraining from interrupting that hell of a show she had just given him.

Layne gasped as he possessively took hold of her, feeling his cock pressing against her and making her flush with a renewed flame of desire. The heat of his breath against her neck as he uttered those last few words to her had her feeling like putty.

Dropping his hand away from her throat, Gage pushed her up against an empty space on the wall, using his large and muscular body to keep her held there. His foot kicked her legs apart, giving him more access to her heated cunt. His fingers dipped between her legs to her slick folds, spreading them as he positioned the head of his cock at her entrance. Taking hold of her hands and lacing their fingers together, he pinned her palms against the wall above her head.

She whimpered as she felt him so close, yet not inside her. "Please," she begged.

Holding her hands tightly, he didn't need to hear her say more. He thrust himself deep inside of her, getting his dick encased in the warmth of those tight walls. Gage let his primal side take over, not waiting after he pulled back and rammed himself into her again. Aggressively, he kept pumping his cock into her.

Layne cried out as his length pushed against the tightness of her body, delightfully stretching her with his size. Her hands squeezed around his fingers while his body began to feed her pleasure. "Fuck! Yes!" She tilted her head back against his chest, letting him rip away any thoughts of all the negative events that had transpired.

Gage bowed his head down, deeply inhaling the sweet scent of her skin as his mouth roughly sucked at the flesh on the side of her throat. His heavy breaths scorched her skin while he gave her the fucking they both deserved after surviving hell together. When he observed a red patch left behind on her neck from his mouth's efforts, his teeth proudly nipped at it. He panted through his groans as his hips furiously worked at slamming himself into her body.

Both of them needed this stress relief, a way to let go of everything that had been weighing heavily on them. Layne's body clamped down on Gage's cock as she cursed out when another orgasm tore through her, leaving her gasping for air as her body squirmed between him and the wall in front of her.

"That's it, baby, fucking come all over my cock." His husky voice dropped low as he kept pushing his dick into her, driving past the tensions of her release, trying to lock down around his length. Grunting through his efforts, his rhythm began to struggle.

She pressed her forehead to the wall as she tried to float back down from her spike of ecstasy. "Gage, I want you to come in my ass," Layne murmured with the last bits of energy she had left in her, hoping he'd hear her.

Oh, he heard her, and he damn near lost control of his climax. He pulled out of her, withdrawing his hands from hers. His fingers found the base of the plug still secured inside her ass and eased it out of her. "What my Lucky Charm wants, she's going to get."

Only having one goal, he discarded the toy onto the floor and shifted her position away from the wall to bend her over. With his cock freshly coated in her cum, he pushed the tip into the puckered hole that had been stretched by the plug. "You ready, baby? This is gonna be quick and dirty." The expanse of each of his hands grabbed a handful of her ass cheeks to steady her body in anticipation of his full entry.

Her palms pressed to the floor as she stood there, already reveling in the initial push of just the round head of his cock in her. Layne nodded her head, "Mmhmm."

Gage sank his cock deeply into her, his fingers digging into her as his grasp tightened. Groaning loudly as he felt the reluctant stretch of the muscle wrapping around him, he felt a tingle travel down his spine. "Fuck!" He withdrew and thrust into her again, yanking her hips back to meet his own. He repeated himself while he moaned out, "Fuck!" He said it several more times, with each frantic and hard shove into her body.

Her body bounced with each impact of his hips, driving his length into her ass. The swell of pleasure had her moans joining him in a sexual symphony.

As he warned, it didn't take long before there was a

final plunge of his dick into her. He yelled out, and his throbbing length released the pressure that had been building up. Ropes of cum shot from the tip, filling up the tight space he was nestled into. His hips rolled up against her with each spurt of his release. Heavily panting, he remained seated inside of her as he looked up at the ceiling and closed his eyes for a second, feeling the satisfaction of ecstasy wash over him.

Gage gradually regained his composure, his heart still pounding away inside his chest. Sliding out of her, he happily grinned, seeing his efforts leaking from the hole he had just fucked like a goddamn animal.

He eased Layne upright and turned her to face him. Her face was beautifully flushed, and her emerald hues filled with sated desire. His smile stretched broadly across his face. Gage rested his hand on the side of her face, his light brown eyes taking a mental snapshot of what heaven on earth looked like.

"Have I told you how much I love you? That felt amazing." Layne stood on her tiptoes to lovingly kiss him, to which he pulled her up against him as he met her mouth with a more tender hunger. Allowing some time for them to linger in the moment before he broke the kiss, he leaned down and scooped her up into his arms.

Layne was carried over to the tub, where Gage carefully stepped in and lowered them both down into the steamy water. He shifted her so she was seated in his lap and leaning back against him. She sighed in total relaxation, closing her eyes while she rested her hands on his broad thighs.

They sat there together in the glow of the sunset coming in through the massive window to their right as it dipped below the skyline of the city. Gage took his time making sure that he lathered every inch of her body with soap, washing away all their sweat, fluids, and burdens. It was the best therapy ever for them both.

He leaned back against the side of the tub, willing to hold her for as long as she needed. "Baby, I could spend all night like this with you." He gently kissed the back of her head, hoping he'd always be able to take away her troubles.

Chapter Four

NO NEWS

"I'm dying," Joey grunted. "The food here tastes like Layne cooked it." He tossed the plastic fork down on the tray in front of him. The plate housed what could only be described as slop in a shape that might resemble the food it was supposed to be.

"Fuck you!" Layne's hand smacked his leg at the offensive statement.

It had been a little over three weeks of listening to Joey bitch about still being stuck in the hospital. If it wasn't the food, it was the bed, the lack of anything to do, and most importantly, the lack of sex. At least his chest tube had been removed, and he had been transitioned from the Intensive Care Unit into a regular room as of last week. It granted him a little more freedom and space.

Joey winked at her. "My cock is right here. Mount up, Layney." In response, he got one of those eye rolls from her that made his sexually deprived dick begin to perk up.

Gage laughed as he looked over at Layne and shrugged.

"Baby, you have many talents, but cooking is definitely not one of them. There's a reason why Rebecca is always stocking up your freezer with meals."

Layne pointed a finger at Gage. "Don't you start." Her eyes went back to Joey as he sat there in his bed, and she took another bite from her granola bar. After swallowing, she sternly spoke to him, "I told you, you're not getting anything until you're cleared for physical activity. I don't need my last memories of you to be performing CPR on you while your dick is still in me."

Sitting on the spare seat next to a circular table across from Layne and Joey, Gage smirked with pride. "Don't worry, bro. I've been keeping her pussy busy for you." He was all too happy to point it out.

Glaring at his brother, Joey grumbled and shook his head. Other than the moment inside the church, he hadn't even been able to give his wife a proper fucking, and it was leaving him with the worst case of blue balls. He would rather go down drowning in Layne's pussy than via gunshot, that was for sure.

Intentionally, he changed the topic. If they continued talking about sex, he would be tempted to say fuck it and jerk off right there in front of them both.

Approaching the topic cautiously after Layne's last blow-up over her brother, his chocolate-colored eyes looked at Layne, trying to keep his gaze above her shoulders. "Any news on where Liam is holed up?"

She pulled her legs up onto the chair she was sitting in at Joey's bedside as she nibbled at the nut and oat snack in her hand. Shaking her head, she spoke with clear frustration, "No. There's been nothing from the guys on tracking him down. He's gotta be hiding out somewhere. I had Ethan check out his old place down in Tribeca, but it doesn't look like it's been touched since he got arrested." At the same time Ethan had scoped the place out, he had helped her coordinate getting Liam's crap out of there and into storage for the time being.

Gage raised a brow, "Do we even know when he got out? I thought he didn't make bail."

She shrugged. "I didn't think he did either, but both the court clerk and Department of Corrections aren't being cooperative in giving me any information."

Joey blew out a breath of air angrily. "Motherfucker better be prepared when I get out of here. I don't care what rock he is hiding under; I'm going to track his ass down."

Pulling a knee to her chest and resting her chin on top of it, she looked over at him. "And do what, Joey? Give him another chance to finish the job?" She frowned, hating that they were in this situation at all. Despite being her little brother, Liam had shattered the last of her shaky bond with him the day he aimed his weapon at her.

Quickly replacing Joey's feeling of horniness was his rage at the little shithead. "I don't give a fuck, Layne! Sitting here and doing nothing keeps you an open target."

Lifting her chin off her knee, she reflected the irritation right back at him. "I'm not sitting here and doing nothing! Jesus Christ! I've been trying to juggle business, worrying about you, and this entire fucking Liam disaster. What else do you want me to do, huh? If he was smart, he has left the damn country already." Wasn't that wishful thinking?

Deciding to play referee, Gage got up from his chair and walked over to them. "Alright, let's just chill the hell out for a second, okay?" He looked at Layne. "We know you've got a lot going on; nobody is suggesting you handle this all on your own." Then, he turned to Joey. "She's not going to be a target as long as I've got eyes on her. We'll find him."

Just as she was going to tell Gage she didn't need him constantly keeping eyes on her, the same nurse with the dark hair Layne had met up in the ICU walked in with a bright and bubbly smile on her face. "Hope I'm not interrupting; I just need to swap in some fresh fluids." Her hand motioned to the bags leading into Joey's IV.

Joey nodded, "Yeah, go ahead." It would at least give him the opportunity to simmer down a little.

The conversation between the three of them paused with the nurse now present. The general public didn't need to be privy to the plotting and conspiring of her brother's ultimate demise.

Layne felt her phone vibrating in her pocket. She reached in for it and pulled it out, seeing an unknown number on the screen, not an uncommon occurrence given the clientele she worked with. "I need to take this." There was a strong hope that maybe one of her associates had uncovered something useful.

She stood from her seat and walked away from them both, keeping her back to them. Layne stopped and stood at the small table where Gage had left the last half of his lunch, his wallet, and his keys scattered across it.

Answering the call, she placed the phone to her ear. "Hello?"

A dark and harsh voice spoke quietly, "Don't say a damn thing. I would hate for one of the nurses to fuck up and introduce a deadly air embolism into fuckface's vein." Liam's voice on the other end of the call sent a chill down her spine.

Glancing back over her shoulder, the nurse was seemingly having a pleasant conversation with the guys. Layne looked back down at the table in front of her as she placed a hand on her hip and bit her tongue. She wanted nothing more than to lay into him with all the hate-filled words she could come up with.

It was clear he knew precisely where she was and who she was with. She couldn't be sure if he was bluffing or not, but after almost losing Joey once, she wasn't going to take the risk of it happening again.

When she said nothing further, Liam continued speaking. "We need to meet and talk." He gave a thoughtful pause before continuing, "Unless you'd rather I find someone else worthy of paying the price on your behalf since your freak of a husband didn't have the good sense to die?"

Layne's body tensed from head to toe with her anger. Her hand squeezed tighter onto her hip to prevent the trembling from her emotions from being visible while adrenaline surged to prompt her heart to gallop in her chest. She tried to swallow down the knot in her throat, but no matter how many times she attempted, it remained lodged there. "Just give me the details." She had chosen her words carefully to not draw any attention from Joey or Gage to the conversation.

The malicious chuckle on the other end of the line made her want to put her fist through a window. Liam responded to her request, "Thirty minutes, House of the Chinese Dragon. Have the good sense to come alone and don't be late, okay? We are long overdue for a little brother-sister bonding time. I would hate to feel like I need to make good on my promises to finally get you to listen."

Being familiar with the restaurant, she knew it would be a tight timeframe to make it down there in half an hour. She didn't even have her damn car here since Gage had insisted on driving her all over the place. "Sure thing."

Before Liam hung up, he left her with a short and artificially sweet goodbye, "See you soon, sis."

Keeping the phone to her ear even after Liam ended the call, she turned around and walked past the guys. On her way by, she pointed to her phone and then out to the hallway to indicate she was going to finish the call right outside Joey's room. She got a nod from each of them in acknowledgment before disappearing from their sight.

Not long after Layne stepped out, the nurse's pager went off, and she glanced down at it. Quickly, she finished up her work of swapping out some bags and making sure that Joey's vitals were all on point before she presumably left to see the next patient.

Joey rubbed his hands over his face tiredly. "I can't sit in this place any longer. It's driving me fucking insane. Not being able to see or touch Layne any time I wake up in the middle of the night is a damn nightmare."

Gage sighed, "I told you, I've got this. Did they give you an idea of when you're being released?" He leaned back against a wall comfortably.

Shaking his head, Joey responded, "If all continues to look good, in the next two weeks. Apparently, I've been healing like a fucking badass." He proudly smiled. "The doctor said on the 15th, I think." Then, it hit him, his smile faded, and he groaned. "Fuuuck." He tilted his head back against his pillow.

Gage's eyes widened with a bit of concern at the sudden shift in Joey's demeanor. "What is it?"

Joey frowned and pulled his head upright again. "That's the anniversary of Layne's mother's death." His fingers combed through his dirty blonde hair. "Goddammit. I have to be out of here before then."

He saw the look on Gage's face, which indicated that while he was empathetic about the gravity of the day itself, his brother was clueless about what it meant for their girl. Joey further explained, "She's going to be a fucking wreck that day, she always is. I'm talking about drinking to find the bottom of the barrel and then some. With everything going on, I have to be there for her this time."

"We'll figure it out, man. I'll talk to the doctor, get him to clear you, and we can both find a way to keep her… preoccupied that day." Gage paused and looked at his watch, "She's been on the phone for twenty minutes."

"Fuck, I hope that means it was good news." Joey shook his head, feeling doubtful.

Gage walked over to the round table where all his

belongings were. He grabbed a bag of gummy bears and then paused, tilting his head. "Huh."

Joey raised a brow, "Hm?"

His brother turned with a puzzled and concerned look on his face. "My keys were right here." Gage patted the pockets of his jeans to make sure he hadn't put the set of keys back in them. Each pocket turned up empty.

"Fucking hell." He dropped the bag of gummies down onto the table and jogged out of the room into the hallway. He saw nothing but medical staff and visitors milling about. There was no sign of Layne.

Jumping to the same conclusion as Gage, Joey cursed and shoved the sheets off of himself as he got out of bed. He ripped the tape off where the IV fed into the back of his hand, then pulled the line out. There wasn't even a wince at the pain, which paled in comparison to everything else he had already been through.

If Layne took off, it wasn't for anything good, and Joey wasn't going to wait until he was discharged to get the hell out of this godforsaken hospital. They would have to detain him against his will and have all of the New York Army National Guard posted at the door.

Chapter Five

KUNG PAO CHICKEN

The entire drive into Chinatown had been riddled with enough stress to leave her sweating by the time she finally parked Gage's Jeep. The damn thing had been making a rattling noise inside the dash the entire trip, driving her fucking insane when her nerves were already on edge. He had enough money to live in a ridiculously swanky condo in Hudson Yards but couldn't let go of a rusty piece of shit Jeep? Luckily, he had reinstalled the doors on it after listening to her bitch for an hour about her hair getting whipped around and tangled into the worst knots she had ever dealt with in her life.

Before she left the hospital, she turned off her cell phone to force all calls to go straight to voicemail. She would have to answer to the guys later about taking off, but this was her decision to make. Layne already saw the price Joey had nearly paid, and hell, if she was going to drag either of them further into this shitshow. Liam was her brother, and that made it her problem.

Layne walked down to the little Chinese restaurant half a block from where she parked. The House of the Chinese Dragon was tucked between two other retail spaces. On one side of it was an Asian grocery store, and on the other side? It was what could be called a massage parlor with a very ill-reputed area of expertise.

This wasn't a randomly selected takeout place. Their father, Scott O'Reilly, had made a tradition of taking them here whenever there was something to celebrate. It didn't have to be good grades or a birthday, but he was known to bring them down here after winning a fistfight, closing a deal under the table, or even after their first kill. It was a way of finding comfort in family and food.

As she stared up at the sign written in two languages with the image of a dragon sprawled over the top of it, this place no longer brought the joy and nostalgia it once did. Having her baby, Glock, tucked into the back of her jeans made her feel less anxious but didn't seem to prevent her palms from feeling clammy. She wiped them against the sides of her pants one more time before walking inside the restaurant.

It maintained a rather eye-catching and spacious interior for in-house dining. The little Buddha statue by the door was the first thing she recognized when she entered. Music lightly played in the background like little chimes being struck to mimic cheerful sounds of nature. Inside was just as she recalled, lots of red and black splashed across the decorations and multiple pieces of artwork of dragons in various styles. At the back corner table—her father's favorite—was Liam.

Reminding herself that they were in a public space, she hoped that it would be the one piece of security that would allow this to be as fruitful of a discussion as it possibly could be. Was Liam stupid enough to start a gunfight in public? She was hoping not, but after what transpired on her wedding day, she wouldn't put it past him.

Layne walked past the other tables, most of them full of hungry patrons. Once she was within three feet of the table, Liam looked at her with an at-ease smile. She didn't bother giving him one in return. He may have been happy to see her disregarding all the red alarms sounding in her head, but she wanted nothing but to come in here with a stick of dynamite to shove up his ass.

He looked the way he always had in some ways but different in others. His smug fucking face was laced with signs of an ugly heart turned black. His auburn hair was no longer in a messy heap on his head but smoothly styled with an off-center part. Liam's hazel eyes seemed darker in an unsettling way, with less of the green popping through the brown. The clothes he wore now looked like he owned a Fortune 100 company. The black tie paired with his custom designer suit was screaming for her to tighten it until he choked to death. Did he think he was Dad? He was far from it, in her not-so-humble opinion.

"I was beginning to think you weren't going to show. You had two minutes to spare." He took a slow sip from the small ceramic cup in his hand, swallowing down the serving of green tea. "Are you going to sit or just stand there glaring at me?"

Layne pulled a chair out for herself opposite him and

plunked down into it. She crossed one leg over the other and crossed her arms in front of her stomach. "Nice suit. A little out of your budget, though, isn't it?" She had been monitoring all the cash, including what was set aside for Liam before he had gotten arrested. His name wasn't listed on any of the accounts, so he had to be getting funds elsewhere.

He grinned at her as one of his hands ran down the smooth material of the jacket. "You like it? I reached out to Dad's old tailor, and he hooked me up."

So, he really was trying to emulate Dad, wasn't he?

"Where did you get the cash?" Her voice was flat in an effort not to let her emotions boil up to a full rage just yet. Flipping the fuck out and scaring all the innocent bystanders was not going to be in her best interest.

He sat back in his seat; his eyes remained on her. "Well, no thanks to you, I had to make a few business deals of my own. Knowing that Dad left everything to you, I took a few proactive steps to ensure that I had some rainy-day funds. I made a few friends, did a little negotiating, and kept those important details to myself." Liam shrugged like it was as much of a common practice as opening a savings account.

There were so many questions she wanted answers to, with the biggest one being whether he wanted his body buried or cremated. Layne sat there, looking far more casually dressed in her jeans and snug-fitting black button-up blouse. The loose waves of her chestnut hair hung down a couple of inches past her breasts. The light above the table caused Gage's gold necklace around her neck to shimmer subtly.

"What's the point of all this, Li?" The first hints of pain tainted her words. She shook her head in disappointment. It wasn't just him she was disappointed in, but herself for somehow never seeing it coming down to this. "The money was there, all you had to do was work for it. I didn't ask for a whole hell of a lot from you."

The corners of his mouth twitched in amusement. "You think this was about money? Cute, Layne. Real cute." He set his cup of tea down on the red linen tablecloth. "Where do you want to begin? For starters, Mom dies, and you shack up with the man responsible for it."

Her facial expression slipped, indicating her surprise at his knowledge of Joey's involvement in their mother's demise. In turn, Liam grinned menacingly as he continued to explain, "Yeah, I know all about it. After realizing you were falling to your knees for our masked friend's dick, I did some research. It wasn't easy, but I see why Dad never traced it back during the hiring process. That fucker has some friends in high places."

He shifted in his seat with a smirk, "Did you know that he was fucking the former mayor's daughter at one point before blowing her dad away on his way out the door? I bet the cum was still freshly smeared over her thighs. Sheesh, he knows how to pick jobs with benefits. I'm almost jealous."

She recalled a contract Joey had taken and executed on the retired mayor back after Eric Ellis had been eliminated. He wouldn't have betrayed her, would he?

Layne gritted her teeth, trying her best not to take anything Liam was saying to heart. There was no telling if he was lying out of his ass or telling the truth. Even if he was being honest for once, she was never ignorant of what type of work Joey often was contracted for. Yet, that little tidbit about the mayor's daughter refused to be unheard.

She shook her head and pushed her chair back to stand up. Liam smirked. "You may want to sit back down until I'm finished." He jutted his chin in the direction of a table near the door. "You see that man in the Yankees cap? All he has to do is make the call, and my contacts at the hospital will make sure that there is an unfortunate incident of gross medical malpractice."

He motioned at another table closer to them. "That one there is always looking for a reason to strangle a pretty face to death. When he heard you nearly drowned once, you should have seen how quickly he nearly busted the zipper of his pants with his erection. The way he's been looking at you since you walked in the door, I would say he might even have a crush on you."

She glanced at both the referenced men. The Yankee fan's face was obscured by the shadows of his location in the restaurant while he had his nose buried behind a newspaper. As for the other man, she was sure to remember his face in the event she ever saw that fucker again. Begrudgingly, she sat back down. This time, she let her anger and hatred start to seep into her eyes, no longer trying to host a composed front. "Fucking talk quicker then," Layne spat out impatiently.

Liam was more than happy to draw this out as long as he wanted, knowing he had her full attention for as long as he wanted it. "In addition to your poor taste in men, you ended up fucking me out of a very beneficial deal with Eric Ellis. I stood to take control of several of his business ventures, plus one more for every baby he knocked you up with."

God, she was thankful she wasn't ordering food, or else she would have projectile vomited across the table at the thought of procreating with Eric. She wasn't looking for any offspring with anybody, and Liam was a prime example of why birth control was a life necessity.

"I knew one day you might find evidence that Dad left you everything, but I never expected you to seriously try to take control of it all. I'm glad I began making plans to ensure I could take back what has always been rightfully mine." With the way Liam was now glaring at her, this was the part that burned him up the most. Layne had what he wanted and what he thought he deserved. How toddler-like of him.

She shifted in her seat, refusing to interrupt him and draw this out any longer than necessary.

Liam continued droning on, "Did you know that Kristill had this special ability to suck the information out of just about anyone? Quite literally, her blow jobs were that phenomenal. I'm kind of regretting my decision to kill her when she threatened to tell you everything." He had the nerve to look remorseful.

"I digress, though. Based on her talented efforts, when I found out you would be beating the crap out of some fucker for information months ago, I thought having her tip off the cops would get you busted and thrown behind bars." He shook his head with disappointment that it hadn't gone that way at all.

"I had to change up my strategy after that. Thanks to that beautifully sloppy mouth of hers, the judge granted me release on my own recognizance. After that, it was smooth sailing, dropping a few pennies into several pockets to keep it all very hush-hush. I wanted our reunion to be a surprise. Shooting your husband instead of you was just a happy little accident." His smile was filled with anything but warmth upon his last statement.

Layne leaned over in her seat after she memorized every damn word he was saying to her. She spoke through her clenched jaw, "Fuck. You. You're a goddamn embarrassment to our family name."

Her brother sat there for a second in silence before he also leaned in closer from the other side of the table, lowering his voice. "As the Upper East Side whore, who really is the embarrassment here?"

The temptation to reach back for her gun and off him in the middle of the restaurant was growing by the second. She ran quick calculations on the likelihood of ending up in prison without either Joey or Gage, and it wasn't odds she wanted to take. But hell, if it wasn't an enticing thought.

Layne eased back into her seat. "Why the hell am I here, then? What do you want?"

Seeing her back down from the edge of her temper, ready to explode, he also sat back. "Everything. Every asset, every dollar, and all the damn respect that I've been owed. If I get that, I'll give you a once-in-a-lifetime opportunity to leave New York and never come back."

He was the worst fucking liar. "Why don't you just try shooting me again? Because you're not getting any of those things from me." She had clawed her way from the bottom to get where she was. Layne wasn't about to give it up because her brother suddenly found his balls and showed up to the game.

"Oh, believe me, Layne, I will, and I won't miss. I'm being gracious enough to try and make this as peaceful of a transition as possible. Now that you know how serious I am, I'm hoping you will come to your senses." He plucked up a fortune cookie off a plate in the middle of the table and cracked it open. Pulling the little paper message out, he barked out a laugh. "Shit, it seems that even my fortune knows I'm destined for greatness."

When Liam tossed the rectangular piece of paper at her, she rolled her eyes and looked at the message typed on it, 'There can only be one crown found through greatness in forming unexpected alliances.' Well, this was the biggest piece of vague bullshit she had read from an all-foreseeing cookie.

Her brother checked his phone before tucking it into the interior breast pocket of his suit. "As much as I would love to stay here and discuss this further, I have some clients who are waiting on me. I will be in touch but just know one more thing. If you start taking too long to come to terms with this, I won't hesitate to forcefully take everything you have one asset at a time. If it comes to that point, I will find more creative and personal methods to persuade you to cooperate."

Liam got out of his seat and straightened out his suit

jacket, smoothing his hands over the front of it. He came over to her side, placing one hand on the back of her chair and the other on the edge of the table. Bowing his head down, he whispered to her, "I heard Rebecca is still single; do you think she still has that middle-school crush on me?"

That was the tipping point. Her anger spilled over the edge, and she began to rise from her seat, ready to break her hand on his face a thousand times over. Her brother anticipated as much and grabbed her roughly by the back of the neck, forcing her back down into her seat.

Keeping his words quiet, he snarled into her ear. "Fucking try me, Layne. I've made a lot more friends than you even realize. I could blow your damn brains out right now, then sit down for some kung pao chicken, and nobody here would blink a damn eye."

She winced as his grasp on her painfully tightened. Just when she thought maybe her head would pop off her shoulders like a broken bobblehead, his hand released her, leaving a red mark behind on her fair skin.

He straightened up and gave her a pleasant smile like they just had the best time catching up. "This was nice; I'm looking forward to our next chat sometime soon. Enjoy the rest of your day, sis." Liam nodded to the two men he had drawn attention to earlier, and both got up from their respective tables. The three of them left the Chinese restaurant, leaving Layne behind.

Layne sat there hoping to feel a sense of relief now that he was gone, but that sense of dread never lifted.

Chapter Six

CONFESSIONS

ayne sat there inside Gage's Jeep, staring at her phone cradled in her palm. The logo popped up on the screen as it powered back on. Moments after it booted up, the backlogged text messages from the group chat between her, Gage, and Joey began to pour in.

GAGE

Where are you?

JOEY

Answer your damn phone.

GAGE

Layne?

Baby, we need to know you're safe.

JOEY

Layne, so help me.

Where the fuck did you go??

Give us something to work with.

GAGE

You don't get to get up and ditch us like you're the only one capable of making decisions in this relationship!

THIS IS FUCKING BULLSHIT!!

That's when the texts stopped coming in from Gage. Joey had sent several more repeating things he had already said. It had been the only thing they could do without more information on her whereabouts. Gage tended to be more patient with her, so the fact he had lost his shit in the chat had her shrinking down lower into a darker headspace than she was already in.

Layne leaned forward in the driver's seat, resting her forehead against the worn and faded leather-wrapped steering wheel. She tried to rein in all the competing emotions of guilt, stress, fear, and anger. She knew that leaving without saying a word to either of them was less than fair, but risking their lives thanks to her brother's newfound penchant for retribution was also unfair. Seeing Joey on the cusp of death was an image that would never leave her and one she never wished to see again.

Her phone began ringing in her hand. Lifting her head upright, she saw Gage's name sprawled across the top of the screen. She frowned, preparing to get an earful. Her finger swiped, and she answered, "Hey, I'm okay." She figured reassuring him she wasn't lying dead in an alley somewhere probably was at the top of the list of things to say.

Waiting for Gage to scream or even say anything at all felt like an eternity.

He blew out a breath of air into the phone. "What the hell, Layne?" His tone wasn't loud or angry but was full of a wearisome relief.

When she wasn't greeted with the same level of aggression he had reflected in his last texts to her, she hoped it meant he would give her the chance to explain herself.

"Look, I'm sorry I didn't say anything. I can explain, but I can't talk about it while you're still there at the hospital. Tell Joey I didn't have a choice or time to spare." The last thing she wanted was for either of them to think that she had worried them without good reason. "I can come back to the hospital to pick you up, then fill you in." Not knowing where Liam had prying ears, Layne didn't dare risk saying anything out loud about his continued threats directed at those she loved the most.

Gage responded, "Don't bother. I got a ride back to your place; I hoped maybe you'd show up here. Just… Just come home, and we can talk about it. I'll let Joey know you're alright."

She nodded, even though he couldn't see it. "Thanks. I'll be there in twenty."

When Gage hung up with Layne, he shook his head, still pissed off. He had the call on speaker so Joey could listen as they both stood there in the living room of O'Reilly Manor.

"She better have a damn good excuse for this shit." He looked over at Joey. The last time she had gone missing had been at the hands of the she-bitch, Danielle Spencer. That had been enough hell for him to endure for years to come.

Joey perched himself on the arm of the sofa, arms

crossed in front of his chest. "Let me deal with it when she gets here." His hand lifted to pinch the bridge of his nose as the sound of her voice had given him hope that whatever had pulled her away left her unscathed.

Shaking his head, Gage shoved his phone into his pocket. "No, this is a problem for all three of us." He let his thoughts begin to unravel and get the better of him again. "Fuck! What was going through her head to take off like that? Is she trying to get herself killed?"

All Joey could do was shrug as he was wondering the same things as his brother. He knew Layne, he knew her weak spots, and that meant Liam likely knew them as well. If he had anything to do with what had drawn her out into the open, he feared this wouldn't be the last time.

Finally, Joey stood up from his spot on the sofa and walked over to Gage. "You can't push her too hard until we know what happened. She'll push back and then shut down entirely."

Gage didn't like it, but he knew the last thing they wanted was for her to feel like she wasn't safe to confide in him and Joey. They both loved her deeply, more than life itself, and their feelings for her had no contingencies. If she was getting pulled into a shitty situation, they were going to dive into it with her. The tricky part was getting her to understand and accept that.

The entire drive back uptown, Layne was caught up in her thoughts. Was it worth fighting this battle with Liam? What were her options when the risks involved some incredibly hefty costs? What went on when Joey took his contracts? The second her doubts about Joey's loyalty to her heart sprang up inside her mind; she felt a pang of guilt for even questioning his faithfulness. But…

She parked the Jeep out front and walked up the porch steps slowly. Each step was slower than the last as she approached the front door with dread of the conversation she was going to have with Gage.

Pushing the door open and walking in, she called out, "Gage?" She shut the door behind her.

"I'm in here," he called from the living room.

Layne walked through the foyer and into the living room, where she saw him sitting on one of the ottomans that paired with an oversized chair. He was leaning forward with his elbows on his knees. His tender eyes looked up to gaze at her, still reflecting the pain of her disappearance and the disappointment in the lack of her trust to confide in him.

Her face fell, and her heart crumpled as she saw the way he was still struggling with what she had done and put him through. She began her heartfelt apology, "I'm so, so sorry, Gage. I couldn't…"

That's when a hand came and grabbed her hip from behind, turning her around to come face-to-face with Joey.

"Couldn't what, Layney?" He guided her backward until the wall was flush with her spine, and he was leaning into her space with his other hand braced against the wall.

From the light scent of soap and the sight of his dirty blonde hair still damp, he must have just gotten out of the shower. The rest of him was dressed in a pair of jeans and a long-sleeved crimson tee. It had been far too long since she had seen him in anything from the bland and unflattering hospital gown.

Her eyes widened in disbelief that she was seeing him standing there before her in the home they shared. He should have still been in the hospital; he wasn't slated to be released for a couple of weeks. Blinking several times through the shock of it all, she glanced over at Gage, who was now getting up off of the ottoman to join them both.

Joey's hand left her hip and cupped her jaw, turning her attention back to him. "Eyes on me. You couldn't what, Layne? Couldn't be bothered to tell us where you were running off to? Couldn't care less what the hell we would think? Go ahead, explain to us what you couldn't do."

Layne's mind was still stuck on processing his presence before her. "They discharged you?"

Gage spoke up from a step behind his brother, "He discharged himself when we didn't know where the fuck you were."

She pitched herself forward into Joey's chest, wrapping her arms around his waist as immense relief overcame her. "Thank God!" Her eyes squeezed shut tightly as she inhaled the hint of leather and sage that had been missing the entire time he had been a patient at the hospital. Having him home again gave her back a little peace of mind.

The very sudden and emotional reaction had been unexpected. Joey had been ready for her to barrage him with her headstrong attitude about why she had done what she had. He had been prepared to hear her tout something along the lines of being capable of defending herself in dangerous situations. He hadn't expected her to fall victim to a softer set of emotions.

His arms embraced her upper body, holding her close despite the lack of answers about her whereabouts. Joey sighed, and his voice softened as he pressed a kiss to the top of her head. As angry as he was about her choices, it felt good to wrap his arms around her again without all the excess medical equipment getting in the way.

When she was ready, she pulled her head from his chest with her stunning green eyes soaked with her recently shed tears. She sniffled and rushed to erase them from her face with the backs of her fingers. "Sorry..."

"Baby," Gage moved to the side of them. "Don't be sorry; we just need to know what the hell happened." His hand came to the small of her back and gently rubbed it to help soothe whatever feelings had those pretty little eyes tearing up.

She shook her head and looked down. Without hesitation, Joey's fingers captured her chin and tilted her head back up. The concern was painted across his face. "There's nothing the three of us can't figure out," he assured her.

"I underestimated Liam." She went to lower her face again, but Joey's hold on her chin prevented her from hiding herself from either of them. "This is all my fault; I should have seen the signs. He's been making moves since God knows when. At this point, I'm beginning to question whether or not he has been plotting shit since he was born."

At the mention of Liam, Gage's jaw tensed, and his eyes darkened with fury. "Please tell me you didn't take off on us to go meet up with him. Not after what he did."

Layne didn't need to say anything. When her eyes looked at Gage apologetically, it had him grumbling under his breath, "Son of a bitch."

Joey shot a hard glance at Gage, warning him to keep himself in check. Then, he looked at Layne and ran his fingers along the side of her face before sliding them into the depths of her brunette locks. "None of this is your fault. If I ever hear you say that again, I will wash your mouth out with my cock every night for a month straight."

He pulled her mouth up to his before whispering against her lips, "And before you get too excited about that prospect, I should add that it won't be getting buried in other parts of you afterward."

Closing his grasp on a handful of her hair, he remained painfully close to the pale pink of her lips. "Do you under-stand me, Layney?"

As quiet as a mouse, she uttered her response, "Yes." It was hard to tell if Joey was bluffing or not, the man had yet to show any amount of restraint when it came to fucking her. However, she enjoyed his cock in her too much to find out just how much he was willing to stick to his word.

"Good. Now," he released her hair and leaned back away from her without ever gracing her with the kiss she had been expecting. "Go sit your ass down and tell us everything."

Both her brows lifted the second he retreated from her. "You're not even going to bother giving me a kiss?"

"If I put my mouth on you right now, the only discus-sion that will end up taking place is going to be you screaming out my name." One thing Joey didn't have was an infinite amount of control. After a few weeks of going without so much as a hand-job from her, he barely trusted himself to be in the same room as her without yanking her pants down and jackhammering into her.

When she looked over at Gage for some level of backup, he merely shrugged at her. "Don't look at me, Lucky Charm. You're going to have a lot to answer for when I get my hands on you."

Great. She knew she had some explanations to make, but she hardly expected to have them both keeping their distance from her in the interim.

Layne took up a spot in the center of the couch. They both followed, and while Gage seemed to prefer standing, Joey sat across the way in a plush armchair. Both sets of brown eyes were on her, patiently waiting for her to lay everything out on the table.

She started from the moment that Liam had called her and walked them through everything up until the time he left the House of the Chinese Dragon. Neither of the guys interrupted her, though, at some points, it looked like Joey was going to put his fist through the glass coffee table in front of him.

"I couldn't risk it, not knowing whether or not he could actually follow through on his threats." Layne sank back into the couch now that she had retold the entire incident.

Gage squinted his eyes in confusion, trying to follow Liam's logic. "Wait. Besides the part where he's a whiny bitch unable to cope with you being in charge, part of this whole damn thing is because he's pissed thinking that Joey executed a contract on your mom?" He scoffed in disbelief.

She shifted uncomfortably, as did Joey. It wasn't a topic they often discussed. They had talked about it enough times to work through the painful realities of it. Layne had gotten to a place where she was able to redirect the blame onto the man who had given the orders, Michael Franzetti. If it hadn't been Joey, it would have just been someone else.

Noticing the awkward silence that fell upon both Layne and Joey, Gage blinked several times in disbelief. He looked at Joey. "Seriously? That's fucked up."

Joey cleared his throat to try and push past the lingering guilt over it. "It was long before I knew Layne." There wasn't a day that passed where he didn't regret that entire fucking contract.

Shifting his attention back over to Layne, Gage now better understood Joey's insistence about being there for Layne on her mother's death anniversary.

Layne busied her hands with a strand of her hair between her fingers as she thought about what else Liam had said about Joey's past. It was something she had deemed unnecessary to bring up during the rundown. "Yeah, so, that's about it. He left it pretty fuckin' vague on when he expected me to get my affairs in order. It could be tomorrow, or it could be three months from now, for all I know."

Standing, Joey pulled out his phone from his pocket and began texting quickly. "I'll get Brandon working on seeing what he can find out about the two other guys that showed up to the lunch date with Liam." After several more taps of the screen, he sent the request over and returned the device to where it came from.

Having a better understanding of why Layne had done what she had, Gage came over to sit next to her on the couch. "Baby," he placed a hand on her thigh. "I'm sorry I lost it. I know you want to make sure everybody is safe, but you can't do that when you don't have someone watching your back."

"He's right, Layne. This can't be an ongoing thing. If Liam knows hanging this threat over your head will lure you to him, he will keep playing that card for as long as he can," Joey piped up, also rising and joining them on the couch on the other side of her.

She looked at them both, wondering how she got so lucky. Two men who loved her to a fault. Two men who would never rest when it came to her protection. Two men who were way too close to her to have any sense at all. Layne wondered how soon her luck would turn bad if she didn't start playing some Russian roulette.

Chapter Seven

HELLO & GOODBYE

"Joey! Fuck! Joey!" Layne cried out as his hips slammed into her again.

After they discussed Layne's little disappearing act to have a chat with Liam, it seemed the air shifted around them quicker than an approaching hurricane. When she leaned over Joey to place her gun and its holster on the side table, his most primal instincts had taken over. The way her body brushed against him in that innocent movement, the light curve of her back that led over her ass which was all but short of presenting itself in front of him, and the quiet groan she made as her arm stretched to reach over to the table on his left. Joey's restraint promptly left the building.

His cock had dictated that it find itself deep inside of her with such an urgency that when he grabbed Layne, the startled look on her face drove him even further into a frenzy. He had tossed her onto her stomach on the sofa and yanked her pants down enough to expose the sight of her pussy that he would happily risk a torturous death for. Joey barely waited for a breath after opening his jeans and pulling out his aggressive hard-on before he shoved himself inside her like a man who had been stranded in the goddamn Sahara, and her body was the oasis he needed to survive.

Layne felt his hands tightly gripping her hips for dear life as he rammed his steel-like cock into her. Her pleasure immediately blindsided her, leaving her moaning out intensely without so much as a chance to ask him what he was doing. His rough entry had her cunt aching as it stretched around him. Yet, all of it was welcomed after the medically mandated hiatus.

He hadn't been the only one that had missed this. While Gage had been more than happy to tend to all of her needs, he still wasn't Joey. Each De Luca had their own particular flavor, and she couldn't handle not having a little bit of both swirled together in her life.

Standing in front of the couch, Gage was giving his brother the moment to satisfy himself with Layne, but he was sure as hell staying for the show. His hand was fisting his cock as he watched their girl get her pussy claimed in a moment of heated passion. "Goddamn, baby," he groaned. "You're taking Joey's cock so well." His brother sure as hell wasn't going easy on her, but Layne still welcomed him with open arms, er…legs.

Kneeling behind Layne while he roughly fucked her from behind, Joey groaned out. "That's right, Layney." He panted hard at the physical exertion on his still-recovering body. He growled, pushing at his limits, "Take this cock like my good fucking girl." Despite getting winded, he didn't give a damn if his heart exploded, he was going to get his fix of her one way or another.

Each harsh thrust into her had her body lurching forward, only to have Joey's grasp pull her hips right back against him. There was no escaping the mounting pressure that was building deep inside her core. Every collision of their bodies had his dick crashing against her sweet spot.

Her hands clawed at the cushions underneath her as her body trembled with the rapidly approaching climax. She whimpered his name as she teetered right on the border of divine release.

That's when Joey smirked and sank himself into her again. "You better show me how much you enjoy getting fucked by your husband while Daddy Gage watches." His hand reached down to grab her hair enough to turn her head so she could see Gage handling his swords in a smooth corkscrew motion.

Joey rolled his hips into her again, watching her face as it showed signs of slipping right off the ledge of ecstasy. Her vocalized orgasm filled the room and was music to his damn ears. His cock was throbbing, and he had barely made it this far along without blowing his load, so when he felt Layne's walls clamp down around him, he knew he was done for.

Her body pushed and pulled at him simultaneously as she fell into the crashing waves of her release. She wasn't even sure what words poured out of her mouth or if they were even words at all.

With Layne's body coming for him, Joey hastily got the

final few thrusts into her before he joined in the blissful state of relief. His dick pulsed as he filled her depths with his hot seed.

When it was all said and done, Joey was still trying to catch his damn breath. It felt like he had just run a marathon—untrained. Oh, but it had been worth it.

His hand patted Layne's ass after he pulled out of her with a satisfied sigh. He fell back onto his ass and let the couch give him the rest he needed.

That was Gage's cue that he was up. He came over to her and eased her from the couch, not intending to make her well-worked cunt take any more dick today. He smiled at her and got her down on her knees in front of him, his thick cock in front of her face already primed by the efforts of his hand.

"Alright, baby, let me see you swallow my swords." Gage grinned at her, his thumb tugging at the bottom of her chin to draw her mouth open.

Late the following night, the three of them showed up at Rebecca's apartment. Layne was doing her best to ignore the soreness from Joey's pounding into her yesterday as she walked. Firmly, she rapped her knuckles against her best friend's door.

There was the sound of the scurrying on the other side of the door, Rebecca called out, "Be right there!"

Layne's heart already ached that it was coming down to this, but it was in everyone's best interest. She couldn't afford to be selfish when Liam was out there ready to prey on anybody who held value to Layne.

Rebecca turned the lock from the other side before swinging the door open. Her face was full of emotion as she saw Layne standing there, mirroring the same feelings. Joey and Gage stood at Layne's back, giving the girls enough space to greet one another.

"Are you ready?" Layne looked down at a few bags sitting just right inside the doorway. Maybe if she just focused on the checklist of things in her head, she could avoid turning both of them into a sappy puddle of emotions.

That all went out the window as Rebecca immediately grabbed onto Layne and squeezed her into a hug that was tighter than life itself. Layne rested her head on Rebecca's shoulder as she shut her eyes, returning the hug equally tight.

"I told myself I wasn't going to cry," Rebecca gave a half-hearted giggle overtop a partial sob.

Layne sniffled, trying to ignore the tears welling up behind her closed lids. All Layne could do was nod, afraid that if she said anything, she would lose her already shaky composure.

When Rebecca pulled back, she noted Layne's fingers were already trying to erase any evidence of the tears that had begun to slip from her green hues. She frowned, not liking the way this situation had Layne in such a pained state.

"I shouldn't be leaving you like this," Rebecca tried to push back on Layne's demand that she pack her bags and indefinitely go live with her mother several states away.

Immediately, Layne straightened up and snapped her guarded exterior back into place. "Rebecca, you are getting on the train, and don't you dare say otherwise."

Her best friend's voice wavered underneath the weight of the thought of abandoning someone whom she held such a tight bond with. "I want to be here for you." The blue eyes looking at Layne right now were filled with the pain of the unknown, swirling with concern and sadness.

Layne stood there in silence as she tried to find the words to make her friend understand why it was necessary for her to suddenly pick up and leave. The breath of her inhale was rocky but managed to smooth out when it was exhaled. "I don't know what is going to happen. Liam is no longer who I thought he was; he has threatened everyone and anyone in my world. I'll be damned if I let you get caught in his crossfire. I can't deal with him when I'm worried about who will end up as collateral. I won't do it, Rebecca."

Frowning, Rebecca still felt a sense of disbelief that it was all coming to this. Liam may have been the asshole little brother, but it was hard to imagine that he would fall this far down the path of depravity.

Joey spoke up, trying to give them both a gentle reminder, "We need to get going if we are going to make it there on time."

Following up on that, Gage came to the doorway. "I'll get your bags."

After collecting Rebecca's luggage, they all went back

down to Joey's car. Rebecca climbed into the backseat first. Before Layne joined her, Gage paused her with his hand on her shoulder.

"It's only temporary." He ran his hand up along the side of her neck before stroking his thumb across her cheek tenderly. It killed him to see Layne making the difficult decision of parting ways with a piece of her heart, not knowing what was going to happen after this was all done and over.

Layne stared into his gentle eyes, and she wanted more than anything to believe him. "I hope so." She ducked into the backseat.

After each of the guys took up the seats up front, Joey drove them to Penn Station. The air was thick with silence the entire trip. Rebecca reached over and held Layne's hand tightly. It was the only communication needed between them.

Once they were inside the busy train station, Layne stood in front of Rebecca. "I know there's a lot up in the air right now, so I want you to take this." She reached into her coat pocket and pulled out a thick envelope. "It should be more than enough to pay the bills for a few months."

Rebecca shook her head adamantly. "Layne…I can't take this." Her hand pushed the envelope back toward Layne.

"No, you can. Please, Rebecca." Layne reached over, grabbed her friend's hand, and placed the money-filled envelope into her palm. "It's the least I can do for uprooting you away from your life here so suddenly."

Reluctantly, her friend accepted the wad of cash safely

secured in the envelope. Shoving it into one of her bags, she gratefully looked at Layne. "I plan on giving every dollar in here straight back to you when I come back."

Forcing a light smile past the looming goodbyes quickly approaching them, Layne leaned in for one last hug. "And I will still argue with you when you do."

A barely coherent voice came over the speaker system, announcing the boarding for Rebecca's train. Rebecca squeezed Layne even tighter than she had earlier. "Be safe."

Layne responded with as much reassurance as she could muster, "I always am."

"Fucking liar," Rebecca quickly retorted with a grin.

They both shared a soft laugh to overshadow the grim truth.

Releasing the woman she considered a sister, Layne shooed her with her hand. "Get outta here before you miss your train."

Drawing in a breath to find the courage to go through with this, Rebecca looked at the two men standing close by. "You two better take care of her." She wagged a finger at them threateningly.

Joey grinned. "Don't worry, Rebecca, she's in good hands."

"As long as she listens to us for once," Gage smirked, then shot a look at Layne.

Rebecca put on her bravest face, readjusted the strap of her bag over her shoulder, and pulled her miniature suitcase with her as she took the first steps towards the stairs leading down to the platform. Before she was out of sight, she looked back at Layne and blew her a kiss.

Without a second thought, Layne blew one right back. She didn't want to imagine if this was her bestie's last memory of their time together, but Layne sure as hell hoped it would be a positive one.

She stood there long after Rebecca disappeared down the steps to get on that train down to Baltimore. "Now is your chance to join her if either of you want a ticket out. I'm not going to ask either of you to stay here with me, knowing how messy this is going to get."

Layne knew it was a long shot, but she wished they would both take her up on the offer. If she didn't need to worry about either man's safety, maybe there was a chance she could keep her head screwed on straight.

"Always and forever, Layney. You're not getting rid of me that easily." Joey's hand slid across her upper back to rest on her shoulder.

Gage's hand did the same and rested on her opposite shoulder. "You're my Lucky Charm, that's not something that you just leave behind. I'm afraid you're stuck with me too, baby."

She slowly nodded. "Okay, then. Let's find out what other fucked up plans Liam has."

Chapter Eight

FAMILY DISPUTES

Layne groaned, rubbing the heels of her palms over her eyes as she sat at her desk. It was nearly three in the damn morning. She knew she was burning the candle at both ends but couldn't find it within herself to give a fuck and surrender to her body's demands for rest. Time was of the essence if she was playing catch-up on whatever strategy Liam had been concocting for months if not years.

She had snuck out of bed in her black joggers and matching cropped camisole, leaving Joey soundly asleep while he caught up on his still much-needed rest and recovery. Despite his reassurances, he was nowhere near back to his prime after the shooting.

As for her other love, Gage was likely wrapping up at Cassidy's Chains about now, the recently renamed strip club-turned-night club. Whether he intended to come back here or just crash at his condo was always a toss-up on any given night.

After speaking with her senior advisor, Thomas, earlier in the evening, it was noted that the relations between her alliances were getting dicey. Contradicting reports were coming in about who did and did not support Layne after the misfortune of events the day she and Joey were married. Some factions thought Liam's move was ballsy enough that perhaps he was a worthy connection to side with. Regardless of Thomas' words of comfort, this would all blow over in time; she didn't feel any less stressed out. All her hard work to get where she was, and now Liam's emergence was fucking it to hell and back.

Now, here she was listening to Jonathan, her prized political negotiator, about how another faction was refusing to do so much as keep their eyes or ears open for Liam and whatever crew he was working with. How was it that no one could tell her the extent of what he had managed to pull together underneath her nose? He had gone dark, and nobody knew a thing? She found that fucking hard to believe.

"There's nothing I can do about it," Jonathan apologized for the umpteenth time on the other end of the phone that lay on top of her desk on speaker. He continued, "The Holskis are claiming that they don't want involvement in a family dispute."

"*Family dispute?!*" she shrieked. Great, just fucking great. Another flakey-ass criminal organization was going to turn a blind eye. Trying to reel herself back in, she lowered the volume of her voice. "Keep putting pressure on them, make whatever negotiations you have to. I don't care what the hell it costs, we can't afford to lose support right now."

After their goodbyes, Layne hung up and pushed away from the desk. She walked over to the window that overlooked the street out front. It was as empty as the room she was standing in.

Alone with her thoughts, she got lost in the web of hypotheticals being woven in her brain. Were any of them going to be left standing at the end of this? Could she pull the trigger to end her brother's life? Maybe if she gave herself up, Joey and Gage would have a chance at survival.

Her train of thought was interrupted as her cell phone began ringing from its position on her desk. Layne rushed over and answered, "Yes?"

Silence.

"Hello?" Her voice carried the crankiness from her lack of sleep. She double-checked to make sure the call was still connected before she repeated herself.

More silence.

She turned her back to the door so she could perch her ass on the edge of her desk. "Oh, for fucks sake," she was prepared to hang up until she heard the silence breaking on the other end.

Liam's laughter echoed in the receiver like he had just delivered the world's funniest punchline. "Jesus Christ, Layne. You sound stressed. You should learn to let loose a bit. Go get a massage or some shit."

If she hadn't been dealing with high blood pressure before, she sure as hell was now when she heard him on the other end of the line.

"What the fuck do you want?" she muttered tiredly.

"Just checking in on my big sister, making sure you're doing okay. Is that a crime?" Liam nearly had her convinced for a split second that he gave a damn.

Looking at the clock hung on the wall, she forced out her exhale. "Given what time it is, yes."

"Hmph," Liam seemed to take offense. "I guess I will get straight to the point. Have you decided if you're going to be surrendering control of all your assets to me?"

"I've been a little busy. I know this might be difficult for you to understand, Liam, but running this business requires a lot of work. So, if you'd—"

The phone was taken right out of her hand. When she gazed at the thief, Gage stood there with fire blazing in his eyes as he put the phone to his ear. She had never even heard him come in.

His massive hand looked like it was about to crush her cell as his body filled with palpable tension. "Look here, shithead. You come fuckin' near her again; I will kill you. You call her again, I will kill you. You so much as mention her name, I will kill you. Do you get my drift?"

Layne dropped down onto her feet from her seat on her desk and attempted to pry the phone from Gage.

Easily keeping it out of reach from her, he pointed at her and then the chair aggressively. He mouthed the word 'sit' with such force she nearly heard it shouted from his thoughts.

Slowly, she sank into the office chair as she waited for Gage to conclude his talk with her brother.

Gage was greeted with Liam's sniggering. "Oh, you must be the other one I've been hearing so much about. Couldn't find a woman of your own, so you had to settle for passing my sister back and forth between you and your brother? Seems real fuckin' pathetic if you ask me."

The twitching in Gage's jaw was visible despite the dim lighting of the office. His anger was rolling off of him and very quickly filling the room. He responded through clenched teeth, "That's a lot of big talk from a little fucking man."

Liam's cocky attitude danced along his words, "Tell *Layne* she better start making up her mind on what she wants." His emphasis on his sister's name was clearly intentional after Gage's threat. "I've got far less patience than she does, and I have my eyes set on taking back a lot of things that belong to me."

Before Gage could snap back, the call went silent as Liam disconnected. He looked at the phone before dropping it down onto her desk. "Goddamn asshole!"

Layne sat there staring at him, unsure of what to say to ease him down.

The brown hues of his eyes were filled with the darkness of his current mood. "I don't want you fucking talking to him again. Not without Joey or me present. God knows what bullshit he's going to start filling your head with. Do you understand me?"

He rubbed a hand over his short blonde beard, the frustration painted all over his face. His eyes shifted to Layne when she began to get up from her seat. "Just go upstairs and get to bed, it's late." There wasn't much pleasantry in his voice as he ordered her to leave like a child being sent to bed.

Trying to provide a level of comfort, she softly spoke as she reached out a hand to his tensed arm, "Gage—"

Jerking his arm out of her reach, he raised his voice. "What?!" The sharpness of the word cut through her as it bounced off the walls of the room. "I don't need you to be a brat right now!"

Gage was normally her source of comfort when things were stressful, but hearing him lash out at her made her second-guess all she wanted to say. She shook her head, deciding it wasn't worth saying anything at all. Instead, she pushed past him on her way to leave the office.

After seeing the hurt he inflicted reflecting in her eyes, his face softened, and a pang of guilt struck his heart. "Layne, baby…" He only needed to break into a light jog for his longer legs to catch up to her shorter strides. His hand gently took her elbow before she was able to get past the office door.

He gently pulled her up to him. "I'm sorry. You didn't deserve that."

She wiggled her elbow from his hand, doing what she did best, and withdrew from uncomfortable conversations and feelings. "It's fine. I'm going to bed like you told me to." The attitude saturated her tone, indicating all was not as fine as she wanted it to seem.

He picked up on it, seeing right through the veil she was trying to hide behind. "No, you're not. You're going to bed because you're pissed." Gage frowned at her, realizing that they were all dealing with short fuses around here, and he was no exception.

Layne tried to laugh it off as a ridiculous notion, but it fell flat and unconvincing. She crossed her arms in front of her to help bolster her defenses that she was holding her shit together. "Whatever you say, Gage."

God help him, he wanted to shake her by her shoulders when her stubbornness flared up like this. Instead, he opted for a different approach and smirked at her.

His hand slid up the front of her throat. "That's right. When your Daddy tells you to do something, you do it." Gage's voice dropped into a low and gravelly tone that made her knees weak.

Her eyes lifted to meet his, struggling to maintain the heat of her anger. "I'm not in the mood." Her voice was already betraying how much his touch was taming her temper.

Gage brought his mouth to her ear as his grasp on her tightened slowly, "Did I ask if you were in the mood? Be a good girl and meet me in the movie room in five minutes." His lips nibbled at the bottom of her ear lobe before he pulled back and released his hand from her neck.

She felt him give her ass a nudge of encouragement to get moving. Still irritated with his outburst at her, she huffed but turned slowly and left the room. Despite the temptation to ignore his request, she opted to hit the bathroom before going to the room that housed the scaled-down movie theater.

He was there waiting for her, lounging back in one of the double-wide leather recliners with a remote in his hand.

"If you're expecting to get laid, you've got another thing coming," she warned him.

A goofy grin spread across his face. "If *you're* expecting to get laid, *you've* got another thing coming," he parroted back at her. His hand patted the vacant space next to him.

Tilting her head in confusion at his comments, she warily approached. Climbing into the seat to his right, she drew her legs up onto the recliner with her as she got comfortable.

Leaning over, Gage's arm wrapped around her shoulders and drew her in close while his left hand grabbed a blanket and draped it over both their laps. Using the remote, he turned on the digital movie projector, illuminating the screen with the opening credits of Layne's favorite movie.

Seeing that he finally gave in to watching her favorite cult classic from the eighties with her, a small piece of her attitude faded away.

Reclining the oversized seat back, he squeezed her against his side, allowing her to rest her head on his shoulder. "Comfy?" He smiled lightly at her.

Layne nodded. It was hard not to be comfortable when he was securely holding her, and the faint scent of his toasted vanilla cologne was wafting over her.

"I shouldn't have yelled at you," his apology was full of remorse for the hurt he inflicted on her. The only pain he ever wanted to bring her was the type that was paired with intensely gratifying pleasure. His hand rubbed over her arm soothingly.

Not hearing her jumping to forgive him, he realized he had a little more work to do.

Lightly sighing, he ran his hand down over her side. "The thought of ever watching you slip through my fingers would have me battling the darkest of demons. I may not deserve you, Layne, but I will never stop fiercely loving you."

She tilted her head to look up at him as he made his heartwarming profession to her. His words were so full of raw honesty backed by his love that Layne couldn't help but allow the rest of her anger to melt away.

Her hand reached up and pulled his face down to hers, accepting his apology with her lips connecting to his. Her tongue easily pushed into his mouth, exploring the addictive taste of him.

Falling into the sweet caress of her mouth against his, he knew all the bruises to his heart from years gone by were well on their way to fading for good, and it was all due to the woman currently in his arms.

Layne's lips drifted from his after several tender moments, her hand stroking over the side of his scruffy cheek. Without the obstruction of her defenses, her eyes shimmered despite the only light coming off the movie screen. "If I ever slip through your fingers, it's because I feel most at home in your heart."

Relieved that there was still hope they could make it through the ongoing nightmare Liam pitched them into, Gage showered her with several more kisses to erase the invisible wounds his words had created after the rare moment of losing his temper.

Once they both settled back on the cozy dual recliner, it wasn't any longer than ten minutes before Layne was lulled to sleep with the movie still playing on the big screen in front of them. Gage's hold never fell away from her as she passed out, listening to the sound of his heart beating in his chest.

Chapter Nine

GASOLINE

After Sean's grotesque passing, McGregor's no longer held the same atmosphere and appeal it used to. Maybe Layne was just projecting her feelings, but the joint used to hold a sense of home and belonging that had seemingly been torn from it. Sean not only had been the face everyone saw behind the bar but his dry humor and work ethic turned the joint into a safe haven for many.

With such a presence now missing, Layne had a hell of a time finding the right owner to replace the man who had been the backbone of this establishment for as long as she had been alive.

It had been sheer luck that Jillian, Sean's niece, was looking to move back to the city. She was every bit of a spitfire that Layne was. Turned out she had experience managing a bar in the rougher parts of Chicago for several years. But when Jillian got homesick, she put up the dive bar for sale and decided the Big Apple was where her heart was.

At first, Layne was wary of Jillian's ability to turn a blind eye to the seedy business transactions that occurred at McGregor's Pub. However, in the first week that she was running things, it was made clear she was a perfect fit.

Layne and Ethan had been meeting to discuss business as usual when a disgruntled drunk not only disparaged Ethan's favorite waitress but refused to leave her a tip. Layne's senior enforcer didn't take kindly to it and, in a move of stupidity, ended up stabbing the man's hand and pinning it to the table with a steak knife. It took everything Layne had not to do the same to Ethan for his lack of awareness and unsound judgment.

Jillian's reaction had been outrage, but not because a member of Layne's crew had just blatantly attacked one of the patrons. No, she had been pissed because of the mess the drunkard's blood left on the table. Ethan had been made to apologize to Jillian and forced to clean up after his moment of indiscretion. Layne had never seen the table so shiny and clean in the entire history of McGregor's.

Currently, with the anniversary of Shannon O'Reilly's death only days away, Layne was checking the accounting records earlier in the month than usual. This was going to be the first year that Layne didn't show up to her favorite pub for her annual inebriated shitshow.

While Jillian seemed to fit in with the rest of the criminally inclined crowd, Layne didn't feel comfortable exposing the more vulnerable side of herself. This year, with Sean's presence no longer there, it would just add to the dark hole she planned to dive into.

"What are you looking for? Those are the books from months ago," Joey asked as he sat back in his chair with a bottle of cheap beer in his hand.

After the day Layne had suddenly taken off from the hospital, Joey and Gage had made it clear that she wasn't going anywhere without either of them. She would have been more agreeable to a thousand papercuts than having her guys risking their lives for her. But arguing with them had gotten her nowhere; the stubborn assholes dug their heels in just as much as she typically did. Only they used it to their advantage that there were two of them and only one of her. So here Joey was, keeping a watchful eye over her.

Layne had dragged the box of records down from the second floor to a table in the back and was now combing through each of them. "Trying to figure out if I'm as crazy as I feel," she responded with heavy distraction lingering underneath her words that indicated she was mostly talking to herself.

She flipped another page, scanning each line for the very thing that had raised red flags the day Sean was killed.

Joey's hand reached out and stopped her from turning another page. The skull on the back of his hand was staring right at her. Layne looked over at him, "What are you doing?"

"You've hardly said more than a few sentences to me since you got back from meeting with Liam." His look grew serious as he tried to read through the masked expression on her face.

She rolled her eyes. "I disagree." Layne attempted to pry his hand from the book, but he was determined to leave it there. She would have had better luck trying to lift a two-ton vehicle than getting him to budge.

Taking a measured breath, he shook his head. "Sentences that revolve around you moaning out 'God, yes, Joey' don't count." He set the beer bottle on the table in front of him, wiping the condensation it left on his hand on the thigh of his jeans.

Not that he was complaining about both of them getting their insatiable fixes of one another, but she had been incredibly more guarded than normal. It was her raising of defenses that he knew so well that had him the most concerned about what was going on in her head. If her thoughts were spiraling, he needed to put a stop to it.

With a blank look on her face, Layne stared at him, waiting for him to say more. When he refused to back down, she let out a huff. "I'm just trying to figure shit out. The sooner we can resolve this fucking situation with Liam, the sooner we will all get back to normal." It wasn't a total lie, but it wasn't the thing that had been chewing away at her typically steadfast foundation.

It didn't seem that Joey was buying what she was selling as he inched his chair closer to hers. When she attempted to lean back, his hand was suddenly on the back of her neck, forcing her to stay right where she was. "Layney, I was shot in the goddamn chest, not bashed over the head. Do you think I can't tell when you're putting up your barricades? I'm going to give you this one chance to answer my question. What has you pulling away from me?"

The way he asked that question of her tore a little hole in her heart. He may not have been a man who wore his emotions on his sleeve, but she knew him well enough to hear the pain in his words. Her hand came up behind her neck to rest on the back of his hand, which was refusing to let her run and hide from this conversation. After several unsuccessful attempts of her fingers to peel his grasp off of her, she finally dropped her hand back into her lap.

Seeing his lips part to follow up on his unanswered question, she quickly let the words tumble out of her mouth. "I wish you had left the city the same night that Rebecca did."

Joey's hand loosened up its hold on her. "What?" His hand shifted from holding onto the back of her neck firmly, now to gently cradling it. The rich tones of his brown eyes reflected a series of emotions, including one that made her feel guilty for even voicing her confession.

"Please don't look at me like that." She frowned. "I can't think straight with you around. I don't know what to believe anymore, and I can't stand that it was you bleeding all over the church steps that day when it was supposed to be me."

At first, she wasn't sure if he was pissed at her honesty or if he was simply in disbelief that she laid it all out for him. Perhaps it was both.

Deciding to leave the heavy conversation there, she pushed her chair back to get up from her seat. His hand fell away from her neck when she stood. It wasn't more than a fraction of a second before his hand wrapped around hers, ensuring she didn't walk away from him.

He pulled her closer until his other arm drew her down to take a seat on his thigh. "Layne, I want you to listen to me." Both his arms wrapped around her waist, holding her securely.

"I know what you're going to say." She braced herself for him to tell her she was being ridiculous and that she needed to suck it up and deal.

He scoffed. "Are you going to shut the hell up and let me talk?" Joey paused, waiting for her to decide if she was going to let him get out what he needed to tell her.

After a few seconds, he continued, "Do you feel this?" His hand lifted hers to rest on his chest directly over his heart. The light pulse of the muscle circulating blood throughout his body thumped against her palm. "You're the only one that will ever have the power to make it stop beating. That's the only thing you ever need to believe."

Feeling the strong beating beneath her hand it grounded her anxious thoughts. Layne leaned over and pressed her forehead to his, trying to focus on the steady rhythm of his heartbeat. "That's what scares me. You're caught up in all of this mess because of me."

"And I would do it all over again. The day I sat down next to you on that stool over there," he pointed over at the line of stools up against the bar, "was the luckiest day of my life."

"Look at you being all sentimental," she teased lightly.

Joey grinned at her, taking her face with both of his hands. "Now, this is the part where I'm going to tell you to suck it up. You're better than this. Don't try to put out your fire because you're worried about me or anyone else. I want you to pour fuckin' gasoline on that bitch."

A smile cracked at the corners of her mouth.

It was the way her lips curved that he saw the piece of her that had been shaken up after his brush with death beginning to fade to make room for the feisty Irish girl to return. "Speaking of sucking things up, I have something else you can use your mouth on while you're at it," his words lowered into a growl.

Immediately, her hand smacked his shoulder. "You're an ass. You should have quit while you were ahead." She laughed.

He smirked, "There's my girl." He pulled her face to him as his lips possessively locked onto her own.

Layne's hands balled up his shirt as she leaned into the kiss, passionately wrestling with him for control. Her need for more of him escalated quickly as she shifted from being perched on his leg to straddling his lap with her body grinding against him.

It wasn't until Jillian cleared her throat, standing in front of their table with her arms crossed, that Joey and Layne halted their actions.

"You two almost done here? If not, God created these things called alleys you can go fuck in." Jillian motioned at the side door that led outside to the nearest said alley. "I would like to get these books back upstairs before I leave for the day." Her eyes dropped to the accounting records Layne had been perusing.

Biting her lower lip with a sheepish grin, Layne was definitely considering going outside to continue what they had started. Her thumb swiped below Joey's bottom lip, wiping away a bit of leftover saliva from their heated exchange.

She looked over at Jillian as she eased off of Joey's lap and back into her seat. "I am almost done. Just give me a few minutes to finish going through this book, and then we'll be outta here."

Jillian nodded, "Mmhmm," before walking away. She was not entirely convinced the two lovebirds would be able to keep their hands to themselves long enough.

As Layne tried to focus back on the records, her eyes stole a glance over at Joey. Damn, getting through the last few pages of this book was going to take every bit of effort and self-control she had in her. He was sitting back in his chair, legs spread with his hand casually resting on top of the bulge that pushed against the fabric of his jeans.

Telling herself that she could manage to keep her hands to herself for another five minutes, she forced herself to look back down at the book in front of her. Intentionally, she placed an elbow on the table and pressed her fingers to her temple to feebly attempt not to be distracted by him. Where were a set of damn horse blinders when you needed them?

She flipped to the next page, and when she got midway down, she paused. Cocking her head to the right, she blinked a few times.

Abruptly, she popped up from her seat. "This!" Layne snatched up the book, strode over to the bar, and dropped the book down onto the counter in front of Jillian.

She tapped aggressively at the line item that had

captured her attention. "Do you know what this is??" With wide eyes, Layne hoped her hunch was correct.

"Um," Jillian looked down at the transaction that was being brought to her attention. "Your initials next to a payment for $611.24?"

Layne shook her head. "Yes! But it's really not. Have you had any other transactions like this since you've been here?"

Now, the woman was beginning to believe some of the rumors of Layne's unhinged behavior, given how she wasn't making much sense right now. "No, you take your cut straight from the cash reserves."

"Exactly!" She slapped her hand down on the bar. "Son of a bitch! Fuckin' Sean knew I'd question it." Layne unleashed a laugh that bordered on the brink of insanity now that she finally had a breakthrough and not a damn breakdown.

Joey came up behind Layne, laying a hand on the small of her back. "Question what?" He raised a brow, wondering how concerned he should be at the suddenly erratic behavior.

She pointed at the page again. "L.O. Those aren't *my* initials. Sean made sure that I never had my shares recorded in the books. It *has* to be Liam! It would explain how he was getting funds without me or anyone else noticing."

Layne cursed under her breath at both the ingenuity of it and whatever other heinous acts Liam must have resorted to in order to get the money out of Sean. If it had been anybody else checking the books, it would have likely gone unnoticed.

That's when the thought struck her. She only checked the books for a few long-standing clients and left the rest to be checked by the lower ranks of her crew. "Fuck…" Layne pulled her phone out of her pocket, quickly dialing up Ethan.

"Ethan? I need the books checked for every damn client of ours for the last few months. If any of them have records with my initials next to them, I want to know." She paused, listening to his response before cutting him off, "I don't care, get Jonathan or Sam to help you. Get it done, and don't tell anyone else what you're looking for." She tapped the red circle, ending the discussion.

God help her if she discovered any of her clients were still actively funding Liam's ventures. They would see first-hand just how hot her fire could burn.

Chapter Ten

BOGEYMEN

S ame fucking day, different fucking year. Shannon O'Reilly's death would always live on inside her daughter's head. Of all the fucked up things Layne ever witnessed, she couldn't get past the sight of her mom getting into the car on that fateful day. The vibrations that reached inside the house as the explosion went off would never be unfelt. The burst of light as the flames ignited wouldn't ever be extinguished in her mind. The instant when her mother was no longer whole could never be pieced back together in her heart.

Lying on her back, she stared up at her ceiling fan as it made rotation after rotation. The air in the bedroom shifted slightly with each movement of the fan blades cutting through the air. Despite having redecorated the master bedroom upon moving in, this was still the very same room her parents used to retire to at the end of a long day.

"Mom!" Layne bounded into the bedroom on a Friday night after coming home from Rebecca's house. She

launched herself onto her parents' bed, bouncing gently against it after landing on her stomach. Her hands propped her head up under her chin while her legs idly kicked back and forth.

Shannon sat there in bed with a book in her hands, reading glasses perched on the tip of her nose, and her beautiful mane of chestnut hair in a loose braid hanging over her shoulder. She lifted her gaze from the words on the page to her ten-year-old daughter with a smile. Her fingers pulled the thin-framed glasses from her face and rested them between the pages of the novel she had been enjoying, titled "Deadly Bonds."

"Layney, how many times have I told you not to throw yourself onto the bed like that? You're bound to break the frame one of these days." Her mother scolded her gently, still upholding a loving smile.

Layne rolled her eyes at the comment she had heard time and time again and blatantly ignored it. Instead, she dove right into her reason for barging into the bedroom in the first place. "You're not going to believe what happened at Rebecca's tonight." She pushed herself up onto her knees, sitting back on her feet as she began to dive into the story.

With childlike excitement, Layne wildly spilled all the details of the eventful evening. "So, we were playing outside on Rebecca's front steps. She was being so bossy again and wouldn't let me pick what game we were gonna play. She was going to go back inside, but that's when Tilly got out the front door!" Layne's hands dramatically moved with each explanation, especially as she mentioned that her best friend's Scottish terrier made an escape attempt.

Her mother gasped, appearing fully invested in the story her daughter was telling. "Oh my, Layney! Did you get Tilly back?"

Layne popped up onto her feet on the bed, ready to continue explaining while standing on the mattress. However, with a stern look from Shannon and a gesture to sit back down, Layne dropped onto her butt with a mild bounce.

"Yeah, we got Tilly back, but she almost ran out into the street! I ran to go get her, but some nice man managed to scoop her up. He had the COOLEST motorcycle. It had a skull sticker on it and everything!"

Layne grinned as she remembered the stranger. The tall man with the dirty blonde hair had been parked right out front of her friend's house. When he heard both girls shrieking for the little black dog to come back, he stopped what he was doing to snatch up the pup before it ran by him towards the open street filled with oncoming traffic.

He carried Tilly back to Layne, squatting down in front of her as he handed the furry runaway back to her with a polite smile.

"After he gave Tilly back, he told me to be careful and all that jazz, but I'm smarter than that. I wouldn't have run out into the street after her. I told him that, too." Layne declared her intelligence proudly as she wrapped up the retelling of events.

Shannon's smile faltered slightly, forcing the curve to remain on her lips, but the hint of concern filled her eyes.

"That was very kind of him, Layney. But come here for a second." She waved her hand at her daughter to scoot closer.

When Layne crawled over to sit next to her mother in bed, cuddling up against her side, Shannon pulled her into a close hug. "I'm happy that Tilly is okay, but I want you to realize something that I know you might not fully understand. Not every stranger who does a good deed is a good person. Daddy's job can make a lot of people upset sometimes, and we should always be careful who we trust, okay? Even if they seem nice."

Her mother leaned over and placed a kiss on the top of Layne's head. "Now, why don't you go get your pajamas on, come back here, and we can watch a movie together before you go to bed."

Layne remembered that night so clearly. She and her mother cozied up in bed together, laughing at a silly movie until Layne conked out. It had all transpired in the same room she found herself in now. No matter how the paint changed, how the furniture got replaced, or the different voices echoing in the air–these four walls would always contain the bittersweet past.

Being stuck inside her memories, Layne could still hear the sound of the explosion as her mom's existence was wiped from this earth months later. Layne wondered if her mother felt anything. Had she known she was getting blasted to pieces? Was there fear of death? What pain had she suffered? Did she have any regrets?

This year, Layne had so many other thoughts weighing on her as she wondered about how things would be if her mother were still alive today. Would she be supportive of Layne's relationship with Joey and Gage? Would Liam be the same homicidal lunatic he had turned into? There were so many questions she didn't have answers to and never would.

She sighed as she remained there in the empty bed for another fifteen minutes while getting lost in the whirlwind of emotions. Layne assumed that at least one of her men was in the house if not both of them. Joey had been adamant about keeping eyes on her with Liam off his rocker. Gage was being equally protective. The two of them took turns at her side, no matter where she was. She couldn't even shower in peace, but that was because both of the guys had other intentions besides her safety.

If she got up out of bed, she could immediately start raising her blood alcohol levels. Yet, the blankets weighing down on her were very convincing in their efforts to dissuade her from leaving their captivity.

Deciding that caffeine and booze made a better tag team than some Egyptian cotton bedding, she kicked the sheets off herself.

Trudging downstairs in her dark blue boy shorts and gray tank top, she grumbled when she entered the kitchen and saw the coffee pot empty. "What the fuck…"

Layne began to go through the process of preparing a pot of coffee so she could at least pretend to be a shell of a human being today. About the time she hit the button to kick off the brew cycle, she looked around the kitchen. It was quiet. Why had no one made coffee this morning? Where were the guys?

She poked her head around a corner, "Joey?"

No response.

Walking down the hall and to the bottom of the stairs, she called up to the second floor, "Gage?"

Silence.

Shrugging with indifference, she shook her head and walked back to the kitchen. Their presence, or lack thereof, wasn't going to alter her self-destructive agenda for today.

Noticing there was enough coffee in the pot for a single cup, she grabbed a mug and filled it halfway with the wake-up juice. The other half was filled with the good stuff: whiskey. For good measure, she added a splash of Irish cream.

Armed with today's breakfast of champions, she headed back upstairs. Once she returned to the bedroom, she slowly sipped the bitter beverage in her mug as she flipped through her phone, finding no messages from either De Luca brother.

"Whatever." She tossed her phone down onto the bed carelessly. Why should she care if they were going to listen to her and actually leave her alone for the day? Last night, she had threatened them both that she would give up sex for Lent if they interfered with her plans for today. That in and of itself would be the greatest gift they could give her as far as she was concerned.

Before she could take her coffee into bed with her, an unusual sound came from downstairs. It sounded like something had fallen, or had it been knocked over?

Placing the mug on her nightstand, she went to pull her firearm from the corresponding drawer, only to

discover that it wasn't where she had left it. That was…
odd.

Another crash of something downstairs. She tiptoed to the door, straining for any other sounds that would give her a clue of what was transpiring on the first floor. When she heard nothing further, her bare feet carried her down the hall to the top of the stairs as she peered over the railing, looking for anything out of place.

Waiting another moment, she continued to investigate while slowly creeping down the steps. Her paranoia began to grow louder inside her head; anxiety sped up her pulse. On one hand, her brain was yelling at her for stupidly walking closer to potential danger, unarmed. On the other hand? It was telling her to stop overreacting and continue towards the source—it was likely nothing at all. As for the teeny part of her brain that thrived off of danger, it was getting excited like it was the damn Fourth of July.

Her feet met the cool tile at the bottom of the stairs. There were no more sounds, no bogeyman was jumping out at her, and all she was met with were thoughts of her ridiculous imaginings.

The tension in her shoulders finally released, visibly lowering them into a state of ease. This damn old house had too many noises.

Layne turned to go back upstairs, only she was stopped by the looming presence of not one but two bogeymen.

Layne yelped at the sudden appearance of two men clad in dark clothing who had managed to creep up on her. She practically jumped out of her skin at the unexpected sight after settling into a false sense of security.

The man closest to her immediately grabbed her by her arms with a firm grip to prevent her from running off or wildly swinging fists. As her initial shock wore off, her eyes finally observed the obscured faces of the two intruders. One mask with a toothy skull across it and the other with bloody demon canines. Both were unmistakably familiar.

These fuckers had her heart racing inside of her chest, thinking that someone had broken into O'Reilly Manor.

As she opened her mouth to bitch them both out, Mr. Tall-Dark-And-Skull-Masked, who had his hands on her, lifted her and tossed her over his shoulder with ease. Her barely covered ass was up close to his face. His gloved hand gave it a hard smack that echoed across the foyer.

"What in the fuck?!" she yelled out. "Joey, I swear to Christ!" Her hands pushed against the flexed muscles in his back.

As she began to protest loudly, that was when Mr. Demon-Couture-Mask approached. He pulled something from his pocket.

"Open up, baby." His brown eyes glimmered in excitement. Excitement that she was not currently sharing with either of them.

She wrinkled her nose up as she often did when she was riled up. "Gage, I will fu—"

Her words were cut off as he shoved a ball gag into her mouth, securing the straps around the back of her head. He made sure that it was tight enough to remain in place but as comfortable as one could hope for.

When her hands instinctively lifted to pull the gag out

from between her lips, they were ensnared by Gage's hand while his other pulled a set of steel cuffs from Joey's back pocket. With expertise, both of her wrists were detained by the metal rings.

Neither of the guys could understand her muffled ramblings and grunts, but their imaginations filled in the gaps. Layne was less than thrilled they had interrupted a day where she wanted everyone to leave her the fuck alone while she wallowed in misery and obscene amounts of booze.

Gage patted the side of Joey's arm. "She's set."

Joey adjusted her weight on his shoulder. "Be a good girl, Layney, we're going to go take a drive."

Based on the way she smacked her hands against his lower back, she wasn't planning on following directions. He was more than happy to let her throw her fit; it gave him all the more reason to remind her how to be a good girl for them both.

Joey chuckled as he carried her into the garage, where his Challenger awaited them.

Gage got into the backseat first, then helped pull her into the back with him. He was careful not to bump her around too much. However, Layne didn't make it easy for either of them.

Wrapping his arms around her, Gage pulled her into his lap while Joey took up the driver's seat. He smirked behind his mask, knowing his already hard cock was pressing right up against her ass.

"Relax. Today, we're going to make sure you're going to be very well taken care of," Gage whispered into her ear.

The engine of the car began to purr as Joey started it up before pulling out of the garage. His eyes glanced up at the rearview mirror to take a look at Gage and Layne. Thank fuck for the heavily tinted windows. He couldn't imagine being pulled over and explaining to an officer that this was just a casual kidnapping of his wife in an effort to make her day better.

"Layney, I better hear you behaving back there." Joey grinned to himself, trying to consciously pay attention to the road. It wasn't a long drive down to the docks, but his dick was telling him that it wasn't a short enough trip.

With one arm remaining latched around Layne's waist, Gage pulled his mask down enough to use his teeth to yank off one of his gloves. Using his now bare hand with the WRATH tattoo across the back of it, he slid it down over her stomach until it passed underneath the waistband of those tiny boy shorts she had on.

Layne's breath caught as she felt his finger stroke along her crease. She melted back against him.

Gage let out a groan as he felt how much her arousal was coating her already. "Baby, you're so damn wet. Are you getting off on being taken hostage by us?" His finger stroked a circle over her clit.

Her hips pressed down into his lap as her moan vibrated against the silicone sphere lodged between her lips. Layne's ass pushed further against the excitement of his cock.

Hearing that first moan, Joey's hand adjusted his erection in his pants, beginning to regret his decision to be the driver. "That's a good girl, you let Daddy Gage work your cunt." Fuck, he hoped he didn't crash the car before they arrived at their destination.

Skillfully using his fingers, Gage continued to massage circles over her sensitive bundle of nerves. Each movement drew another velvety moan out of Layne. Her ass continued to grind against him, teasing his dick and driving him to stroke her quicker.

The way her heart was pounding in her chest before they left the house had been from the surge of adrenaline. Now, it was the rise of pleasure saturating her body. With her hands bound in front of her at the wrists, she pushed Gage's hand further into her panties, wanting his touch inside of her. Her thighs parted, allowing him more access to her heated core.

Chuckling, Gage pulled his touch back up to her clit. "Mmm," he growled into her ear. "It seems like you've had a bit of an attitude adjustment, Lucky Charm." His fingers made tighter circles over her slick nub, listening to each of her moans grow heavier with the need for release.

Layne whimpered as she felt her climax drawing closer, but still just a breath out of reach. Just as she thought he was going to leave her dangling on the edge, Gage finally dove his hand lower to shove two fingers deep inside of her tight pussy. Curling his fingers, he had no difficulty finding the sensual spot that would have her coming undone.

She cried out as her pleasure spilled across her body, squirming against him as she came. Gage's arm tightened around her so he could selfishly take delight in the way her body writhed in his hold. Each of her loud moans was dampened by the obstruction he had placed in her mouth, only making him harder at how her ecstasy couldn't be fully silenced.

"Fuck, baby. Coming so soon?" He wiggled his fingers inside of her tauntingly to extend the clutch her orgasm had on her. "We haven't even gotten started." Tauntingly, he pushed his hips up, driving the solid bulge of his cock against the center of her ass.

She panted hard as she laid back against his chest, her breaths being forced past the sides of the gag. Layne shut her eyes, allowing herself to bask in the afterglow while Gage kept his fingers buried deep inside of her. Every so often, she could feel him move them, prompting her body to respond with delightful little shivers across her skin.

Joey found himself placing more pressure on the gas pedal as Gage had their girl already unraveling between her legs.

Chapter Eleven

HAPPY ANNIVERSARY

Arriving at the docks, the tires caused a crunching sound of the gravel underneath the rubber as the car rolled to a stop. Joey parked the Challenger right in front of the same abandoned building where Layne had first encountered the darker side of his occupation. It was the very same day he made the best decision of his life, the day he decided to let her go free instead of carrying out Franzetti's contract on her head.

Joey exited the car, with Gage helping to ease their girl out of the backseat and back over Joey's shoulder. Securing her with one hand, Joey reached into the pocket of his black tactical pants with the other. He grabbed a set of keys and tossed them over to Gage, who snatched them from midair and unlocked the building, allowing his brother to enter with Layne first.

With less resistance in the afterglow of her orgasm, Layne kept herself steady by holding onto the back of Joey's shirt. She still wanted to give them both an earful for interfering with her plans for today, but it was pointless to try when they couldn't comprehend her past the gag firmly lodged in her mouth.

The door clicked shut behind the three of them once they were inside. The interior of the building hadn't changed much from a few years ago. It still looked just as abandoned but with more cobwebs and the same musty and ancient office furniture.

Layne was slid off of Joey's shoulder and down onto a chair, wrists still held captive by the handcuffs Gage had slapped on her. Being upright, she could more easily see a few of the differences in the room from the last time she had been in it. The air mattress on the floor was the most obvious addition, and next to it was a cooler.

They didn't bother securing her to the chair, both of them confident in their abilities to prevent her from running off. The bigger threat was how much she was going to lash out at either one of them before they were done here. Further validating their confidence, when she went to stand up, Gage came behind her and pushed down on her shoulders to get her ass back in the seat.

The boots Joey was wearing softly thudded against the floor as he double-checked several of the locks and windows before circling back to stand in front of her. With his face still obscured by his hallmark skeleton mask, his eyes were truly what gave his lust-filled intentions away.

Gage's hands remained pressing onto her shoulders to keep her in one place; the way his fingers massaged the muscles of her upper back, he was doing his best to relax her.

Joey leaned over with his hands braced against his thighs as he stared at Layne. "It's not often anyone gets second chances, Layney, but when the opportunity presents itself, I've learned not to turn it down. Do you recognize where we are right now?"

Not bothering to fight the obstruction in her mouth, she simply nodded at him. How could she forget anything about the fateful day he entered her life? It was the day their story began.

"Good." His eyes glanced at Gage, and he gave a curt nod. The gesture prompted his brother to loosen up the straps of the ball gag until it was removed from her mouth and returned to Gage's pocket. If she got mouthy again, it would be easily accessible.

Layne opened and closed her mouth several times to ease the ache from her jaw. Her cuffed hands came up to wipe the trail of saliva away from her chin. "This is fucking ridiculous. I told you both last night that I just wanted to be left alone for one goddamn day."

Gage's hand wrapped itself around her hair and tugged her head back. "Baby, it's not your turn to talk yet." He leaned over and pressed his mouth to hers with a softness that was in stark contrast to what would look like a rather grim sight to an outsider: two masked men holding a woman hostage in an abandoned building.

After that tender kiss, Gage smirked at her. "But if you prefer one of us to fill your mouth with something other than the gag, we will be more than happy to oblige."

When Gage eased up on Layne's hair, her attention was drawn back to Joey. He moved his hands to the top of her bare thighs while squatting down in front of her. "Now, be a good girl and tell me what I want to know." His hands squeezed onto the tops of her legs, digging in firmly with his fingers to make sure he had her attention.

"If the question is if you're both in such deep shit right now, then yes. You better pray when I get these cuffs off that both of you are miles away." She rolled her eyes with a fierce attitude and shook her head at their audacity of going to this extreme length. On a day when she always woke up in a foul mood, they hadn't exactly made it any better. Well, except the orgasm on the way here hadn't been half bad…

Joey laughed. "There's the part of you I love the most. All the attitude and confidence behind your words, even when you're not in a position to be pitching threats."

He leaned in and whispered into her ear, "Do you think I don't know you well enough to be several steps ahead of you? I bet you were confused when your gun wasn't in the nightstand drawer earlier, huh?" He had already been shot once by an O'Reilly; he wasn't looking to make it two-for-two when they caught her off guard at the house earlier.

She huffed out a breath in frustration. "You know today of all days is my one day for myself. It's not about you."

Tugging his mask down, Joey leaned down and dragged several rows of kisses up over the soft skin of her inner thigh as he inched closer to her center. His thin layer of scruff brushed against her body as he murmured, "That's where you're wrong, Layney." His hands forced her legs apart wider as his final kiss was pressed to the damp fabric of her boy shorts.

Behind her, Gage tossed his mask and gloves down onto the floor. Each of his large hands ran over her shoulders and down onto her chest until he slid them into the top of her tank top. His palms found her firm and round tits and began to knead them in his grasp.

Layne quietly fought the moan her body wanted to respond with at both of their touches. The weight of her desire began to impact her breathing as her heart sped up and her core pulsed with desire. Her damn body was trying to betray her again.

Continuing, Joey pulled his face away from between her legs to peer up at her, "Today is about me, it's about you, and going forward, it's going to be about the three of us." The warm pools of his espresso eyes were full of certainty and promises. "Are you going to be a good girl for us? Today can be all about allowing us to worship every fuckin' inch of your body until you've come so far undone that there's nothing left of you for us to take. All you have to do is say the words, Layney."

Still, with his hands down the front of her tank top, Gage's fingers pinched her stiff nipples, twisting them between his fingers. It elicited a gasp from her as her body shifted under his touch. Each tug at her body had her hardheaded attitude faltering.

While Layne was struggling to be amenable to the new terms of what this day was going to be about, Joey's hand commanded her attention as it grabbed under her jaw.

"I asked a question, you know what happens when I ask twice," his gravelly voice deepened into the cusp of a growl. His other hand dropped between her legs, grabbing at her thinly covered pussy.

Lustful thoughts were already filling her eyes as one set of hands continued their exploration and play of her breasts, but when Joey introduced his rough handling of her body, all she could think about was hunting down her next release.

Layne's full lips parted in anticipation of the gasp pulled right out of her. Losing a battle she wasn't sure she even wanted to win, she whispered, "Make me your good girl." Her voice was breathy from the shameless desire that had eaten away her self-control.

Joey smirked before sliding his mask back into place; his eyes glanced at Gage, who pulled back from Layne, bearing a grin brimming with excitement at the playtime they were all going to have together.

She was promptly pulled to her feet as Joey lifted her arms above her head and lowered them around his neck. Her cuffed wrists ensured that she wouldn't be escaping the proximity of his body.

Coming up behind her, Gage put his hands to better use by yanking her boy shorts down from her hips until they fell to the floor. Once his job was done there, he left to find the bag he had dropped off in a corner earlier.

Impatiently yanking at his belt, Joey's hands opened up his pants before pulling out his impressively-sized dick that ached to fuck the ever-loving shit out of her. His hands grabbed onto the back of her thighs and hoisted her up until her legs wrapped around his waist.

Layne's arms tightened around his neck as her ankles

locked behind him. His cock was already teasing the slick entrance of her body. She stared at his mask-covered face as he walked with her until her back hit a wall.

"Don't hold back," she instructed him. If either of them wanted to make today not about her emotional wreckage, it needed the physical intensity to shatter the mental barriers.

"Oh, I wasn't planning on being gentle, Layney. I plan to fuck you like I just stole you." He drove his cock roughly into her, proving his point. He groaned as he felt her tightness squeeze around him.

She tilted her head back against the wall as she loudly moaned out as he forced her body to mold around him. Her nails clawed into his upper back, finding any part of him to latch onto.

His hips drew back and pushed into her again, the head of his cock attempting to spear straight through her. The way her arousal warmed his cock, he wanted nothing more than to forever live buried deep inside her.

Despite the mask covering the lower half of his face, she could still feel the heat of his breath against the skin of her neck as he panted with his efforts. Equally, her labored breaths were expelled as she continued to voice out the intensity of the pleasure he was giving her.

"You should have taken my dick just like this the first time we were here together." His hands squeezed onto her legs tighter. Allowing his lust to drive his movements, he sped up his thrusts to keep fueling both of their needs. Roughly, he claimed her body, his hips nearly bruising in their intensity as he used his strength to take her.

Barely able to keep up with her breaths between her

moans, she gasped at the thought of if she and Joey had caved to their desires the same day they had met. "I-I… I would have never given it to you."

She groaned out as the tip of his cock stroked over the sweet spot deep within her core. With every shove of his hard length into her, he was pulling at the string wrapped around her release, getting closer to unraveling it.

Lifting a hand, Joey tugged his mask down and then snatched up her throat in his grasp. "Don't lie to me; you would have let me fuck this insatiable pussy of yours however I wanted."

His lips feverishly kissed her lips, swallowing up her moans hungrily. The strength of his hand squeezed around her throat, placing enough pressure to have her feel the slowing of blood on the way to her brain before releasing the hold. Joey repeated the process of squeezing and releasing several more times as his hips drove into her.

With the power of his thrusts jolting her against the wall, her body quickly ramped up towards its climax. "Fuck, Joey! I-I'm gonna come!" Her body was already wildly squirming against him as her insides trembled.

Joey dropped his hand from her neck down to her hip, where his other hand joined it, steadying her body so he could continue fucking her even harder there against the wall.

He growled into her ear, "You're gonna suck your cum off my cock when I'm done with you. You better be fuckin' hungry." His teeth caught the bottom of her ear lobe, giving it a possessive nibble.

The metal links holding her wrists together pulled

against the back of Joey's neck as her body tensed around him. His words were just enough to pull the trigger to fire off her orgasm. The walls of her pussy clenched onto him as her release spilled over his cock, coating every thick inch of him.

Gage was finishing the last few touches of his setup over by the air mattress when he heard Layne's screams of ecstasy as she came for Joey. Listening to her moans while Joey had her wrapped around his dick had been a sweet form of torture. He was more than ready to have his turn with her, and the way his erection was fighting against the confines of his pants had him tempted to reach in and take the matter into his own hand.

As Layne's high began to clear enough that she wasn't holding Joey's dick hostage inside of her, he pulled back, fighting the urge to blow his load into her pussy.

Joey groaned as the cool air outside of Layne's body met the wet skin of his cum covered dick. Moving quickly, he let her down on her feet and ducked out from the circle of her arms. He grinned, urging her down onto her knees, "Show me how much you enjoy tasting yourself on my cock."

Layne sank to her knees, her hands holding the fabric of his boxer briefs away from his dick, still standing at full attention. Her cum shone against his skin, mixing in with his clear precum leaking from the tip of his length.

Her tongue snaked out and stroked a long line along the underside of his cock. The flavor of her mildly sweet juices mixed with the taste of his flesh.

With one hand braced against the wall in front of him,

Joey dropped the other to the back of her head. "Layney," he groaned as his cock twitched when her tongue made contact with him. "You better not be fuckin' teasing me down there." He tilted his head to look down at her.

She smirked and looked up through her dark lashes at him. "Would I ever tease you?" The hint of snarkiness tainted her words.

His hand fisted her hair. "Open up, smartass," he ordered.

Opening up her mouth wide, she drew him into her mouth, sealing her lips around him. Sliding her mouth down over his length, she taunted him with the dance of her tongue.

The sensation of her sucking on him while her tongue did its wicked movements had Joey hissing out a string of curses. Layne's head bobbed back and forth along his cock, cleaning him of all the evidence of her release.

Trapped in pleasure's passage of time, it didn't feel like long before Layne's throat was squeezing around him, prompting his hand to firmly push her head even closer to him as he groaned loudly, "Fuuuck!"

Several thick spurts of his seed shot down into her throat, quickly filling up her mouth before she swallowed his release.

Layne slowly pulled her mouth from him, sitting back on her feet as she looked up at him with swollen lips, flushed cheeks, and a satisfied smile.

Heavily breathing, Joey weakly smiled at her before leaning over and helping her onto her feet. He pulled out a key to her handcuffs and popped them open, releasing her wrists from the steel bracelets.

Joey's finger and thumb held onto her chin gently as he looked into her eyes. To think he had been so lucky to fall head over heels for the woman in front of him on this day a few years ago had him wishing for nothing else in life.

He leaned over and lovingly captured her lips momentarily before whispering against her mouth, "Happy Anniversary, Layne."

Chapter Twelve

FOUNTAIN OF YOUTH

After the tender moment shared between them, Joey glanced over his shoulder at Gage, who had given them space for Layne's first fuck of the day and certainly not her last.

Noting that his brother looked ready for his shot, he looked back at Layne and smirked, knowing that her day with them was only beginning. They promised her that they would make this day about the three of them together. That was a promise they planned to deliver–in spades.

Gage approached, taking Layne's hand with his. Without a word, he led her over to the air mattress. "Baby, now it's your Daddy's turn to take care of you." He stopped at the edge of the makeshift bed and faced her. His hands grabbed the bottom of her shirt and lifted, removing the last piece of her clothing. It left just the golden chain of his collar around her slender neck.

His boyish smile spread across his face as his eyes trailed over her fit figure on display before him. Everything about her captivated him, from the currently tousled locks of chestnut hair hanging down past her shoulders with the ends brushing past the sides of her perky breasts to the petite figure that was home to the unique soul that called to his own. Tying it all together was her captivating set of royal emerald eyes that glowed with every ounce of her spirited personality.

Her hands went to the zipper of Gage's black hoodie and began to slide it down. When his inked hand with the rose on it halted her about halfway, she looked up at him with confusion clouding her face.

Lifting her hand to his lips, he gently kissed each of her fingertips. "Not yet. Take a seat." He nodded over at the air mattress.

Layne hesitated, wondering just what his intentions were. The man standing before her didn't budge as he patiently waited for her to comply. She got down onto the mattress, feeling the air shift underneath her weight, Layne crawled to the center and took a seat while leaning back on her hands.

He stepped to the cooler and retrieved a partially frozen bottle of water from it. Gage removed the top and discarded it into the depths of the room, where it rolled off to join other random debris left behind in the abandoned building.

Joey took up a seat in the chair Layne had been in earlier while he recovered from his efforts with their girl. Slowly, he began easing out of his clothes, starting with his boots, while he casually watched the interactions between the two in front of him.

Kneeling between her ankles, Gage beckoned her with

his finger to lean closer to him. When she did as she was told, her arms hanging down between her thighs, he placed two fingers under her chin and tilted her head back slightly. "Part those lips for me, baby. I can't have you getting dehydrated this early on."

There he was—her caretaker—always making sure she was in a healthy state, whether it was physically or otherwise. Layne smiled at him and opened up her mouth. Gage slowly poured the frigid liquid into her mouth until there was enough for her to swallow down. He repeated the action until he was satisfied she had consumed enough.

"Thank you, Sir." Her eyes sparkled as she gave him her full attention.

Gage proudly smiled that his bratty Lucky Charm was actually using her manners for once. "You're welcome, baby. Now lie back so I can quench my thirst."

Partially leaning back on her elbows, she rubbed her leg suggestively against his hip with a grin. "Last I checked, you are a bit overdressed for the occasion."

It seemed her good behavior was short-lived as her inner brat made an appearance. He grabbed her leg that was rubbing up against him and yanked her forward several inches so she fell the rest of the way on her back.

Dragging the bottom of the cold water bottle down over her abs, he watched as she sucked in her stomach in response to the icy sensation against her skin. Gage continued the movement south and noticed her breath cease momentarily as the chilled plastic hovered closer to her center.

"What were you saying? That *almost* sounded like you

were trying to tell me I don't know what pleases my girl." A devilish smile crossed his lips.

Layne lifted her head to watch as the frigid object threatened to come into contact with her heated folds. "Gage, that wasn't—"

With his grip still firmly on her leg, he lowered the bottle down over her pussy, immediately finding gratification in how her squeak interrupted her protest. "Is that how you address me?" He removed the bottle from her sensitive flesh.

She dropped her head back down onto the mattress as she blew out a breath of air. Shaking her head in response, "No, Sir."

Gage smiled, released her leg, and gave her inner thigh a pat. "Better. Go ahead and spread your legs, baby. I want to make sure I don't leave any part of you untasted."

Biting her lower lip to prevent herself from making another sassy remark, she parted her legs enough for him to have all the access to her body he could want.

The dark brown hues of his eyes soaked in the sight before him, filling up with a desire to have her falling apart at his doing. He leaned down, his lips just barely brushed against her folds as he spoke. "Your pussy is gorgeous when it's so swollen after taking Joey's cock."

He held onto her hip with one hand while his other hand remained on the plastic bottle with frosty condensation forming on the outside of it. Gage's tongue came forth and ran along her crease, reveling in the taste of her arousal.

Layne moaned out quietly, needing more contact from

him as he took things slowly. When she thought he was going in for another lick, she felt the sting of the ice-cold water running over her clit. Her hips instinctively jerked at the unexpected sensation, but Gage's strong grasp kept her steady.

As she gasped in surprise, she felt an immediate warmth from Gage's mouth, sucking the water from her pussy. There was a drastic change from cold to warm that had her body reacting to a new type of tortuous pleasure.

Hearing Layne react favorably to the temperature play, he hummed in approval against her core, drawing out another satisfied moan from her. Gage's mouth drank away the chill thoroughly, allowing himself to feast on her body. He continued the cycle of spilling the water over her body's most sensitive areas before melting away the bite of the cold using the strokes of his tongue.

The back and forth of him pulling her sensations to both ends of the spectrum had her in a frenzy of whimpers and moans.

While his tongue swirled over her small bundle of nerves, working her up hard, he ditched his hold on the partially frozen bottle he had been holding in his hand. It fell off to the side and rolled a few feet away from the bed. Gage nipped at her clit, adding in another type of pleasurable pain.

She cried out, "Please, Daddy, I need to come!" Her hands tugged at the sheets on either side of her.

Knowing damn well his fingers and the silver rings on them, were cold as hell from holding onto the water for so long, Gage shoved two fingers deep inside of her for another added layer of contrasting sensations. The depths of her warm pussy heated his fingers while her body soaked the cold from them.

"Fuck!" she repeated several times. Layne shook as the opposing temperatures hurdled her into her release. The tight walls of her center locked down on his icy fingers in the process. Her back arched up from the mattress as her hips pushed against his face.

Gage continued to lap at her cunt while he thrust his fingers deep inside of her, the silver rings held the cooler temperatures much longer and rubbed just beyond the entrance of her pussy. The tips of his fingers eagerly stroked and pushed at the special area far within her. Not letting her orgasm fade off, he continued to use his fingers to fuck her while she was making the most beautifully feral sounds.

His voice thick with need, he glanced up at her, "Baby, I told you I was goddamn thirsty. Now, I'm going to need you to give me more to drink." With quick and deep movements, his fingers curled inside of her, keeping her ecstasy at its highest levels.

She could hardly breathe as each moan tore out of her throat. Her body continued to tremble and tense up with each of his movements. "I...I..." Before she could complete the thought into anything coherent, Gage latched his mouth back down on her clit, roughly sucking at it while his fingers continued to press into her.

Layne's eyes rolled back into her head briefly as she cried out, and her body crashed into another vicious climax.

This time, as she came, a stream of liquid spilled from her body.

Swiftly, Gage removed his fingers and began to drink straight from her tap as the mild taste of her body's oasis delighted his taste buds. He swallowed down every last drop while she squirmed against the movement of his mouth.

When he finished, he lifted his head and saw Layne lying there heavily, panting with a sheen of sweat over her flushed body. He sat up on his knees and began removing his clothes. "Baby, I'm so proud of you. You taste fuckin' magical when you squirt for me." He was pretty sure he had been drinking from the Fountain of Youth while she had been falling into the abyss of obscene pleasures.

Quickly shoving off the last of his clothes from his body, Gage lowered himself over her, allowing the swollen tip of his tattooed cock to push against her entrance.

His SPQR medallion necklace hung down from around his neck, where it dragged over the length of hers while his hand stroked the side of her face. "And for being such a good girl, you are going to get a reward." He smiled down at the breathless expression on her face in awe of the beauty he saw lying there underneath him.

Layne's endless pools stared up at him, still clouded by the high of her releases. Her eyes glanced down the length of his body, drawing in the sight of his chest muscles flexing as he propped himself up above her. His cut abs were on display down to the start of the ink at the bottom of his V and led onto the broadswords painted over his hardened length hovering at the opening to her aching pussy.

"Eyes up here, beautiful," he instructed. When she complied and looked up into his tender espresso eyes, Gage slowly pushed himself inside her.

Her hands slid up over his large biceps, over the tops of his shoulders, and onto his upper back as she moaned out. The soreness between her legs fed into extra sensitivity as he stretched her cunt to fill her completely.

Barely audible, she whispered his name on the tail end of her moan, "Gage…"

"Yeah, Lucky Charm?" He rolled his hips into her, the head of his cock driving back into her.

Uncertainty was splashed across her face, and her mind began to drift into thoughts of events of the past despite the efforts of both her men. "I don't know if I can take much more."

"You're already trying to tap out on us, baby?" He lowered his mouth down to her ear and whispered, "C'mon, Layne, your pussy was made to take both of us. The way your cunt is wrapped around my dick right now tells me it wants to continue being used." He kissed her neck right below her ear. "Just keep your focus on what feels good."

Layne's fingers slid up the back of his neck, burying themselves into the short, ashen blonde hair on the back of his head. Her hips pressed up against him, encouraging him to keep going.

Gage planted several kisses along the length of her neck, his hips beginning to pick up the pace of driving himself deep into her. He groaned as her slick walls stroked him with each thrust.

He looked back over his shoulder at Joey, smirking, "How's it look watching me fuck your wife?"

Joey had fully undressed himself and was lounging back in the chair, his cock was already recovered enough and back to being half erect, watching and hearing Layne as she took Gage. He continued slow but sure strokes of his hand on his rapidly swelling dick. He grinned at his brother's question, "She still looks like she's missing something."

"Oh?" Gage turned his attention back to Layne. "Did you hear that, baby? He thinks you're not being worked hard enough."

Breathlessly, knowing she was flirting with the line of her body's limits with all their affections, she blurted out, "Fuck you, Joey."

That got her a chuckle from him in response and a stoppage in Gage's movements. Joey responded with a devilish grin, "If you're offering, Layney, I'm not about to turn it down."

Using the strength of his hands, Gage quickly rolled them both over onto their sides while still buried inside her. He grabbed her leg, pulling it over the outside of his hip. Swiftly, his open palm slammed down on her ass cheek, leaving a stinging red glow.

Giving a surprised squeak, Layne's hips pushed against him as she jolted from the spank he had just given her.

Smiling, Gage looked at her with delight. "One of these days, I'll be able to smack that sass out of you." Though, he secretly hoped it wouldn't be anytime soon.

Joey rose from his seat and strode over to a bag next to

the cooler. Reaching in, he pulled out a bottle of lube, slathering it over his thick cock in preparation for diving into his favorite part of her–that round ass of hers.

Soon, she could feel the bed dip under Joey's weight as he joined the two of them, his hand came to the indent of her waist as he pressed his chest to her back. Gage's hard cock gave a taunting nudge deeper into her while Layne felt the steel-like erection from Joey nudging between her ass cheeks.

The stubble from Joey's face lightly scratched against the back of her shoulder as he kissed it. His hand slid over her stomach and upward to grab a handful of one of her breasts. His fingers pinched and rolled her nipple between his fingers.

The depth of his gravelly voice vibrated against her soft skin as he spoke, "Layney, I swear to God, I will never grow tired of fucking this perfectly tight ass of yours. Now, be a good girl and beg for both of your holes to be full. I know you can sound goddamn needy when you want to."

She moaned out as Joey's fingers toyed with her stiff nipple, and he teased her back entrance with the tip of his cock. "Please, I need both of my Daddies filling me up; I need to be fucked like your good girl." Her voice was heavy with her desire as her body ached to be full from the waist down.

Joey's hand left her breast and slid up to her throat, wrapping around it possessively. "I can't wait to hear you scream as we make you fuckin' come so hard that you'll never question who the fuck you are ever again." His hand tightened around her neck as his eyes flicked over to Gage with a nod.

Smiling as he saw Joey gear up to push into Layne's back entrance, Gage looked at their girl. "You're Layne motherfucking De Luca."

In a smooth motion, the head of Joey's swollen cock inched into the tight space of her ass. Sweeping over him immediately was the pleasure of her body squeezing around his throbbing cock, causing him to curse. He pushed into her until he was fully seated inside, the familiar tightness that came with their girl taking both their cocks had him reeling already.

As Layne's lips parted to moan out, Gage shoved two fingers into her mouth, forcing her moan to get cut off as she gagged on the two large digits. He groaned as it caused her pussy to strangle his cock, barely allowing him to draw back and drive back into her. "Fuck, baby, you better pray for your birth control. I'm going to fill you with so much of my damn cum that you'll be leaking for days."

In tandem, both De Luca men hungrily indulged in taking her body in a coordinated rhythm. Joey's hips bucked against her ass as he nipped at the side of her neck as his cock claimed her body. "You'll always be ours, Layney," he huskily spoke into her ear.

Both the guys used their hands to play with her body's ability to utilize oxygen. They alternated between Joey's hold on the outside of her throat and Gage's fingers trying to find the back of it; she gasped for air intermittently as they allowed moments of reprieve and recovery. Each time their hands took control, her body squirmed wildly between them as the sharp escalation of extreme pleasure overtook her.

The room was filled with sounds of bodies smacking against one another, heavy panting, and feral sounds of ecstasy as they all chased after their needs.

Layne's hand scratched over Gage's chest, clawing at it while yanking on the silver necklace he always wore. Her other hand had her nails biting into the back of Joey's hand on her. Her green eyes watering from all the breath play while they both continued slamming their large cocks into her with fierce determination.

Seeing a burst of starlight behind her eyes, she screamed out as her release tore through her very existence. Gage removed his fingers from her mouth, allowing them both to revel in the sounds she made. Her pussy had Gage's cock in a vise grip, and her ass locked down onto Joey's dick.

After she tumbled off the cliff into a state of unparalleled bliss, Gage roared out as his cock pulsed and ropes of his hot cum shot forth deep inside of her. Each spurt continued to fill her up until there was no part of her inside that wasn't drowning with his release.

Joey growled as he wrapped himself around Layne's back, his own climax erupting out of him violently. He whimpered as he filled her ass with his seed and was overcome with intense satisfaction in every part of his body.

All of them were still tangled up together, Layne sandwiched between the men who laid their claim to not just her body but her heart.

None of them had to say a word as they lay there listening to the heavy breaths and pounding heartbeats of one another.

Chapter Thirteen

IN CASE OF EMERGENCY

Perhaps it wasn't a five-star hotel and sex by candlelight, but the efforts both Joey and Gage made to diminish the morbid association that day held for Layne had been one for the books. Instead of attempting to pretend that it was any other day of the year, Joey reminded her that it had been the start of their story together. Gage's involvement gave her hope for the future that he was in this for the long haul to meet her every need.

Spending all their energy on carnal pleasures for a day in an abandoned building down at the docks may not have earned the label of being hopelessly romantic, but it was meaningful to the woman who bound them all together.

Several days had passed, and Layne still felt like every muscle in her body had been put through the wringer by both guys, not that she was complaining. Gage had insisted on treating her like a goddess worth pampering, knowing how much her body needed the recovery.

Sitting in the center of Gage's bed cross-legged with

her laptop in front of her, phone to her right, and her earbuds lodged in her ears, she growled in frustration.

"Thomas, there's evidence he was fucking stealing from my businesses all this time. Liam's been stealing from *me*. I want to know why it's taken this long to get answers!" She swiped her fingers across the trackpad on her computer, scrutinizing every record available to her.

Listening to her trusted advisor spout off a million reasons why it so easily slipped under the radar was giving her a dull headache at the base of her skull. Her fingers smoothed away the wrinkles between her eyebrows that were evidence of her annoyance.

Her eyes lifted from her computer screen as Gage entered the bedroom with a plate of food. Quickly, she minimized one of the windows on the computer. The last thing she wanted was for either of her guys to ask more questions when they didn't need to know the answers.

Gage was wearing one of his slate gray dress shirts and a pair of jeans. Right above the left pocket of the shirt was embroidered silver thread with the initials 'C.C.' for his kink-inspired night club, Cassidy's Chains.

Approaching the bed, he set the plate down on the night table for her, a grilled chicken wrap and a handful of chips neatly piled on it.

Layne's hand shooed him away even though she couldn't recall the last meal she had eaten. At her dismissive gesture, Gage's face went stern.

She continued to focus on her conversation with Thomas, who explained further that Liam's whereabouts were still unknown, and they were no closer to figuring out his next moves.

"So, we've got jack shit? This is fucking unbelievable; it's *Liam,* for God's sake!" The heat of her words caused a shameful silence on the other end of the line. "Tell Sammy, Ethan, and Jonathan to meet me at the Brass Mirror tonight at eight, and they better have good fuckin' news." Her finger firmly tapped the end call button on her phone before plucking her earbuds from her ears.

It wasn't until Gage's hand gripped her jaw that she realized he hadn't left the room. His hand turned her head to face him.

"Open." He commanded as his other hand held half of the wrap he had brought her.

Still irritated with the lack of details on who her brother was coordinating with to have him feeling so confident in his ability to snatch back the family business, she pushed the wrap Gage was offering away from her face. "I'm not hungry. I'll eat later."

Not approving of her response, Gage kept his hand firmly attached to her jaw. "I wasn't asking," he paused before continuing, "unless you want me to find out just how much punishment your ass can take."

That had her attention as the stubborn look in her eyes faded to a softer and more wanton glow. Layne would be lying to herself if she didn't admit to flirting with the idea of defying him one more time just to see what sort of discipline he had in mind. The rumble from her stomach quickly chased away the bratty consideration.

Layne parted her lips, and Gage brought the sandwich

to her mouth for her to bite into, smiling proudly. "That's my good girl."

When Joey and Layne arrived at her covert and elite gambling club, the Brass Mirror, it was packed with members obscenely wagering away their trust funds and generational savings. Each of the tables was full, seating the richest and dirtiest fucks the city had living in it. Scantily clad waitresses moved from table to table, taking drink orders and dirty one-liners with a smile.

Despite not barging into the room commanding attention, there was a large portion of eyes drawn to her when she stepped foot inside. There wasn't a single soul that didn't know who she was and her reputation for not putting up with anyone's bullshit when it came to the denizens of the criminal underbelly.

After Russell Spencer's assets were seized by her associates and he found a permanent home at the bottom of the Hudson River, Layne had a lot fewer issues with the other factions. Despite being one of the few females to have ever broken into the upper echelons, the other leaders rarely questioned how far she would go to back up her promises—or threats.

Joey's company tonight had been at his insistence. This makeshift casino was entirely under her control; anyone who tried to start shit here would have to be mentally unstable. Yet, it was an argument she lost the moment Joey had his hands on her. Goddamn, hormones were her weak spot.

His hand grazed across the small of her back. "I will be right over there," he tipped his head in the direction of the high-top table at the far end of the bar.

Layne smiled and nodded in acknowledgment. "I'll find you when I'm done."

Thank God he had been able to compromise on not being buried up her ass tonight, figuratively speaking. Instead, he was capable of granting her the space she needed to yell at these assholes who worked for her and were supposed to be finding out more information on her delusional sibling.

Scanning the room, she saw Sammy sit back in his chair at a poker table, unleashing a hearty laugh as the dealer shoved a pile of chips his way. The other men at the table with him all groaned, seeing the Full House laid out in front of her senior associate.

Sammy's cocky smile was full of pride as he sat forward to collect his bounty. "Sorry, fuckers, guess you just can't keep up with the pro," he said as he organized the slew of chips in front of him.

She came up behind Sammy, leaning over and plucking a few black chips off the top of the stack in front of him and pocketed them. When he snapped his head around, his hazel eyes were fired up, and he was ready to unleash a tirade of profanities at a woman touching his money. When he recognized Layne, his expression eased, and tensions quickly faded.

As one of the top men who worked for her, Sammy was

used to Layne's high expectations and even higher attitude. He ran his hand over his slicked-back raven locks, realizing it was time to get to business.

"You're early," he pointed out. The light above the table glinted off the face of his Rolex on his wrist as he cashed out his chips and stood from his seat.

With displeasure in her voice, "And you were sitting here fucking off. Where are the other two?"

Straightening out the jacket of his black suit that matched the darkness of his hair, he shrugged. "Last I saw, Ethan was flirting with one of the waitresses, and Jonathan was yapping on his phone."

His mixture of brown and green hues shifted as he scanned the room for his partners in crime. Noticing Joey at the table near the bar, he gave a small nod in polite form to his boss's husband and got a nod in return.

"How's he feeling?" Sammy looked at Layne, the genuine concern painted over his olive complexion.

Not bothering to look at Sammy, she continued to keep an eye out for the other two. Layne answered his question, "As good as anyone can expect after giving death the middle finger."

Immediately, she picked out Ethan by his hulking size as he came out of the restroom. His fingers were buttoning up the last button of his gray vest over his white dress shirt. Close behind him, also coming from the single-person bathroom, was the head cocktail waitress at the Mirror.

Layne's green eyes locked onto Ethan's sapphire hues, and he immediately quickened his strides over to her.

People parted like the Red Sea to avoid getting bulldozed by him on his beeline to her.

When he stopped in front of Layne, he gave a large smile, showing off his pearly whites, "Was just wrapping up… business."

She raised a hand to fend off any further details. "If you keep fucking every waitress at every damn place we do business, I'm not going to be held responsible for the fallout when they all find out about one another." Layne shook her head, trying not to picture the day ten women came after her lead enforcer. One woman scorned was bad enough, but a herd of them? He was just begging to get raked over the coals.

"What? Melissa's a sweet girl; we were just having a chat while she was on her break." Ethan smirked, knowing his lie was as plain as the sleeve of tattoos on his ripped arms.

Now that she had two of her three head honchos, she just needed to track down her top-tier negotiator, Jonathan.

"Why don't you both go grab the table in the back? I will see where the hell Johnny-Boy is." She pulled her phone from her pocket, but before she could even unlock it, a hand came onto her shoulder from behind.

"I think this still qualifies as fashionably late," Jonathan's voice smoothly spoke up as he came around to her side. Then, when he saw the pissed-off look on Layne's face, he winced, "Or not." He dropped his hand away from her and back down to his side into the pocket of his black dress slacks.

At the very back was a private room, though it wasn't

very private as the room had glass walls on two of the four sides. The only level of privacy it offered was from eavesdroppers' prying ears.

Once they were all seated at the round table inside the cozy gathering spot, Layne sat back in the plush armchair and looked at the three men before her.

"I'm going to say this once. I expect fucking results, and I haven't seen shit from any of you except excuses," her eyes darted to Jonathan to shift the blame on him for all the piss poor explanations he had given her. "Horrible judgment calls," her gaze moved to Ethan, knocking his brash actions. "And a whole bunch of nothing." She stared at the last of the bunch, Sammy.

It was Sammy who tried to defend himself first, "Layne, there's not a trail to follo—"

Her hands slammed down onto the table in small fists as she rose to her feet and snapped at him. "He's not a fucking ghost! There's a fucking trail somewhere! I don't give a shit if you have to talk to every goddamn hooker in the five boroughs! *Somebody* knows *something*!"

Lord help her, she wanted to shoot the next person who tried to tell anything less than helpful to her current situation.

It wasn't just the lack of action and information that had her anger topping out, but the stress that, at any moment, Liam could strike again, and she wouldn't see it coming. He had already managed to take her by surprise twice; she didn't want to be caught off guard a charming third time.

Jonathan immediately went into mediator mode and

raised both of his hands in front of him. "Let's just take a moment here to evaluate everything."

She tilted her head as she stared at her prime negotiator, a mostly clean-cut-looking guy. His dark brown was always styled into place, and just the faintest semblance of a goatee around his mouth.

"What's there to evaluate? I feel like a sitting duck, all I've got is twenty-four-seven security detail up my ass and the realization that Liam has been stealing from me. What part of that should make me feel good about where we are currently at, huh?"

Met with blank stares for a moment, all she could hear was her pulse roaring in her ears as her blood pressure rose in conjunction with her temper.

"What do you want us to do?" Ethan shifted in his seat as he posed the question to her.

Layne hung her head down as she shut her eyes, trying to think past her swirling emotions. Refusing to sit back down, she spoke through gritted teeth, "Someone get me a fucking name. The name of someone who can help me. I don't care who they are or where they're from."

When she lifted her head and opened her eyes, they were all still sitting there with solemn looks on their damn faces.

"NOW!" She barked at them, wondering what they were waiting for.

Sam was the first to push out of his chair and leave the room, followed quickly by Jonathan.

Ethan was slow to make his way out, stopping and whispering to her, "Liam always finds a way to fuck himself over; we'll find something sooner or later." Then, there was hesitation as his voice caught as though he was about to say something more.

Layne looked up at the broad and muscular man at her side. His longer locks of blonde hair hung down out of place in front of his eyes.

"What else?" she said defeatedly, expecting another dose of bad news.

Unsure of what lengths Layne was willing to go to or how desperate she was feeling, he hesitated in directing her towards a wild card. Ethan cleared his throat. "There's a high roller at table fifteen, the one that looks like he's had five too many plastic surgeries. He knows a guy that might be able to help."

The faintest glimmer of hope began to chase away her frustration. "What type of guy?"

"Just," he sighed, "a guy that I've heard that has methods that would have sent Eric Ellis crying to his mommy. Some Russian dipshit, not anyone I would want watching my back."

Of course, it was a deranged Russian—those assholes always seemed to have a screw loose. This bit of information sounded both promising and terrifying.

Seeing the gears turning in Layne's head, Ethan frowned and placed a hand on top of hers. "Only for use in case of emergency, Layne. I'm serious."

She gave a slow nod as she took it all under consideration.

"Thanks, E. I appreciate it." Layne offered him a light

smile before he did the same and left her there with her considerations of what she should do.

Once she composed herself and pulled her big boss bitch panties on, she headed over to table fifteen. Sure enough, there was some man who should have looked old enough to be her grandfather, yet his face was stretched so tight that the jazzercise leotards from the eighties would have been jealous.

When she approached, she lifted a finger to the attendant at the roulette table, prompting a pause in action. Layne pulled up a seat next to the man Ethan directed her to.

Mr. Shiny Plastic Face glanced over at her and grunted.

Layne leaned against the edge of the table as she faced him. "I don't think I need to introduce myself. I need the name of someone who's known to get results, and I'm told you're the man who is going to give it to me."

The fucker laughed like she was running a standup comedy joint here. The other players at the table even knew that had been a mistake, and all seemed to lean back in their chairs.

Her cheeks grew warm with the flare of her irritation. Not in the mood to play fucking games with some rich asshole, she snatched the back of his head and slammed it forward into the table.

The impact had chips rattling and skittering in several directions. She made sure his face met the table two more times before holding his bloodied mug down against it.

She leaned in and harshly spoke to him, "The goddamn name. *Now*."

Whimpering at the superficial damage she had done to his precious face he treasured so much, he stuttered out, "M-my… pocket, left pocket. His card is in my wallet."

Pinning his head down, she went in search of the wallet. When she retrieved it, she opened it one-handedly, thumbing out a small black card from one of the slots. Layne released the gambler while she looked over the glossy cardstock with nothing but the initials 'D.P.' and a QR code on it.

"This him?" She showed the card to the man who was fumbling for cocktail napkins for the laceration above the bridge of his nose that was forking blood down both sides of his nose.

"Y-yes," he muttered.

"Thanks for your cooperation." Layne tossed the worn leather wallet onto the roulette wheel. After tucking the card away safely into her pocket, she motioned to a security guard to get the pathetic mess of a man out of her club.

Her eyes found Joey sitting at the table he had promised he'd be occupying. His soul-capturing brown eyes stared at her after the minor show of violence she had just put on. Layne's heart both swelled and ached; he was worth every last emergency call and last-ditch effort. Hell, if she wasn't going to make a deal with every devil, demon, and god if it meant preventing the two loves of her life from sacrificing themselves for her.

Chapter Fourteen

JOB OFFER

Sunrise. Sundown. Rinse and repeat. There had been no word from her trusted trio of associates, and it left her questioning whether doomsday would arrive sooner or later. There was no question it would arrive at some point.

Gage had forbidden her from talking with Liam, which had been easy enough since her brother hadn't bothered her since their last phone call. It was either a blessing or curse that she didn't have Liam chirping in her ear. But the silence? It was fucking unnerving.

Layne had kept the information about the unhinged Russian contact to herself. There was no need to get one or both De Lucas riled up over her consideration of involving a potentially risky third party. Not to mention, no matter how many attempts she made to get the QR code to work on the business card, it kept giving her various errors. They weren't your standard 404 errors when the webpage no longer existed; the errors had such foreign code to her that she was pretty sure she had been trying to break into the Matrix.

"Have you heard back from…" Joey grimaced before saying Brandon's cringy hacker name, "Cowboy?"

Layne pulled another dress from the rack inside the high-end clothing store, looking it over, she shook her head. "No, he said he should have something soon though. He's just running through the street cameras looking for any sign of Liam and his two miscreants coming or going from the Chinese restaurant."

She turned and raised the black satin cocktail dress for Gage to see. "Yes or no?"

Gage immediately shook his head and gave a thumbs down. "Baby, while anything you pick is going to look amazing on the floor, I think you're better off with some-thing that makes you stand out in the crowd. Everyone needs to know that you're with me and to bow down to the fucking Queen of New York." He grinned proudly.

"You said the theme is 'Blackout,' and everyone was going to be wearing all black!" Layne exclaimed in exas-peration as she roughly returned the hanger to the silver hook it came from. Black dresses blended in with a crowd no matter which way you cut it. This was one of the reasons she loathed dress shopping without Rebecca.

Cassidy's Chains was hosting its official Grand Opening party in a month despite already being open for business full-time. The party was invitation only, and Gage was determined to make it one hell of an upscale bash.

Smirking, Gage reached over and pulled another dress from the rack. "How about this one?" He waggled his eyebrows suggestively at her, looking oh-so-hopeful for her acquiescence.

Layne looked at the thin strip of fabric being marketed as a dress and placed a hand on her hip. "Are you kidding me? Wearing tinfoil would be more appealing." She shook her head and went back to flipping through the options in search of another black dress.

Gage chuckled and shrugged before returning the dress to where it came from.

Accompanying Layne shopping wasn't high on Joey's list of favorite things to do, but they had turned their group date into shopping, dinner, and a show. He leaned against a wall, crossing his arms in front of his chest.

Feeling his phone vibrate, a notification in his pocket, Joey dug it out and looked at the message that had just come in. "Jonathan says he might have something of interest."

She shifted her attention over to Joey; her curiosity was immediately piqued at the first sign of life from one of her worker bees. "Tell him after we leave here, we are heading to Qwerty for dinner; he can debrief me before we eat."

Clearing his throat, Gage chimed in, "*After* we eat. Anything related to your brother pisses you off, and then you bitch you're not hungry. So, he can tell you after you have something in your stomach."

With a frustrated groan, Layne rolled her eyes. "So, I can be pissed and nauseous throughout the show?"

"After dinner then," Joey confirmed, taking Gage's side as he texted the details over to Jonathan. If she was worried about the topic of Liam souring her mood tonight, he had plans to counteract that. Plans that involved having her squirming in her seat during the show.

His eyes glanced over at Layne, lustfully thinking of all the ways to make sure she was aptly distracted during the highly-rated acrobat show they planned to attend. It wasn't some family-friendly circus show, this one was advertised as quite the opposite, with darker themes of seduction and the magnificence of the human body.

Joey dropped his cell back into his pocket. As he was about to get comfortable against the wall, something caught his eye. He promptly walked over to a rack several down from Layne, selecting a dress from it, and he returned to them both.

"This one." The hanger dangled from Joey's fingers and suspended from it was a striking crimson dress.

Her eyes were immediately drawn to the beauty of the garment. While she thought it was stunning, it wasn't even close to the party's dress code. "Joey, it's red."

Gage immediately let out an appreciative whistle. "It's perfect." He smiled broadly, immediately falling in love with the shape of the dress. His dick was stirring to life in his pants, just thinking about how it would cling to Layne's body and how the color would match her spirit. Dress code be damned.

Despite her protests, both Joey and Gage refused to consider any other dress but the one Joey had selected. Once again, the De Luca brothers outvoted her.

After they left the store, they all had a delicious meal together at the oddly named upscale restaurant and micro-brewery.

At the end of the meal, Jonathan arrived at their table. He stole an unused chair from the next table over and dragged it to the empty space between Gage and Layne.

Standing, Gage's hand took the back of the chair her associate brought over. "Take my seat."

The two men stared at one another in a battle of intimidation before Jonathan looked to Layne for her opinion. Gage didn't bother waiting for input from anyone; he immediately occupied the chair right next to Layne. He didn't give a fuck who the pretty boy thought he was; he didn't want anyone coming between him and his girl.

"Looks like you're taking Gage's seat." Layne shrugged.

Doubling down, Gage draped his arm along the back of Layne's chair and flashed a shit-eating grin.

With Joey seated on the other side of Layne, he smirked, knowing damn well he would have done the same exact thing as his brother. Well, maybe he would have done it a bit more aggressively and shoved Jonathan down into the seat.

Layne took a large sip from the frosted pint glass filled with a beer that had hoppy notes of citrus and pine. It carried enough of an alcohol content that she was feeling less tense than she had at the start of dinner.

Not able to wait another minute to hear whatever was discovered, she prompted him, "Spill it." Her eyes set on the man who was supposed to be a diplomatic guru and curator of navigating the toughest conversations.

Jonathan subtly wiped his palms against the thighs of his pants. "He purchased 430 East 84th Street."

She damn near dropped her beer. If it hadn't been for Gage's quick reflexes that took the glass from her hand and set it on the table in front of her, it would have ended all over the front of her blouse and jeans.

"Motherfucker," Joey grumbled, recognizing the address of the residence of one very deceased Eric Ellis. Layne had put the piece of real estate on the market months ago and recently off-loaded it with the acceptance of a generous offer.

The disbelief threaded through each of Layne's words, "What? It was sold to a corporation; it was plain as day on the settlement papers."

Her associate apologetically scrunched his eyebrows together as he looked at her. "SVO & Son Enterprises? It's just a placeholder, Layne. Liam's the sole owner."

Once again, her brother had flown under her radar. "Scott Vance O'Reilly and Son Enterprises," she muttered at the realization. This time, it was so blatantly under her nose that he had done it, she was pretty sure Liam's ego right now was the biggest it ever had been.

Gage's hand squeezed her thigh supportively. "He's fucked in the head, baby. He's trying to emulate your dad and live out whatever skewed sense of what could have been."

Joey looked over at Layne with pain and anger filling his eyes at how things were getting so much worse and not looking any better. He should have thrown Liam in the trunk of Shannon O'Reilly's car before it blew to pieces if he had been graced with the foresight to know how the youngest of the O'Reilly clan would haunt him so many years later.

Looking over at Jonathan, Joey cut to the chase, "What's he want with Eric's property?"

"Don't know. Your guess is as good as mine." Jonathan shrugged before looking over at Layne. "There's one more thing."

The way her stomach was beginning to churn, she was regretting the burger she had consumed twenty minutes ago. Her eyes narrowed at Jonathan, wondering what the hell else could be dumped on her.

"He…" her associate paused to choose his words carefully. "He called Sammy earlier. Sam didn't want to say anything to you, not after our meeting at the Brass Mirror. He made me swear not to tell you, but..."

Her eyes went from the warm green of a grassy knoll on a summer day to the shadowy moss on rocks at the bottom of an oceanside cliff. "Tell. Me. What?" Layne squeezed her words out past her clenched jaw as she leaned forward.

"Liam offered Sam a job." His visible discomfort as he shifted in his seat indicated that this wasn't a job involving doing grocery checkout at the supermarket.

A lump formed in Layne's throat, and both De Lucas on either side of her had their tensions inflating a thickness in the air around their table.

All eyes were on Jonathan; everyone on edge, waiting.

"Um, he turned it down, but… Liam offered Sam a well-paid spot on his team if Sam would, I quote, 'force his dick in you until you were broken and bleeding.'" It was clear from the shade of beet red that Jonathan's cheeks were now turning that he hadn't wanted to deliver this message either.

Gage nearly flipped the damn table over the second he shot up onto his feet, ready to brutally slaughter the messenger.

As the words sank in, Layne sat there feeling like the walls were closing in all around her.

Joey's rage followed closely behind his brother's, but he had the clarity not to take it out on Jonathan.

In the depths of her soul, Layne wanted to believe that those words never came out of Liam's mouth. Yet, all she could hear was her brother's twisted laughter inside of her head. She squeezed her eyes shut, trying to force all the thoughts back into a tiny black box inside of her where she never had to acknowledge they existed.

When her eyelids popped back open, Joey was ripping Gage off of her associate, who appeared so shaken that she would be surprised if he hadn't pissed his pants.

Getting in Jonathan's face, Gage spat out threat after threat, "If any of you fuckers ever consider laying a goddamn finger on her, I will fucking toss you into a bath of nitric acid and watch you rot!" He clenched onto the front of Jonathan's shirt, gave him several harsh shakes, and refused to let go.

She fought the urge to look around at the gawkers who were watching the scene they were causing in the otherwise tame atmosphere. Instead, she focused on reeling in her thoughts within the unraveling chaos in her small little world there at the table.

Attempting to force the trembling sensation in her limbs to cease, she got onto her feet. She put a hand each on Joey and Gage to draw their attention. Maybe it was the pleading look in her eyes or the draining of color from her face, but the hold on Jonathan's shirt was relinquished, and Gage allowed Joey to pull him back a few steps.

Her head was spinning, so when she spoke to her associate, who was sitting there wide-eyed, she wasn't even sure how much of what she said was intelligible. "Find out why—why he bought the house."

She backed up a couple of steps and grabbed her jacket off the back of her chair on her hurried exit from the restaurant. Gage followed directly behind her, leaving Joey glaring at Jonathan.

"The next time you have any information on that fuck-face, you bring it to me first." There was no need for Joey to tack on an 'or else' to his demand, the deadly cold stare he gave was enough to make a corpse shiver.

Chapter Fifteen

LET THE GAMES BEGIN

The crisp air outside the restaurant had been more refreshing than the beer she had been drinking inside. The breeze swept away some of the panic that had been attempting to pull her under.

She pushed her arms into the sleeves of her cargo-style jacket, her hands pulling her long brunette tresses out from underneath the back of it afterward.

Layne remained standing out front, watching the hustle and bustle of the people on the sidewalk. The microbrewery, Qwerty, was basically in the center of the busiest section of Times Square. Even with the evening quickly falling over the city, the massive number of electronic signs lit up the area like it was high noon.

A pair of strong arms came down around her, pulling her back into the safety and warmth of Gage's chest. His face nuzzled into the side of her neck, lightly kissing over the soft skin and inhaling the scent of her soap.

"How are you doing, Lucky Charm?" His voice was

just loud enough for her to hear but gentle enough not to come off as startling.

She swallowed down another piece of her anxiety. "I'm fine."

Gage's arms squeezed around her, wishing they could make everything right in her world.

Stepping outside right as Layne responded, Joey came around to face her. He cradled her face in his hands. "Layney, we all know that's bullshit. It's okay if—"

With a bit more forcefulness in her tone, she repeated herself, "I said I'm fine. If he wants to give me more reason to hate him, he's only making my life easier."

It was the answer she wanted them to hear, not the one she wanted to scream into the void. Trying to blow by the topic of her asshole sibling, she stepped out from between the two men. "We're going to be late for the show."

Allowing her to create space for herself, Gage dropped his arms from around her, and Joey's fingertips glided across her cheeks as she began to walk into the flow of foot traffic.

Layne led the way, with Joey and Gage quietly conversing two strides behind her. Both of them made sure they had a set of eyes on her back.

Joey leaned over, whispering to his brother, "Have you heard back from any of your buddies if they've discovered any other shifts amongst the other factions?"

Gage shook his head. "Nothing. Have you made the call?"

Inhaling deeply with a slow exhale, Joey also shook his

head. "I'm trying to avoid it. It's a favor I don't want to ask unless we get desperate."

"Joe, this shit isn't going to de-escalate itself. He already tried to shoot her once."

Grunting at the memory of the pain of having a bullet lodged in his chest, Joey's hand rubbed the fresh scar over his heart. "Don't have to remind me."

They all passed by a set of doors that led from a theater. Timing as it was, a show was just letting out, and a sea of people came pouring from the double doors. The human stampede came between Layne and the guys, separating them further and obscuring Joey and Gage's view of their girl.

Joey yelled out, "Layne, hold up!" His words were lost over the sound of boisterous conversations of the audience that had just left the theater.

"Fuck," Gage muttered as he tried to push through the crowd.

When both guys got past the sudden surge of people, they still couldn't lay eyes on where Layne had wandered off to.

"She probably is still heading straight for the show's venue," Joey attempted to reason.

The two of them stepped off to the side, out of the flow of pedestrian traffic. Gage took out his phone and was in the process of pulling up Layne's location when a seemingly old homeless man with a Yankees ball cap approached them.

The strange man was hunched over and wobbly on his two feet. The brim of the cap shrouded his face, but visible was his peppered beard, which was unkempt and scraggly as it extended several inches below his chin.

With an unsure and meek voice, the disheveled man leaned in towards Gage, "P-please, excuse me. Could you spare some money? I could use some food."

Barely sparing the man a glance and irritated with the homeless man's shitty timing, Joey placed a hand on the vagrant's chest to stop him from getting closer to Gage. "Sorry, man, can't help." Joey continued to peer over at the phone in Gage's hand.

Gage's impatience grew by the second as he waited for Layne's blue dot to appear on the phone's digital map. Just as it did, the stranger tried to pull the phone from his hands.

"Maybe I could use your phone instead?" The strange man's strangely clean hands tugged at the device Gage was holding.

Defensively, Gage grabbed the dude's wrist and took back possession of his phone. He flung the man's hand away from him.

Angrily, Gage shouted, "Back the fuck up, mother-fucker! What the hell is wrong with you?!" Jesus, he had never seen a homeless person so damn brazen before.

Joey huffed and, pulled a twenty from his pocket and tossed it at the guy. "Here, get the hell outta here asshole!"

The man fumbled for the bill and began to profusely thank them both, trying to shake their hands and grace them with all the blessings in the world.

When the crazy beggar went on his way, Joey looked over at Gage's phone. "Got eyes on her?"

With a nod, Gage zoomed in on her location and then

looked up at their surroundings. "She should be right over there," his finger pointing towards the mob of tourists filling the heart of the popular sightseeing destination.

"Fuckin' Times Square," Joey muttered at the insanely busy area that made this place a nightmare to traverse.

***

Feeling the sudden herd of people behind her, Layne stopped and looked back. Her eyes were unable to locate either Joey or Gage. "Great…"

After feeling a figure knock into her shoulder, she stumbled a half step before a painful grip curled around her bicep. Her head spun around to face whoever was holding onto her, to be greeted with the face of the last person she wished to see tonight.

Liam's lips curled into a forced smile. "Keep walking." He yanked her close to his side.

Before she could protest, underneath the coverage of her jacket, she felt the unforgiving metal tip of a blade digging into her side. It was positioned perfectly between her fourth and fifth ribs, if he wanted to drive it into her heart, he easily could have.

Her brother leaned over and whispered into her ear as he led her farther away from her dutiful protectors, "At least fuckin' smile like you're happy to see me."

When her scowl didn't leave her face, more pressure was applied to the knife placed at her side.

Layne snarled as she mustered as much of a damn smile

as he was going to get from her. "I'll be happy to see you when you're lying in a coffin."

As they walked into the thick crowd of the tourist area, he came to a stop right in the middle of the most densely populated section and also the most public. Times Tower, the twenty-five-story building with its iconic three-hundred-and-fifty-foot LED screen, loomed over them. The colors of the changing advertisements flashed across both their faces.

Her eyes quickly surveyed the busy surroundings. She scanned the area for Joey and Gage, assessed opportunities for a swift getaway, and noted the occasional police officer performing their public safety duties. Nothing was in her favor; Joey and Gage were lost in the crowd, the foot traffic was too thick and unpredictable, and murdering her brother in the middle of Times Square would be a publicity nightmare in the best-case scenario—battling homicide charges was the worst case. This was all assuming she wasn't stabbed to death first.

Keeping close to her, Liam's painful grip never let up. He kept his face inches from hers. "Did you get my message, Layne?"

She glared at him. "What message?"

Liam snickered, clearly getting off on the games he was playing that had been concocted inside his demented mind. "The message that there isn't anyone who I'm not willing to turn against you. Everybody has their price, and I have the funds to pay it."

"Go fuck yourself, Li. Not everyone in my inner circle can be bought." Trying to pull her body away from the threat of being stabbed was unsuccessful, and the tip poked through the thin layer of her shirt and then pierced the first layers of skin. Her hardened exterior faltered for the first time. Layne sharply inhaled as she winced, feeling the light tickle of a drop of her blood begin to drip down her side.

Her brother's face displayed wicked amusement at getting that brief reflection of her pain from her.

"Oh, you mean fuck boys one and two? Are you sure they're as loyal to you as they say?" He cocked his head at her, hazel eyes staring into her own and beating at the door of her soul's resiliency.

When she refused to respond, she was sure he was going to shove the blade between her ribs as the pressure continued to painfully increase.

"Check your phone." His weapon pulled back on the threat to impale her, but only just enough that she could breathe a little easier.

The urge to take her chances of making national headlines by blowing her brother away in Times Square was looking more and more appealing. However, she followed his instructions, and her hand slowly pulled her phone from her jacket pocket. Her eyes glanced down at the screen, where a notification from an unknown number was waiting for her.

"Go on, Layne, check your messages," Liam urged with nearly giddy excitement.

Using her thumb to unlock the phone and check the latest message, her fingers could barely conceal their trembling. When she pulled up the text, it only contained pictures.

The first picture was of a young woman in her early twenties with a large pregnant belly. Layne didn't recognize the girl at all. "So what? Do you need the birds and the bees to be explained to you?"

"Don't you know who that is? That's Mackenzie Pearce, the daughter of the tragically murdered Mayor Pearce. She's due with a baby boy any day now." The way Liam pretended he cared made Layne's disgust come to a head.

Her thoughts reeled back to when Joey had taken the contract on the retired mayor's head a little over eight months ago.

"You said it was an in-and-out job," Layne looked at Joey as he came into the living room, coming home later than expected.

He tossed his work duffle onto the floor next to the sofa, and his words came out strained with irritation, "It would have been, but apparently, his daughter was visiting for the holiday and was staying over."

Layne lifted a brow. "So, what did you do?"

Joey's hand pinched the bridge of his nose. "What the hell do you think? I took care of it–of her."

She blinked several times at him at his snippy response and uncharacteristically bad mood.

"I'm going upstairs to shower and go to bed." He left her there without so much as an apology or effort to smooth over his shortness with her.

Normally, after he finished a contract, he wanted nothing more than to curl up with her and relax. Not this time.

Coming back to the present with the image of the woman in front of her, she felt conflicted with all the things her heart knew about Joey and what her brain was trying to rationalize.

Liam lowered his voice to ask his next question, "How confident are you that he bothered using protection when he was fucking her?"

Layne pressed her lips together in a hard line, trying to combat the intrusive thoughts riddling her core with doubts. Joey had never bothered using a condom when he was with her, and since she was on birth control, she had never questioned it before now.

She tried to move past all the scenarios trying to infiltrate her mind by swiping to the next picture in the message.

The next image was of Gage and two attractive women inside his club. Looking closer at the surroundings, it was sometime after the renovations were done to convert Cassidy's Cave into Cassidy's Chains. Each woman was perched on one of his knees with his hands holding each of them around their waists. They were leaning in close to him, their fucking tits practically up in his face and their hands resting right on top of his damn crotch like they owned it.

Her brother frowned. "I'm sorry, sis. You deserve better. You can't possibly expect them to stick to one partner when you won't do the same." He watched as he saw the gradual decline in the faith of her two guys in her eyes filled with unshed tears.

Trying to come up with good reasons for the stories

behind both pictures was becoming a losing battle. Her hand shakily turned the screen off, yet she could see both photos popping up in her mind still.

Sniffling back her emotions, her eyes looked at Liam, and shook her head firmly. "It doesn't change what you've done." Internally, she grasped for any straw of anger to chase back her rattled insecurities.

Liam shrugged and tapped the knife idly against her ribcage. "When you're ready to fall in line, I will be waiting. You had your chance to hand everything over to me and take your leave quietly. Now? Things have to get messy so that you can learn your lesson."

In the distance, over the dull roar of the crowd, she heard her name being shouted. Her attention was drawn away from Liam as she looked frantically for a familiar face or two. The first pair of chocolate eyes she met was Gage's, followed by the coffee hues belonging to Joey.

Realizing his time with Layne was up, Liam withdrew the threatening blade from her side and released his painful hold on her arm. No sooner had he done both of those things than he thrust the knife down into the muscle of her thigh.

Layne gasped as she felt the cold steel enter her leg, when she looked down, there was a goddamn pocket knife in her body. Well, fuck. That wasn't supposed to be there, was it? The searing pain quickly followed the sight her brain was trying to wrap itself around.

When she looked back up, Liam was already quickly blending back into the movement of people all around her.

Ragged breaths escaped her as the pain and rage fused together in her veins.

Both her men had rushed to her the second they saw Liam leering over their girl. From their angle, they only saw a movement from Liam before Layne flinched and hunched over. The coward took off quickly thereafter.

"Layne!" Joey appeared at her side first.

Losing all sense in the hurricane of her feelings, she was already pulling out her Glock. Layne was prepared to empty her goddamn clip if it meant there was a chance of one bullet finding its way into Liam's skull.

Coming to her other side, Gage's hand abruptly shoved her arm back down, quickly pulling the firearm from her grasp and tucking it inside the front of his waistband underneath his shirt. He harshly whispered in her ear, "Hey! What the hell are you doing?"

"That fucking, son of a bitch, asshole!" The anger in her voice was enhanced by both the physical and emotional pain she was experiencing. She went to take a step to go after Liam, forgetting there was a fucking pocket knife stuck in her. Layne stumbled as the pain reminded her of that small but important fact.

Joey's hands caught her by her arm and waist. He looked down at Liam's parting gift and cursed under his breath. "Gage, we gotta get her out of here." He glanced around them, hoping between the both of them, they could cloak Layne's injury with their massive frames until they got someplace private.

Gage wrapped an arm around her. "Baby, just hold onto me."

She winced as the pain just seemed to blossom across her entire thigh now that her adrenaline was slowly fading. Feeling both of their hands on her, images flashed across her memory of the images on her phone.

"Don't touch me!" She snapped at them, shoving their hands away.

Seeing her lash out at both of them as they tried to help took them by surprise.

Her gaze fell back down to her leg, and the blood soaked into her jeans. "Fuck!" Layne groaned as her hand went to the handle of the knife, wrapping around it, ready to yank it out.

"Whoa, whoa, whoa." Joey took both her hands before she did something stupid. "Just stop, Layne. Look at me and fucking think for a damn second."

While she was directing her vicious stare at Joey, it was Gage who began tying the arms of his jacket around Layne's hips to cover the glaring injury before anyone else noticed.

As clouded as her head was, filled with a myriad of emotions ranging from highs to lows, Layne still recognized that she couldn't just stand there in her current state. "Call Jonathan and have him come here to pick me up and bring me to Dr. Patty's."

Gage tightened the knot of the jacket around her hips and looked over at Joey, hoping he wasn't the only one of them confused by her request for one of her associates.

Not seeing any indication that Joey knew what the fuck was going on, Gage reached over to try to hold her face. "Look at me, Layne," his tone soft in hopes she wouldn't verbally or physically lash out again. "Let us help you, baby. I don't know what happened, but we need to get you patched up."

The tug of emotions in her eyes was causing them to fill with watery frustration and pain. "I don't want you to do anything except call Jonathan and have him come get me." Her voice shook. Jonathan wasn't her first choice, but he was likely the next best one, given she knew he had been in the area after their discussion at the restaurant.

Joey's irritation was clear as he spoke under his breath, "This is fucking insane." Regardless, he pulled out his phone and called her associate as requested.

While he gave Jonathan directions, he and Gage assisted Layne to the nearest side street that was mostly out of the public eye. She stubbornly tried to refuse as much of their help as possible. Gage finally bit the bullet and risked suffering her wrath when he wrapped an arm around her waist and all but damn carried her the last few steps against his side.

Refusing to make eye contact with either De Luca brother, she silently leaned back against the side of a building while they waited for Layne's ride to arrive. Not accepting any further assistance, she used Gage's jacket to help stem the bleeding until she got proper medical attention.

Layne looked down at the knife buried in her left quadriceps. Her chin quivered as she saw the silver inscription lasered into the black handle.

J. De Luca

Chapter Sixteen

PATCHED UP

Her torn and bloodied jeans were in a pile next to her on the patient table inside Dr. Patty Kimmel's in-home clinic. Layne sat there in her underwear, furiously typing on her phone.

Jonathan was doing his best not to directly stare at his half-dressed boss, despite her obvious lack of fucks given.

"Are you sure you don't want me to wait outside?" He asked for the sixth time.

Growing more irritated every time he asked, Layne finally lowered her hands into her lap and looked over at him with exasperation filling her tone. "You want to be useful? Go outside and tell Joey and Gage to go the hell home."

The guys had followed Jonathan's car there to Dr. Patty's house, despite her repeated protests that her associate was more than capable of getting her there in one piece.

Unsure whose fury he would have rather endured in

that moment, it seemed getting out of the room with Layne seemed the wisest decision. Jonathan took the opportunity and immediately scurried out into the hall.

A minute later, Layne could hear the front door close as he went to deliver her message. Did she really think either man lingering out front would listen to him? No, but it at least gave her a few minutes of peace with her thoughts.

She returned to tapping out a few more texts on her phone to her trusted techie, Brandon. From a short stool in front of Layne, the doctor glanced up at her and spoke without judgment in her voice. "You know as well as I do, Layne, that poor man is going to get an earful." She gave a soft chuckle.

Layne sighed. "His damn nervous energy was going to drive me insane if he stayed in here any long—" A hiss of pain escaped her lips as a fresh wave of pain coursed through her thigh.

"Sorry, all done." The woman in front of her finished wrapping the bandage around Layne's leg before getting up from the stool she had been perched on. With a light snapping sound, Dr. Patty removed the latex gloves from her hands and tossed them into a waste basket.

Silence filled the room, but it wasn't until Layne realized that Dr. Patty hadn't moved that she stopped her fingers' swift movements across the screen of her phone. The doctor was standing there with her hip cocked and a hand on her waist, looking at Layne over the tops of her glasses.

"What?" Layne asked in clear confusion as to why she was getting a stern look from her private physician.

Granted, getting stabbed wasn't an ideal visit, though very few of her visits were routine checkups. Layne would like to think she had been a half-decent patient in not punching the crap out of the doctor when the knife had been dislodged from her leg.

Dr. Patty pulled the glasses from her face and perched them on top of her head. "I know the look of trouble in paradise, and I know you. Do you want my non-medical advice?"

"Are you going to give it to me anyway?" Layne had a feeling she knew the answer and expected to hear a long, drawn-out speech about playing nice in the sandbox, not being so damn stubborn, and how everything would be back to normal in a day or so. That was not the talk she got.

"Do they even know why you're pissed off?" She paused and then raised both her brows at Layne. "Do *you* even know why you're pissed off?"

The pointed questions weren't what Layne had expected. She took a moment to carefully mull over what she was asking, then frowned. Layne started to respond, "I..." but then she realized she didn't have a worthy answer.

Layne's eyes watched as the doc moved over to the sink and grabbed an item off the counter. When she returned, she held her hand out to Layne. Lying there in her palm was the pocket knife belonging to Joey that Liam had rudely embedded in her leg.

Taking the weapon from Dr. Patty, she gave a partial attempt at a smile. "Thanks."

Lowering her now empty hand, she continued, "I don't

know Gage as well as I know Joey, but one of those men took a bullet for you. If that doesn't speak to his character, I don't know what does. So, whatever has you in a tizzy, the least you could do is clue them in on it. In all my years of practicing medicine, I have never come across a man who can read a woman's mind except when it comes to one thing. Even then, it's a rarity."

Looking down at the inscription on the knife, Layne nodded. The truth was, both men had taken a bullet for her. Would they be capable of betraying her trust after something like that? What if they really had gone so far as to break their bonds with her? Maybe they both decided that if she got to indulge in more than one partner, then they should be afforded that luxury as well.

Pulling Layne from her thoughts, the woman spoke as she moved to the door, "Just something to think about." She winked and gave a smile to Layne that was filled with kindness and warmth before leaving Layne to get dressed.

After dropping the knife into her jacket pocket, Layne was pulling up her jeans gingerly over her thighs as her phone began to ring. Answering, she pinned the phone to her ear with her shoulder as her fingers buttoned and zipped her pants. "Howdy, Cowboy. I'm guessing you got all my messages?"

Brandon spoke into her ear, and what he said had her straightening up and taking the phone into her hand. "What do you mean the QR code leads to a site that needs a password? It's just a bunch of garbled nonsense when I pull the site up."

Unsurprisingly, Brandon was better at this tech bullshit

than she was and was able to sort through the code to find the access point. Apparently, said portal needed a password. That was incredibly inconvenient.

Great, now she needed something she didn't have in order to contact a guy she didn't know. "Okay, I will work on it. What about the two photos I sent over to you?"

She listened carefully as Brandon explained that the photo of Mackenzie Pearson was legitimate, it was even posted on the girl's socials. He hadn't been able to find anything out about the father-to-be, effectively leaving Layne still questioning Joey's behavior when he was out of her sight.

There was some good news: the photograph of Gage was a complete fabrication, a good one but fake nonetheless. Fucking AI was getting better and better these days.

Cringing and feeling sheepish, Layne groaned at her idiocy for allowing Liam to fucking toy with her head.

Her hacker friend on the phone continued to give her updates on the other things he was working on, including finding out who had been with Liam at the Chinese restaurant. Brandon had been able to pull images of the two individuals and was cross-referencing their identities as he spoke.

She felt some of her stress melt away. "I appreciate the update. Let me know when you have a name or anything else useful." At least they were getting somewhere on finding out more about who was working with Liam.

As Layne said goodbye and hung up, she heard the

front door of Dr. Patty's home aggressively slam shut, followed by heavy stomps approaching the exam room.

Swinging the door open, Joey burst into the room, his voice booming in the quaint space. "What the hell is going on with you?! I'm not taking fucking orders from Jonathan just because you're being too chickenshit to come talk to us yourself!"

She opened her mouth to say something, but he stepped up in front of her, continuing to yell so she couldn't get a word in edgewise.

"When the hell are you going to get it through your thick fucking skull that we are doing every goddamn thing we can to protect your ass and take care of you?! Instead, you keep fighting us tooth, nail, and titty on it!" He kept leaning in towards her with each word he shouted in her face.

In frustration, he let out a growl before continuing his venting, "You are the biggest pain in my ass! I swear to God, if I didn't know better, I'd think you have a fuckin' death wish!"

Layne had enough of his anger being hurtled at her that she finally snapped and began to toss it right back at him. She squared her shoulders, and her hand pushed at his chest as a warning for him to step back.

"Who the fuck do you think you are coming in here acting like you're not as big of a pain in the ass, huh?! You don't get to charge in here, ready to unleash hell on me because you don't like what I'm doing! I didn't ask for either of you to fuckin' hover over me, ready to protect me from a goddamn papercut!" Seeing that he hadn't budged from his position looming over her, she used both hands to shove him this time.

Joey's eyes widened before he pointed at her leg. "You call this a paper cut?!"

Gage came to the doorway of the room right as Layne was beginning to get physical with Joey. As equally frustrated with Layne as his brother was, he had still tried to talk him out of storming in here to wage a war none of them actually wanted. He made another attempt to intervene by firmly speaking up, "Both of you need to calm the fuck down."

With a glance at Gage, Joey sharply responded, "Fuck you! I am fucking calm!"

Layne scoffed at how clearly he was, in fact, not the least bit calm. "Get the hell out of my way. Gage can take me home."

When she went to shove him again, he defensively diverted her hands away with a firm push.

"Now all is good with him 'cause he's not the one calling you out?!" The anger still boiled beneath Joey's skin.

"At least he's not going around knocking up some girl while working a contract!" The words just fumbled out of her mouth before she could realize she was saying them. Sometimes her temper could be a heinous bitch.

Gage's eyes widened enough that they nearly fell out of his head while wondering if he correctly heard what Layne had just said.

Joey froze, standing there slack-jawed like she had just slapped him. His lips moved to try and find a response, but no words fell from him. Stunned by her accusation, he watched as Layne pushed past him and stepped around Gage to leave the room.

"What is she talking about?" Gage looked at his brother, hoping for clarification. He didn't want to murder his own brother, but if what Layne had said was true, he wouldn't hesitate.

Finally snapping out of trying to process what she had just claimed, he shook his head and stalked after her. "I have no fuckin' clue, but I'm about to find out," his voice calmer as he responded to Gage's question on his way by. Gage followed behind, needing the same answers.

Even fueled by her emotions, the fresh wound in her thigh had her moving slower than she would have liked. She had barely gotten to the front door when Joey ran up behind her and grabbed her by the elbow. He didn't let up when she rolled her shoulder to try and pull free from him.

Swinging her around to face him, Joey's confusion was quickly overriding the outrage he had been unleashing moments ago. "Layne! Have you lost your mind? What in the hell are you talking about?"

Her face was flushed, and she refused to meet his eyes. "Just forget it."

"Forget it?!" He caught himself beginning to relight the extremely short fuse he currently had going on. Taking a deep and steady breath, he did his best to ground himself. "Who is knocking up who?" It sounded ridiculous even to ask the question. He lowered his face down, trying to force her to look into his concerned brown hues.

Layne saw the doctor standing at the far end of the hall,

overseeing the scene unfold. The look she was giving Layne reminded her of the one she had given earlier when she had asked what had Layne so upset.

She shifted her eyes from Dr. Patty to look at Joey, who was waiting for her to explain. Layne's emerald eyes were fighting not to fill with tears as she quietly said the name, "You and Mackenzie Pearson."

Joey wrinkled his forehead, becoming more perplexed. "*Mackenzie?*" The way he spoke her name was like it could leave an STD in his mouth. Good God, he wouldn't have touched that twisted bitch no matter how much she paid him.

Explaining further, "Yeah, I mean, it all makes sense. You were so damn off that night you came home from the job and refused to talk about it. You've never been that way after a job–ever." Layne shrugged defeatedly before attempting to pry herself out of his grasp again, only to remain unsuccessful.

He stared at her, trying to wrap his head around what alternate universe Layne thought they were living in. Then, Joey couldn't help it when a laugh bubbled up from his chest at the insanity of it all. He tried to hold it back, but the more his brain envisioned fucking Mackenzie, the next few laughs couldn't be contained.

Layne scowled at him. "I'm glad you find this fucking amusing, asshole." Taking his laughter as a sign of admission, she was damn near the point of kicking him in the balls to see if he thought that shit was funny, too.

His hand released her elbow only so he could take a firm hold of her face with both hands, looking her directly in the eyes. He failed miserably at containing his smile despite his efforts to be serious with her. "Layney, first of all, I'm not putting babies in anybody—not even you. I had that shit snipped years ago."

Seeing Layne's skepticism still etched over her features, he reassured her, "I will go jack off in a cup right now, and Dr. Patty can have it analyzed just to confirm that all I got are blanks."

"Fine, then you're not the father. Congrats." Her voice was completely flat and devoid of any emotion. It still didn't mean that Joey hadn't slept with the dumb hoe.

His thumb rubbed over her cheek, trying to stroke away her doubts. "Second, the reason I was in a bad mood that night wasn't because I had to come home to you after fucking someone else. It's because Mackenzie is a whack job, she's the one who hired me to take out her dad. She wasn't even supposed to be there that night. I was trying to get the job done, and she fucking grabbed my dick—twice." He shuddered at the memory. "Then, when I tied her up to make it look like a home invasion gone wrong–and so she would keep her hands to herself–she kept moaning like a beached whale and begging me to do weird shit to her."

Joey felt dirty even thinking about that night. "Layne, it was the worst contract I've ever taken because I had to deal with her." He was also certain if he had fucked the girl, his dick would have disintegrated into ashes from some undiscovered venereal disease.

Layne's cheeks began to grow hot as Joey began to explain away all her concerns about his faithfulness. All the concerns that had spiraled out of control in her mind, thanks to all the stress Liam's bullshit was causing her.

She sank her teeth into her bottom lip as she scrunched her brows together, realizing that maybe she had overreacted and her possessiveness over the two guys got the better of her. It wasn't like her to jump to conclusions, but nothing about what was going on in her life right now felt normal.

He shook his head at her and brought his mouth down onto hers lovingly to grab her attention for what he had to say next. "Not once since the day I met you has my cock been in another woman, and it never will be. You understand me?"

She nodded. "I'm sorry… Liam had mentioned it; then today, he showed me these pictures to try to show me you both aren't as loyal to me as I thought."

Gage stiffened hearing the source of all the lies being fed to her and grumbled, "That little prick doesn't have shit on me."

Her gaze shifted to settle on Gage while she frowned with embarrassment. "I thought he did; he sent me a picture of you at the club with two girls. It ended up being a fake, but it looked so damn real, and my head was already spinning by that point."

Pulling her into a hug, Joey gave her a hard squeeze and a peck on the forehead before he released her.

Gage took his place, capturing her chin with his fingers as he traced the bottom of her lip with the pad of his thumb. "Layne Nicole De Luca," he spoke with a playful sternness but still used her full name to emphasize how serious he was. "Until there is a day where you no longer want to wear my collar, you are the only woman that exists for me. If you haven't learned that by now, I may need to finally put you on my St. Andrew's cross."

He smirked at her, already thinking how she would look spread for him on the X-frame. Gage leaned in and affectionately locked his mouth onto hers to help wash away any of the fabrications and doubts Liam had tried to fill her head with.

When the sweet moment concluded, she suddenly remembered one more thing. "Oh!" Her hand dove into her jacket pocket and pulled out Joey's pocket knife. "This is yours." Layne offered it to him.

Joey perked up a brow, seeing that it indeed was his knife. Unnerved that Liam had gotten his hands on it and then used it on Layne, his jaw ticked as he swallowed his rage. He had been looking for that knife for several weeks and assumed it was hiding out somewhere in O'Reilly Manor.

Shaking his head, Joey nudged the closed blade back into her hand. "Hold onto it. I'll let you return it to Liam in whatever method you feel he deserves." He didn't want anything responsible for spilling Layne's blood in his possession.

Dr. Patty smiled as she watched Layne with the two men in her life who were bound to her with the utmost devotion. She knew the late Scott O'Reilly would have been so proud of his daughter, no matter how unexpected her life had taken a turn.

Chapter Seventeen

CHAOS

The vision of Layne was ethereal. Her dark brunette locks of hair were being caressed by the wind in a delicate dance. The sun illuminated her fair skin and the white wedding gown she wore. When she looked at him, her breathtaking emerald eyes sparkled as her smile made them shine even brighter.

"Why didn't you kill me, Joey?" Her words didn't match the visage of a goddess he saw before him. They were such harsh words said with such a delicate voice.

Joey stood there, reaching out for her hand. "What are you talking about? Layney, I love you. I would never hurt you." Somehow, her hand was always just out of reach of his fingertips, no matter how far he stretched.

Layne's face became flooded with glittering tears. "But you did. You killed me. You made sure I wasn't in that car. You have signed my death warrant every time you saved me."

He kept running for her, trying to close the distance

between them. All he needed was to hold her. Holding her would make it all okay. Yet, no matter how fast his legs carried him, he never seemed to get any closer to her. "No, that's not true!"

Her sobs echoed in his ears. "You didn't save me this time, did you?" She looked down, and suddenly, crimson blood poured from several small holes in her chest. Holes which were created by bullets he should have taken for her. With profound sadness, she stared at her hands coated in the shiny red liquid of what should never have been spilling so freely from her body.

Joey yelled for her, feeling the painful burn of lactic acid in his legs and the ache of depleted oxygen in his lungs as he ran faster and harder for her. "NO! LAYNE!" He couldn't let her fall into death; he couldn't allow himself to lose her.

Just when he thought he could wrap his arms around her to pull her into the safe embrace of his hold, her body faded into nothing but cold.

The surroundings swirled and shifted, and now he was in the church they had been married in. At the altar were two coffins, one considerably smaller than the other.

When he approached the larger of the caskets, it remained open to reveal Shannon O'Reilly lying there in the peaceful slumber of death. He stepped over to the smaller casket, which had been left closed. Joey's hand reached out and began to lift the lid to see who was inside.

The top half of the coffin opened, and the horrific sight greeted him. A ten-year-old Layne was laid to eternal rest inside. She should have looked innocently angelic and perfect, and yet her body was bruised, and her skin was marred with damage.

The little version of Layne suddenly popped her eyes open like a creepy doll, staring directly at him. "You'll never keep me from my fate. I'm already lost."

He stumbled back, tripping over his own feet. When he fell, he expected to land on his ass—instead, the sensation of falling continued for far longer than should have been possible.

It was the jolt of startling awake from his dream that disrupted the images in his head. Joey's heart was thumping hard in his chest. Partially, he sat up as he struggled to catch his breath while he looked around the bedroom illuminated by the light of the early morning.

At his side and asleep soundly, curled up with her overstuffed pillow, was Layne. The blankets were tangled around her legs, leaving her bandaged thigh exposed to the air without the weight of the sheets on top of it. Her wavy locks of hair were held captive in a loose bun that had become half undone throughout the night.

Joey leaned over and gave the lightest of kisses to her bare shoulder so as to not wake her. He hovered close to her while he did so, drawing in the delicate scent of her body. The smell of freshly picked daisies that had been graced by the sun was what helped remind him that it all had been a nightmare.

He slid out of bed, nakedly walking around the room as quietly as his large form could manage before he located and pulled on a pair of boxer briefs. Joey took his phone off the charger and crept out into the hallway.

Allowing himself to stop tiptoeing after he was well past their bedroom door, he walked down the hall to one of the spare rooms on the second floor of O'Reilly Manor, where he locked himself inside.

There on the screen of his phone was a contact, someone he didn't want to ask a favor of. Gage had been right; there was no de-escalating the Liam situation. They were past the point of no return, and he needed to take measures with consequences be damned.

He pressed the call button and waited for someone to answer on the other end. When the bubbly receptionist picked up, Joey cleared his throat. "Hi, I need to speak to Commissioner Saito."

That afternoon, Joey found himself seated across from New York City's Police Commissioner, Vincent Saito, inside his personal residence on the North Shore of Long Island. As far as Layne was concerned, Joey was on a supply run, and Gage was left in charge of keeping watch over her.

The couch Joey was seated on was the brightest shade of white he had ever seen, and he wondered if it ever saw any use or if it just got replaced any time a stain sullied its blank canvas.

Vince held a short glass made of expensive crystal and filled with even more expensive bourbon in his hand. "Finally decided to cash in your favor, eh?" He raised the glass to his lips and swallowed down a large mouthful of the booze.

Joey rested his ankle on top of a knee as he sat back, trying to find comfort on the piece of furniture that he swore was stuffed with wood chips.

One of the household staff members Vince kept around to keep his home running smoothly brought over an identical glass of amber liquid to Joey. Taking it, Joey nodded politely and rested it on top of his knee.

"Seeing as I helped to pave the path for you to be in your current position, I figured now was as good of a time as any." Joey was keeping everything strictly business, refraining from bringing his private motivations into this discussion.

Vince may have looked like a minivan-driving soccer dad who went camping with his kids every weekend, but that didn't preclude him from being drawn into more sinister methods to get the results he wanted.

Idly swirling the remaining bourbon in his glass, the commissioner took Joey's words under his consideration. "Alright, I'll bite. What are you looking for?"

Trying to play it cool, Joey shrugged before laying it out there, "Where does Liam O'Reilly fall on your radar?"

The sudden laughter from Vince filled the massive space of a living room they were currently occupying. "Your brother-in-law?! Oh man, shit." His hand came to settle on his chest as he tried to gather his composure with a few more chuckles. "Fuck, if you were coming here to talk about anybody, I figured it'd be your wife." There were very few professional contacts who knew the unmasked version of Joey, and Vince was one of them.

Commissioner Saito snickered before he drew another

sip of the bourbon into his mouth. Licking the flavor from his lips, he shook his head. "The O'Reillys have been on the NYPD's radar for some time. I'm pretty sure the Bureau even has their eyes on them."

It wasn't news that Joey was particularly happy to hear, but that's why he was here, wasn't it?

"Your wife is a real piece of work; ya know that?" He whistled in amazement. "The body count she's racked up over the past few years is astounding–according to my sources, anyways." Vince grinned as he sank back into the sofa.

Joey stared at the man who was drunk on power, the power that Joey had helped him achieve. "I'm well aware of my wife's indiscretions. I'm more interested in why the fuck Liam is still on the streets."

Tossing back the remainder of the alcohol in his glass, the commish finally engaged in the more serious side of the matter at hand. "Liam O'Reilly isn't enough of a headline-worthy perp to be focusing the NYPD's resources on. Don't get me wrong, he's not a saint, but from a political stand-point, he's nothing. Layne, on the other hand…"

Dropping his foot from his knee onto the ground, Joey leaned forward with a deadly threat looming in his eyes and a crushing grip on his glass. "You and I had a deal."

Before Joey got too carried away, Vince lifted a hand to halt him right then and there. "Relax. I'm not going back on my word. While nailing Layne would make for head-lines of the century, she's not in any danger from my precincts." The press would have a field day with an attrac-tive young woman in charge of an organized crime unit so violent that it made grown men shiver with either desire or fear.

There was no falling back into a sense of ease for Joey before Vince tacked on one little caveat, "But, I am not the only authority. As I'm sure you've heard, the FBI has helped us get the Unwind and Unorganize Program off the ground. It's only a matter of time before they realize she's not just a pretty face."

Joey consumed his entire serving of the oaky notes of booze in one go. He leaned over and set the glass on the coffee table in front of him. "Liam needs to quickly become one of New York's finest's top priorities."

"And just how do you propose I go about that without zeroing in on Layne, hm? They're from the same family. As you well know, where there is one family member with black blood, there are always more. Apples never fall far from the tree; you get what I'm saying?" The commissioner examined the empty glass hanging from his fingers as the sunlight shone through it in an array of refracted colors.

The hint of frustration reached Joey's voice as he made his point, "That sounds like it's your problem to figure out, not mine. Liam is his own person and responsible for his own actions. There's no reason you can't perform a sting operation focused on someone who shouldn't have left prison in the first place."

Chuckling at the irony, he pointed out to Joey, "Sounds like someone else I know." The commissioner's eyes looked pointedly at Joey before mulling over the idea of a sole sting op on Liam.

Vincent shifted his head from side to side, weighing

every alternative. "I *could*. However, this seems like a hell of a favor to be asking."

Forcing to swallow his growl, Joey's eyes darkened with a glare. "Your biggest opponents to you taking up your current position have been silenced. Do I need to remind you what lengths I had to go to?"

Commissioner Saito leaned forward before laying out his counteroffer, "Here's the best I can do: I can look into it. Get his file reopened and turn it into an active case. It's not a quick turnaround time, though, these things need to be carefully curated." He motioned a finger at Joey's chest. "You know what would speed things up? If you suddenly recalled who put the bullet in your chest."

Well, that wasn't going to fucking happen. He wasn't about to get roped into a fucking political nightmare and put Layne in a position where her allies questioned her ability to keep her mouth shut. Openly working with the police wouldn't accomplish anything but put a strain on her business and both their livelihoods.

Joey stood and approached the man who sat comfortably in his politically powerful position with an air of arrogance wrapped around him. "If I hear the faintest whispers of Layne getting pulled into the scope of things, I guarantee you'll be waking up to a skull in your face in the middle of the fucking night."

Vince stood nowhere close to matching Joey's towering height. "Tread carefully, De Luca. Do you think you're the only one who can execute favors at my request?"

Narrowing his brown eyes, Joey chose his words carefully as he grasped the commissioner's hand in a firm handshake while laying his other hand on his shoulder and whispering into his ear, "Do you think I give a flying fuck about the sloppy assholes who pretend to be bumps in the night? They're pups trying to play amongst the wolves."

He patted the back of the commissioner's shoulder before pulling back and releasing his grip on the man's hand. "I'll be in touch."

Heading out of the room, he heard Vince shout out after him, "If the Feds get involved, it's out of my hands, and all deals are off!"

Joey prayed that it didn't come to that; he'd hate to try and take down the entire damn Government, but for Layne, he'd thrive in all the chaos.

Chapter Eighteen

LUCK

Using a small step stool, she pulled another box from the top shelf of a hallway closet where she kept some of her dad's belongings. She plunked it down on the floor with a huff. Layne sat down next to the box to see if there was anything in there that was useful in trying to predict Liam's next moves.

She lifted the lid of the box and was surprised to find nothing work-related. Instead, she found family photo albums from an era long before cameras were on phones, one where rolls of film had to be processed.

The maroon leather-bound album lying on top still had a thin layer of dust clinging to its front. She pulled it out and opened up to the first page.

Front and center was a rare impromptu O'Reilly family picture. Scott O'Reilly was in a pair of khaki shorts and powder blue polo, a grill filled with burgers and dogs behind him. Smiling proudly, his arm was wrapped around the waist of his vibrantly beautiful wife, Shannon.

The family's matriarch was in a flowy yellow sundress with a brown leather belt wrapped around her waist. Shannon's smile was as bright as the summer day when this photo was taken. Her hands were each resting on one shoulder of her two children standing in front of her.

Layne was giving the biggest, goofiest, and cheesiest-looking smile there ever was at about eight years old. Right next to her was a seven-year-old Liam, sticking his tongue out at the photographer.

Mick tried sputtering out words over his laughter, "L-Liam! Liam, stop sticking your tongue out like that! And Layne, sweetheart, can you give a nice-looking smile?" Their Uncle Mickey made one last failed attempt to wrangle the O'Reilly kids so they could get a decent snapshot during the summer cookout.

Giving up, Mick snapped the picture anyhow with a forced grin. The second he lowered the bulky camera, Layne and Liam went running off into the expanse of Mick's lush green backyard of his summer home.

Layne chased after her brother toward the swing set that was the largest she had ever seen. "Li, wait for me!"

She reached the ladder leading up to the slide at the same time as Liam, they both bumped against one another in an effort to be the first to climb up.

"Layne! I was here first!" Liam griped.

"I'm older!" Layne retorted.

Gaining the advantage of enough footing on the first rung of the ladder, Layne hurried up to the top. She made it down the slide with Liam following behind her moments later.

Not hesitating, Layne ran over to one of the two swings that swayed in the gentle breeze. She flopped her behind onto the blue seat, her hands wrapping around the metal chains that secured it to the wooden frame.

Just beginning to pump her legs to try and gain some momentum, an older child from one of the other families at the barbeque came up behind her and slammed his hands into her back. Layne was knocked right off the swing, landing face down in the grass.

The bully leered down at her like the little shit he was. "This is my favorite swing; girls aren't allowed to use it!"

As Layne pushed herself up onto her feet, Liam came barreling in and shoved the kid. "That's my sister!"

The two boys got into a shoving match while Layne ran back up the hill to tell her mom. The scuffle quickly ended when the boys were separated by one of the other parents in attendance, but not before Liam had landed at least one punch.

Scott took both of his children aside, and he praised Liam for all of his actions before sending him to get some ice on his hand. She stood alone before her father, who was down on a knee looking her in the eyes with disappointment.

"Layne," he started with a shake of his head. "Do you know what you did wrong?"

She frowned as the weight of his words sank into her soul. "No…"

"Not only did you not stick up for yourself, but you ratted out your brother. Don't you ever go snitching on your family again, do you understand me? That is not what

O'Reillys do. I don't care what the hell he does; he's your brother, and you need to support him." Her father stood again, irritated with her choices. *"Go on, get out of here. Go tell your mother to try to get those grass stains out of your nice clothes."*

Layne slammed the photo album shut and tried to vanquish the echoing of her father's words in her head. She wondered if he would be so judgmental of her if he was alive to see what Liam was up to. Layne would like to think he wouldn't be, and not knowing for sure was the most difficult part of his absence in her life.

Sitting on the floor in the middle of the hallway, she took a moment to collect her thoughts. Her hand removed her phone from her back pocket as she brought up a name in her contacts. Layne sat there, allowing the judgment of her dad's ghost to berate her with whispers inside her ear.

Her thumb tapped the call button, and the screen suddenly reflected the damning words, 'Calling Det. Adams…'. The call rang once before Layne heard the footsteps jog up the main stairs at her back. She quickly disconnected the call before pushing herself up onto her feet.

Gage appeared at the top of the stairs and offered her a large smile. "There you are. Thought maybe you were going to try and get the slip on me."

She shoved her phone back into her pocket and shook her head. "No, just trying to go through some things. Miss me?" Layne smiled sweetly at him.

He wrapped his arms around her waist and pulled her up against the front of his body. "Always." Gage leaned over, and the warmth of his mouth washed over the length of her neck. He murmured against her skin, "You always smell so damn good."

She tipped her head back some as he lavished her with his kisses, a light purr rising from her throat. "Mmm, you're one to talk, Mr. Dolce & Gabbana." As much as she teased him about using such a fancy cologne, she couldn't complain about the way the spiced vanilla always perked up her senses.

His hand slipped underneath the shoulder of her shirt and pushed it down along with her bra strap, leaving space for him to continue to get a taste of her. He groaned, knowing that he had come up here for intentions not involving his cock getting some action.

"The way I want to bend you over that stepstool right now and pound into your pussy…" Gage wistfully sighed, his dick fully on board with the temptation as it grew harder in his pants. He pressed one more kiss to the faded scar on her shoulder from her old gunshot wound.

Gage pulled her shirt back into place. "But Sam is waiting for you downstairs."

"Mmm, duty calls then?" Layne's hands rested on his bearded face as she gave him a kiss, letting him know she appreciated all the things he had wanted to do to her. "Maybe afterward, you and I can have our own meeting, and you can convince me just how much you are the right man for the job."

When she went to put the box back onto the closet's shelf, Gage took the box from her and grinned. "I got it, short stuff." He winked at her.

Her hand lightly patted his firm ass in thanks before she

quickly headed downstairs to have a much-needed discussion with Sammy.

Before putting the box back into the closet, Gage peered inside and curiously looked at the photo album right on top. Setting the box on the stool, he flipped to the first page, seeing the old photograph of Layne and her family.

He grinned, having seen that same cheesy smile from Layne on more than one occasion.

Flipping to the next page, the following picture wasn't nearly as heartwarming. The handwritten title 'Layne's 1st Broken Bone After Bike Collision With Liam' was above a picture of Layne with her right ankle in a cast and on a set of crutches.

She looked a little older than the previous picture, but not by much. The thing that caught his attention was Liam's smug face in the background, looking at Layne's bright pink cast. Even without knowing the full story, Gage had a gut feeling that the evil little shit was looking proud of his handiwork.

He closed the photo album before he worked himself up further into a rage. Gage securely put the box of memories back into the closet where it came from.

Downstairs, Layne walked into her office and saw Sammy standing by her bookshelf. His hands were tucked into his pockets as he shifted his stance nervously when she entered.

Based on his clothes, the dress slacks and a casual black button-up, her associate was trying to keep a professional but relaxed image. The tattoos crept up the front of his neck, meeting a silver chain clinging loosely around the base of his throat. "Sorry to drop in on you, Layne."

"It's fine." She walked over to her desk and took her seat behind it. "Gage didn't give you too much trouble, did he?"

Sam looked down in a rare moment of discomfort and shook his head. "Not more than expected." He kept his distance from her while clearing his throat to try and make way for the words. "Look, Layne, I just wanted to let you know that I'd never…"

She cut him off, saving him the awkward words, "I know." Slowly, she exhaled a tired breath. "Liam is doing what Liam does, pushing until he gets the result he wants."

His hazel eyes looked at her with sympathy, seeing that all of this wasn't without its toll on her. Somehow, dealing with people like Russ Spencer and other faction heads came with very little cost to her psyche. Sam may not have been a man with any sort of degree in psychology, but Liam's actions were making more of an impact on her mentally than any other crime lord could.

"You'll get through this." He ran a hand over his thin beard, his fingers tracing over the outline of his mouth. "You just need to treat him like any other jackass that wants to come stomping all over your territory."

She scoffed with a bit of a smile at how he simplified it. "But he's not just any other jackass, Sam. He's my brother. There's no one else out there that has as many years of knowing what makes me tick."

With a nod, he was willing to give her that point. "True,

he may have years of knowing you, but you know what he doesn't have?"

The urge to give a smartass comment as a response was all too tempting, "Fashion sense?"

That drew a chuckle from her associate. "You're not wrong. But, even more importantly, he doesn't have this." He pulled his hand from his pocket and tossed an item onto her desk.

Layne leaned forward, reaching out and examining the small metal object in her fingers. Furrowing her brows together, she glanced over at him. "What's this?"

Proudly smirking, Sam responded with words that were music to her ears, "A name."

Flipping the rectangular box in her hand repeatedly, she finally noticed there was a latch. Popping the little spring mechanism, the container opened, and inside was an empty bullet casing. Layne picked it up, examining the shell between her thumb and forefinger, still unclear what this was supposed to tell her.

She read the words on the bottom of the casing, "Winchester 45 Auto?"

Sam shook his head with a grin. "Do you know what that's from?"

Well, she was guessing a forty-five-caliber pistol based on the imprinted text.

Knowing that he had her hooked at this point, he dropped the crucial piece of information. "That right there," he pointed at the casing in her hand, "is from the bullet that struck Joey."

Her expression immediately changed to one of disbelief

as she stared at her associate. "What?" The question was so quiet that it sounded like she was posing it to no one in particular.

Stepping up to the front of her desk, he leaned over, resting his hands on the edge of it. "And as luck would have it, and with a little help from a friend, the three unique markings left behind from the fired round were able to be traced back to a gun. A gun that has been used repeatedly by a very slippery fellow by the name of Nicholas Orellano. So, the real question is, why would Nick allow Liam to borrow something so sentimental to him?"

The final question really wasn't a question at all. It hardly took any connecting of the dots to assume that this Orellano guy was somehow connected to Liam, perhaps even working with him. Her eyes lit up at finally getting a piece of useful information.

In an unusual and very rare show of girly emotion, she shrieked happily and popped out of her seat. Closing her palm around the shell, Layne clutched to it like it was a piece of treasure. She ran around her desk and threw herself at Sammy. Her arms wrapped around his neck as she gave him a huge hug.

Layne pressed a kiss to his cheek, not giving a fuck how unprofessional it was. He had just proven his worth by delivering this crucial tidbit to her.

Gage rushed into the doorway, having heard Layne's exclamation. Initially, all he saw was Layne up against her associate and Sam's hands on her sides. After the job offer Sam had been pitched by Liam, Gage was ready to beat the shit of the fucker for even breathing wrong at Layne.

Seeing Gage standing there, Sam immediately lifted his hands in the air off of her.

It wasn't until Layne pulled back with that goddamn cheesy smile plastered over her face that he thought twice about going into a blind fury.

"What's going on?" Gage's suspicion tainted each of his words.

Running over to him, Layne gave him several kisses before she showed him the forty-five casing in the center of her palm.

She explained, "Finally, a bit of luck."

Chapter Nineteen

WRATH

G age had wrapped up closing down Cassidy's for the evening with a grumbling appetite in his stomach, and Three Stack Diner had the best grease-laden breakfast, especially at one in the morning. Bonus? It was located two short blocks from the club, making it an easy option for late-night chow.

He pulled open the glass door to the twenty-four-seven diner, the little brass bell chiming to announce his arrival as he did so. It was empty as hell in there. A lone waitress was rolling silverware at the breakfast counter, chairs were neatly tucked in at vacant tables, and you could hear the faint music of the local radio station playing.

The only occupied table was a large horseshoe-shaped booth filled with several guys, all appearing in their late twenties to mid-thirties. All of them trusted friends he had made throughout his business ventures, most visiting from across the river in Jersey.

"Damn, bro. Could you move any slower?" Devon griped at Gage, who was easing out of his seat behind the wheel of his naked Wrangler—doors and top all completely removed.

Pulling out a lockbox from underneath the driver's seat, Gage retrieved a semi-automatic and tucked it into the back of his pants. He shot a glare over at his buddy, who was coming along on this…business opportunity.

Jax climbed out of the backseat over the rear wheel well and jumped down onto his feet. "That's what happens when you get your dick tattooed." He had been the one person Gage had trusted his secret to, and it seemed it was a poor choice in judgment.

As Jax spilled the beans, it earned him the middle finger from Gage.

"Look, I'd like to see how quick you two are when your dick gets stretched out like goddamn salt water taffy and needles jammed into it for over an hour." Gage griped at his friends before joining the other two guys, Isaiah and Hunter, waiting on the sidewalk outside of a rundown rowhome.

Hunter raised a brow. "What are we talking about?"

"Gage had the bright idea to tattoo his dick," Jax smirked, finding any opportunity to spread this entertaining information amongst their group.

Isaiah cringed. "You know, I heard of a guy who did that, and he ended up with a permanent boner for life."

Devon shook his head. "Do I even want to know what you even put on it?"

Gage pulled out his phone, double-checking the address of the house they were supposed to be at. "You that interested in my cock, Dev?"

Laughing, Hunter shared his thoughts, "It probably says 'My Best Friend.'"

The rest of the crew joined with a few chuckles.

Rolling his eyes, Gage retorted, "Says the guy who still lives in his mom's basement and has struck out on the past five girls."

As the five of them took up space there on the sidewalk, a young blonde woman carrying a small bag of groceries approached. She had the sweetest smile as her eyes landed on Gage.

"Excuse me." She slowed her steps as she waited for them all to make space for her to get by.

Without delay, Gage stepped back. When his eyes met hers, he no longer gave a shit about the lingering discomfort of his healing cock. This girl had the most angelic voice he had ever heard, and it stole his words straight from him. His hand shoved Jax back to help make room for her to walk by.

An older woman still in her robe from the house next door came out onto the rickety front porch and shouted, "Rose! Did you remember my cigarettes?!"

While Gage was distracted watching the woman walking by them, Jax leaned over, smacking Gage's stomach with the back of his hand. He whispered, "Bet you'd like to impale that pussy with your swords...Vlad."

Interrupting his flashback, one of the men flagged Gage

down like it wasn't obvious where they were all seated in the otherwise unoccupied joint. All of them were raucously chattering away with one another like a bunch of frat boys after a night of drinking and debauchery.

Once one of his friends noticed his arrival at the edge of the table, the rest of them all greeted him. Several of them shouted out, "Vlad!" welcoming him with giant smiles and laughter.

Rolling his eyes at his nickname that persisted over the years, Gage shook his head and took a seat at the unoccupied end of the booth as several guys scooted over to give him more space. After his pals found out about the three swords tattooed on his dick, he never was able to live down the nickname of Vlad the Impaler.

In total, there were five of them seated here, Gage included.

Everyone had their own beverages and plates in front of each of them. Flagging down the waitress sitting at the counter for a cup of coffee, Gage shared a few laughs at the jokes casually being tossed back and forth.

Jax, the friend he had known the longest, was sitting across from him. He caught Gage's attention. "How's business, man? I'm surprised you switched things up from the titty bar to just another nightclub."

Cradling the lukewarm cup of bitter coffee in his hand, Gage leaned back and shrugged. "It was time to switch things up." He lifted the mug to his lips, drawing in a mouthful of the stale beverage. Maybe it was just another nightclub to outsiders, but he liked to think that its kinky spin carved out a uniquely valuable spot for itself in the Big Apple. So far, the rebrand was paying for itself in spades.

The man to his right, Devon, shook his head and jumped in on the conversation, "Damn, dude. You were surrounded by pussy all day long, why would you give that up? I couldn't do it; I live for that shit."

All Gage could do was shrug. He knew damn well that he could have been drowning in women, and it still wouldn't have satisfied him the way Layne did.

"I know that look," Jax said as he smirked at the revelation. "Fuckin' bastard found himself a keeper."

Isaiah, the guy at the far end, laughed, "Nah, no way. Our Vlad? Pssh, I'll believe it when I see it. She'd have to be one of those innocent and naive starry-eyed aspiring actresses that move into the city every summer." Mockingly, he spoke in a high-pitched feminine tone, "Do you really think I have what it takes? Will you practice this kissing scene with me?" His voice dropped the imitation as he laughed.

Trying to deflect the inquiries into his personal life, Gage fired back at his friend. "Yeah, and when was the last time you got laid, assbutt?"

That got a series of elbow jabs, snorts, and chortling all around the table.

Jax's eyes drifted back to Gage. It seemed that everybody else was easily tossed off the scent by Gage's switch in gears, but not him. Though kudos to Jax that he had the good sense not to steer the conversation back.

After a few more minutes of bullshitting, Gage was

prompted by his former roommate, Hunter. "So, you told us to meet you here to talk about business or some crap. You going to clue us in or what?"

Gage ran his fingers through his short blonde locks; it was now or never. "I'm having a Grand Opening party for the nightclub. I need extra security, people I can trust with my life." His eyes stared at every one of his friends there at the table with him. The heaviness of his gaze communicated just how serious he was.

While Gage knew people who were willing to help in this unsavory business and had helped him previously with Layne, this was different. Things were too close to home, and hell, if he was relying on just anybody to keep his girl safe.

All the guys shared looks amongst themselves, but it was Jax who spoke up first. "Whatever you need. You just tell me when and where."

The rest of his friends nodded in agreement, echoing the same sentiments. Isaiah was quick to reassure Gage he would be there to have his back, "If it weren't for you, my ass would have gotten jumped by those bikers at that bar in Atlantic City. I got you, bro."

Knowing he had to come clean with a few more important details, Gage shoved his now empty coffee mug away from him. "It's not me I'm worried about."

Jax declared his now confirmed suspicions, "I fucking knew it. It's a piece of ass, isn't it?" Feeling smug about his intuitions being on target, he smiled proudly.

Gage's eyes narrowed at his friend's assumption that this was over a one-and-done lay. "She isn't a piece of ass, and she can't know that you're there to keep tabs on her." He would never hear the end of it if Layne knew he was bringing in fresh faces to keep watch over her at the party in addition to himself and Joey. He'd like for the three of them to actually have a night to enjoy themselves without worrying about Liam's sick games.

Devon lifted his brows curiously. "It's one chick. No offense, Vlad, but it doesn't look like you've skipped the gym recently. So why do you need four of us to watch just one of her?"

That made Gage chuckle. Fuck, if these guys even knew how he would have difficulty trusting a goddamn army to keep Layne safe these days.

"It's complicated, just trust me when I tell you I will need you all on your A-game," he explained.

Slapping his hand on the back of Gage's shoulder, Hunter joked, "Aw, trying to make sure the little woman stays in line? You're getting soft on us."

Gage groaned; at this rate, he was going to need to protect his asshole friends from Layne if they behaved like this at the event.

He pulled out his phone and brought up a picture of Layne, laying it down on the center of the table so they could all lean in to see who needed the added insurance of safety.

The photo was a selfie he had snapped of them together while in the hot tub in her backyard one night. Her brown hair piled high on top of her head with a few strands hanging down loose around her face. The fluorescent pink straps of her bikini top contrasted sharply against her pale skin. Her left hand rested on top of his chest as she leaned in against him, pressing the side of her face up against his for the snapshot.

Each of the guys gawked as they stared at the beauty in the picture, a couple of them giving whistles of appreciation.

"Damn, man, I'd want to protect that, too," Devon commented.

Jax leaned in closer before giving an aggressive sigh combined with a groan as he noticed a small detail. "Oh, come the fuck on, man." He pointed at the pic, specifically at Layne's hand, that had her engagement and wedding bands on display. "Tell me you're not banging some guy's wife."

Shrugging, Gage was obviously unbothered. "I told you it was complicated. He's not who I'm worried about; he's well aware of everything that's going on. It's her shithead brother that's the problem."

"You screwing the brother, too?" Isaiah blurted out. Before Gage could correct him, Hunter smacked him upside the back of his head on Gage's behalf. "Ouch! What?" Isaiah initially looked confused as to what he said, then gave a goofy grin. "You never know who wants to be impaled by the mighty Vlad."

In disbelief of Isaiah's commentary, Jax muttered to himself while consuming the rest of his coffee. When he finally collected his thoughts, he gave a resigned sigh. "How much of a problem is the brother? Are we talking about a guy who talks big or one who brings all his low-life friends to come play?"

The memory of the pocketknife sticking out of Layne's leg and the bullet hole in Joey's chest had the emotions running hot through Gage's veins. Trying not to bend and snap the silver butter knife in both his hands that he hadn't recalled picking up, Gage's words came out strained. "The type who deserves the wrath of every damn horror in hell."

Chapter Twenty

SAFETY FIRST

"How's the leg?" Rebecca asked from the other end of the line.

It was on the edge of being a little too cool to be sitting outside in shorts, but it was worth the occasional goosebumps when the wind picked up. Layne looked down at her stab wound; it was just getting to the stage where it began to itch as it healed. Fortunately, Dr. Patty had only needed to do minimal stitching during the initial triage. The blade had felt like it created a foot-long opening when it had gone in but had only left about an inch-wide wound in its wake.

"It's healing. I've had worse," she responded, trying to minimize the incident. "Anything exciting going on down in Baltimore?"

With a giggle and a coy tone, Rebecca drew out her one-word response, "Maaaaybeee."

For a split second, Layne felt like she was living a part of her life that could be considered normal. This was just another talk with her best friend, and she could pretend for a little bit longer that they weren't hundreds of miles away from one another. She could also pretend that her life of crime and danger was nothing but a crafted storyline in a book.

The next thirty minutes were spent listening to Rebecca gush over her new beau. Some guy that shared many of the same interests as her and even had a decent taste in wine. She griped about him liking an opposing football team, but otherwise, he seemed like he was worthy of keeping around.

"Well, don't fall too hard for him until I get the chance to meet him, okay? I got to make sure he's good enough for my bestie," Layne playfully warned Rebecca.

Feeling a text come in from her watch, she noticed it was from her associate, Ethan. Real life was beckoning her back, it seemed.

"I'm sorry, Rebecca, but duty calls. I promise I will check in again in a few weeks, okay?" The apology was heavy in her voice.

The sadness clung to Rebecca's words, "I love you. Be careful."

"I love you more." Layne ended the call with a sigh. Promising to be careful would have felt like a massive lie. She wasn't going to make promises she couldn't keep.

She looked around the small square footage of the backyard of O'Reilly Manor. It was just enough space in a city where any amount of a footprint came at a premium.

Taking a few minutes to shift the gears in her brain, she

looked at Ethan's message and smiled at the way he always attempted to lift her spirits.

ETHAN

Who is your favorite employee?

LAYNE

Depends.

What do you have for me?

ETHAN

Our latex-faced friend suddenly remembered a password.

LAYNE

Suddenly?

ETHAN

After becoming acquainted with the bottom of my boot.

Layne's lips drew upward into a smile. She could only imagine how quickly the man with the Russian contact's calling card cracked under Ethan's physical pressure.

LAYNE

Are you going to keep me waiting?

ETHAN

I want you to answer my question.

She rolled her eyes in minimal annoyance before she texted him the praise he was looking for.

LAYNE

You are my favorite employee.

Don't fuck that shit up.

ETHAN

I knew you loved me most.

Password: 12345

LAYNE

Seriously? 12345?

ETHAN

No, I was just making sure you were
paying attention.

The password for real:
pokayaniye777$SIYLLCAILSCLW

Holy fuckballs, that was a password. Layne copied and pasted that shit over to Cowboy immediately.

No sooner had she sent the password over to her tech guru than the sliding glass door from the house opened. She looked up, and her heart fluttered as she saw Joey step outside to join her.

"You planning on getting ready for tonight?" He asked as he crossed the brick patio to where she was seated on the lounge chair. "I know you take forever and a damn day." He grinned.

That's right, Gage's party was tonight. Gage had been supervising the setup for it all day. She had hardly seen him since he rolled out of bed this morning.

Layne turned, swinging her legs over the side of the chair to put her feet down on the ground. "Yeah, just wanted to finish a few things first."

His hand reached out, his fingers coming up underneath her chin and tilting her head back. Joey's eyes lovingly gazed down into hers. "Promise me something?"

The multitude of shades of green her eyes held were

staring right up at him. "You know I don't make blind promises."

With a light touch, his hand trailed over her jaw and up onto the side of her face, his fingers tangling themselves in her hair. She leaned her face into the palm of his hand.

Joey stood there drinking in the sight of her melting into his hold. His mouth positioned itself in a knowing smile. His ask was so simple, and still, he knew nothing with his wife was ever simple.

"Try to have some fun tonight. Relax. No working and absolutely no worrying. Can you do that for me?" He leaned in, brushing his lips over hers to help sweeten the request.

It was a tall request that she wasn't sure she could give her word on, no matter how much she wanted to. "How can you ask me not to worry after everything that's happened? What if—"

He grinned at her stubbornness and cut her words off, "Don't make me ask twice, Layney." Joey pulled her up onto her feet, tugging her up against him.

Layne dragged her teeth over her bottom lip as she rested her hands on top of his chest. "But it's fun when I do."

His hands slid down her lower back and came to rest on her ass. Joey filled both of his hands with the full curves of her backside. "Get this ass inside and start getting ready before I make us both late to the party."

He looked down at his watch on his wrist. What the hell was taking her so long? Joey had been waiting out front of O'Reilly Manor for what felt like hours but had been more like fifteen minutes.

The front door opened, and Joey's cock hardened the second he laid eyes on Layne.

One dainty little foot after the other stepped over the threshold of the front door onto the front stoop. Her strappy black heels wrapped around her feet and crisscrossed several times over each ankle. Much to the delight of his dick, the rest of her lean legs were left bare.

Layne may have thought the stab wound on her thigh was an eyesore, but it didn't deter him from wanting to kiss and worship every part of her—scars included. The short length of the tight crimson dress had the smallest ruffle at the bottom hem that added an extra feminine flare to the style. It made him want to immediately plunge himself between her thighs.

He had known the outfit would be absolute perfection on her body when he had chosen it, but seeing it on her surpassed his wildest dreams. It adhered to every curve and line of her slender physique. The thin straps looked like he would be able to break them easily with just one pluck of his finger.

Layne's waterfall of chestnut locks of hair naturally hung down around her bare shoulders with a loose mohawk-style French braid down the center of her head.

The Challenger was already running in anticipation of getting them both to Cassidy's Chains ahead of schedule. He was so stunned by the vision he saw emerging from their home that his feet were left cemented to the ground until she was standing right in front of him.

She tried to steady her breath as she soaked in the sight of Joey dressed in a suit that he had no business wearing so well. The all-black ensemble was tailored to each swell of his muscles. The black dress shirt was left without a tie, and the top couple of buttons remained undone, leaving exposed the spread wings of the tattooed birds creeping up his neck.

"Every time you put a suit on—" she began, only to have her words silenced. Joey leaned in and crushed his mouth against hers. His lips nearly bruised her own with the intense need brewing behind them.

His hands roamed over her body, exploring it like he didn't already have every inch committed to memory. The spread of his palms ran down her sides, sliding back to grab at the spheres of her ass in appreciation before coming back around to travel over her hips.

Just as his hand dropped down past the hem of her dress, sliding between her legs, it took everything in her to bring him to a halt. Her hand grabbed onto his wrist as her thighs squeezed together to close off access to where he very much wanted to gain entry.

Layne's words were coming out breathlessly as she forced them past her lips, "You know it's Gage's night, and we promised we wouldn't be late." She wanted nothing more than to break the rules the three of them had set, and maybe she would at the after-party. However, she was doing her best to make sure that Gage also got his dedicated alone time with her.

Groaning in a mixture of disappointment and irritation, Joey knew damn well that he could press the issue and get past Layne's defenses with very little effort. However, they had agreed on solo nights so Layne could get some semblance of physical recovery while trying to keep up with all three of their needs. Given tonight was Gage's big evening, his brother had dibs.

Begrudgingly, he withdrew his hand, knowing it was going to be a long night watching Layne moving her body in a dress that looked like it was painted on. Gage better take advantage of their girl, good enough for the both of them.

She wasn't blind to the disappointment in Joey's eyes, but seeing as he was driving them to the club, perhaps she could find an acceptable compromise. Her hand patted his chest lightly as she walked over to his vehicle.

Joey drew in a deep breath, trying to convince his fucking erection to settle down. He turned and rushed ahead of her to open the passenger door before she got the chance.

Getting into her seat, Layne made sure she strapped herself in before he yelled at her for being reckless about her personal safety. It was going to be a twenty-minute drive in slow city traffic; she hardly expected any large-scale incidents where a seat belt was going to be required.

He rounded the front of the car and got settled before pulling away from the curb. "Remember what I said, Layne. We got everything covered, all you need to do is let Gage show you a good time tonight."

When Joey glanced over at Layne, she was unbuckling

her seat belt. His jaw tensed, hating when she wasn't strapped in. "What are you doing? Put your damn seatbelt back on."

As they slowed for a red light, she gave a smile that said she was up to no good. Her hand ran over the large muscle of his thigh before reaching between his legs and rubbing over his cock that had only partially softened.

"Showing you a good time." Her hand gave another firm massage over the front of his pants before leaning over the console between their seats and working his pants open.

He shifted in his seat, his eyes darting between the mischievous woman now fishing her hand into his pants and the traffic signal ahead of them. "Layne, you need to be buckled up." His voice didn't sound convincing, and with one hand on top of the steering wheel, he wasn't making any effort to stop her with his other hand.

"Joey?" She pulled his long and hard length from his boxer briefs.

The light turned green, and he nearly forgot he needed to press the gas pedal to get the car moving. "What?" He looked down at Layne as her upper half encroached on his space.

"Shut the fuck up and drive." She smirked before she lowered her head and drew his dick into her mouth.

He groaned as his cock was suddenly buried into that tight and warm space past her lips. Joey's hand grasped onto the steering wheel tightly while trying to focus on the road.

Layne hallowed her cheeks while sucking on him like

he was her favorite treat. Her lips applied added pressure in waves as she bobbed her head up and down on him.

Quickly, his spare hand roughly grabbed a handful of hair on the back of her head, guiding her movements as he cursed to himself.

"Fuck, Layney. You and your damn mouth." Joey pressed his hips up into her, feeling the tip of his cock greeting the back of her throat.

Her tongue swirled around his cock, taunting and teasing him as she made every effort to make sure that he had to work at maintaining his focus on the road.

Joey's palm circled the steering wheel as he made a turn that he had nearly forgotten to take. He was constantly torn between watching the road and sneaking glimpses of Layne with her ass in the air while her mouth worked him over.

With his release rapidly approaching, he gave a light growl as his hand pushed her head down on him. The way she gagged around his dick had him barely clinging to his control over his release.

"Ah, fuck! You better not waste a drop of my cum, Layney." His breaths grew ragged as he pulled her head back and forced it back down on his cock several more times.

His knuckles turned white from gripping the steering wheel so tightly. Feeling the tingle at the base of his spine, he pinned her head down on him right before his dick began pulsing. Groaning as his pleasure burst through his body, Joey's hips thrust up into her mouth as he came, shooting lines of his hot seed into the back of her throat.

Each swallow she made with him still buried inside her

had him whimpering and working to catch his breath. His hand released her hair and slid down over her upper back.

"Jesus Christ." He sighed in satisfaction as he relaxed back into the driver's seat. It shocked the hell out of him that he managed to keep the damn car on the road this entire time.

Layne slid her mouth off of him, giving the head of his cock one final lick as she smiled proudly. She shifted back into her seat and pulled her seat belt across her lap.

"Couldn't have you feeling left out all night." Her eyes sparkled, complimenting the flush of her cheeks and the puffiness of her lips that were missing most of her lip gloss after her oral endeavors.

Joey gave her a relaxed grin before he pulled up to the building with a slate blue sign above it bearing the club's new name. Metal chains wrapped around each of the individual handles for aesthetics, and a line wrapped around the block of people waiting to get into Cassidy's Chains.

Before she could open her door, Joey reached over and took her by the back of her neck. With her face turned toward him, he smiled. "I love you." He leaned over and captured her lips in a tender and gentle kiss. If he had made the wrong decision so many years ago, it killed him to think that he would never have found his own piece of heaven.

Chapter Twenty-One

CONNECTED CHAINS

I nside the nightclub, most of the decor that had once screamed strippers and poles had been removed. The stages also had disappeared, except for the one designated for the DJ in the corner.

Along the walls were extensive lines of sofa-like seating with royal blue velvet cushions. Spaced out every couple of feet were small tables placed in front of it. Hung up throughout the space were framed photos of various kinky toys that included everything from your standard BDSM accessories to things a little more… adventurous, peculiar, and unusual.

The lighting was expectedly dim but was accented with the cool glow of blue lights placed around the seating areas, walkways, and bar. A curtain of thick metal chains hung in the entryway that divided the main area of the club where all the drinking and dancing happened to the hallway that led to the private rooms.

An evening of exclusive access to those rooms was

available for a hefty fee. All of the photographs of toys and accessories on the walls of the main club area were made available for use and play. At your own risk and pleasure, of course.

Gage was standing in front of the industrial-looking bar, meeting with his extra security adds before the club officially opened up for everyone to file inside. It was the same crew of friends he had met at the diner around the corner a few nights back. Jax, Devon, Isaiah, and Hunter were all gathered in a loose circle.

Adjusting his earpiece, Jax looked at Gage. "I'll be doing rounds at all the points of entry to make sure there's only one way in here and one way out."

Hunter nodded and reassured Gage that they all had a plan in place, "Don't worry, Vlad. Someone will have eyes on her at all times."

While Devon began to reiterate some of the other minor details of the specific security measures in place, Isaiah smacked his arm several times with the back of his hand.

"Holy... fuck... Dude!" Isaiah's mouth was left hanging open as he stared at the front door.

Devon finally stopped speaking long enough to see what the hell Isaiah was gawking at. When his eyes followed the line of sight, he was also rendered speechless.

Turning his head to see what everyone was distracted by, Hunter raised both of his brows. "Is that...Joey? Your brother?"

Layne and Joey had just entered, being allowed to pass by the dedicated bouncer at the door. Joey's arm was wrapped around her waist, possessively keeping her close to his side. The two of them chatted between themselves as they drifted further into the club.

Isaiah, being the immature one of the group, chuckled. "Oh, man! You've got to be shitting me! You're banging your brother's wife, Vlad!?"

Gage's eyes narrowed. "Say that a little fuckin' louder, why don't you?"

It was Hunter who smacked Isaiah on the back of the head so that Gage didn't have to. "Why don't you ever shut up instead of saying stupid ass things?" He shook his head in annoyance.

To say it was a shock to all of them to see Joey there was an understatement, and that was without knowing the unique circumstances between the three of them.

Layne's eyes were drawn to the sight of Gage standing with several men, all dressed in your typical black security attire. It wasn't the crew standing around him that captured her attention; her eyes were fully focused on Gage.

The way Gage wore his black suit made her realize that she didn't see him dressed up nearly enough. A dark red shirt underneath the jacket complimented the same crimson red of her dress that she wore. Each cut of fabric hugged his bulky muscles, reminding her just how much strength he packed when he wasn't tenderly taking care of her.

Leaving Joey's side and crossing the room, Layne came up to Gage and smiled. "We made it."

Only a step behind her, Joey added, "Barely." He had a massive grin drawn over his face, still reeling from the blowjob he had gotten on the way there.

Locking his hands on her hips, Gage drew her up to him

as his espresso hues admired the sight of her. "Damn." He let out a breath as he allowed himself to soak in every detail of how she showed up looking like a delicious goddess at his disposal.

Lowering his head, Gage slowly worked his mouth over hers, making sure she knew how much he approved of her arriving here looking like a snack he could quickly devour. A hand came up to her face, gently cradling her cheek as his tongue dove into her mouth, ready to get a head start on dessert.

Finally relinquishing her lips before he ended up bending her over the bar, he looked over at Joey. "Why the hell do you look so happy?"

Joey shrugged with a smirk, trying to remain casual about it. "It was a nice drive over here." His hand subtly dropped to adjust his cock that wanted to stiffen up at the replay in his head.

That got him a stern look shot from Layne as she looked over her shoulder. "*Nice*?" It had been a phenomenal blowjob, in her opinion.

Jax cleared his throat, drawing attention to the fact that he and the rest of the guys were still standing there. "We good here?" He looked at Gage for confirmation.

Gage nodded. "Yeah, we're good. The doors should be opening up in about ten minutes."

Fist-bumping a couple of the guys as they dispersed, Gage fully turned to Layne, lifting his hands to hold her face. "You have no idea how excited I am for tonight. I want everyone to know you're mine." He dragged a finger down her throat, tracing over the gold necklace she always wore–his collar that she refused to take off.

Smiling, he stole another kiss from her deliciously swollen lips.

The club music was blasting throughout the entirety of Cassidy's Chains. The bass could be felt through your chest and down into the floor. Everyone was packed onto the dance floor, dancing and having a good time. The drinks were flowing freely as every person seemed to be living carefree.

All the guests were dressed fully in black as the invitation had dictated, except for Layne and Gage. It made it easier to spot Layne from a distance through the crowded space. Not that Joey or Gage allowed her to get more than an arm's length from either of them.

Letting his brother have the majority of the time with their girl, Joey mostly kept an eye on things happening inside the nightclub. Hell, if he was going to let an evening out get ruined by fucking Liam and the war campaign he was on against Layne.

Despite Joey's giving them space, it didn't mean he and Gage hadn't pinned Layne between them during a dance or two. They let her feel both their cocks press against her like steel rods while both their hands explored her scantily clad body with the beat of the music driving each movement.

Gage had ditched his jacket early on, rolling up his sleeves to his elbows, exposing the corded muscles of his forearms. His tattoos sprawled up his arms until they disappeared under his shirt.

Layne had been pleasantly surprised to see a pair of black suspenders leading over the tops of his shoulders and down over the front of his chest. There was just something about the way the stretchy straps clung to his upper body that had her wanting to climb him like a tree.

She finished off the cocktail in her hand, having worked up to a solid buzz. Leaving the glass on a table, her hands grabbed Gage by his suspenders and pulled him back onto the dance floor with her. Layne's hips swayed to the beat of the music as she led him into the center of the crowd.

As she began to dance, she kept her body close up against him. The look in her eyes let him know that no one else in the club existed except him. Seductively, her lithe body rubbed up against him as the music seemed to pulse throughout her moves.

Gage's hand slid onto the back of her neck while the other slowly ran down her back towards the swell of her ass. His body moved with hers while he leaned over and began to drag his mouth over the side of her neck, where there was already the light taste of perspiration against her skin.

His hand glided onto her ass and gripped it possessively as he pulled her tighter sagainst him. The roughness of his hand grabbing her sent a shock of arousal between her thighs as they continued their sensual dance together. Neither of them gave a fuck who saw them behaving like a couple of horny teenagers on the dance floor.

Layne purred in approval as she felt the hard press of

Gage's cock against the front of her lower stomach. Arousal was already soaking her panties, leaving her craving more of him. Her hips pressed up against him, letting him know just how much she needed him.

He continued to grind his dick against her, letting her ache for him a little longer with a playful smirk. Gage kissed his way up to her ear, speaking into it, "Baby, are you ready to take my dick while I fuck your pussy?"

Her hands grabbed the front of his shirt, balling up the fabric in her hands. Moaning out quietly as he whispered to her, she nodded her head. "Yes, please." Layne's breaths were already heavy between her burning desire and her dance movements there with him.

Giving one last squeeze of her ass, he released it so he could grab hold of her hand. "I have a surprise, c'mon."

Layne lightly bit into her lower lip in excitement as Gage tugged her along with him, leading them off the dance floor. They walked through the curtain of metal chains, entering the blue-lit hallway with various doors.

He brought her to one nearly at the very end of the hallway, which had a reserved sign on it. Gage pushed the door open and allowed her to enter first.

Inside the private room was a very similar decor as the rest of the club, there was a small velvet loveseat and a table just big enough for a couple of beverages. Music from the club played from a speaker in the ceiling, adding to the ambiance. The room was cast into a warm glow from a few strategically placed red lights. The most notable item in there was the large x-frame in the corner.

Locking the door behind them for privacy, Gage spoke

up from behind her, "I told you I was going to get you on my St. Andrew's cross."

She barely had enough time to take in the sight of the piece of equipment with its wrist and ankle straps before his hands snatched her by her hips and spun her around to face him.

Gage's finger came up under her chin to angle it up so he could look into those hypnotizing green pools of hers. He grinned and gave his command, "On your knees for me."

Layne had an intense ache between her thighs for him, and now, seeing him shift into his dominating side had her wanting to leap right onto him. She lowered herself down onto her knees in front of him, never breaking eye contact.

He slid the straps of his suspenders off, letting them hang down at his sides as he began unbuttoning his dress shirt. All the while, he stared down at the beauty kneeling at his feet.

"Do you want to be fucked on my cross, Lucky Charm?" He yanked the bottom of his shirt out from his pants before removing it entirely from his upper body.

With her hands resting on top of her bare thighs, she spoke up with a breathy voice, "Yes, Sir." Her eyes watched as he bared his chest to her, his silver Roman legion necklace hanging down between his pecs.

He tossed his shirt over onto the sofa to his right. "Such a good girl, always wanting my cock," he praised.

Gage stood staring down at Layne, admiring the view as each breath she took had her breasts pushing against the neckline of her dress. "You know how hard my cock has been for you all night? I've been dying to get you in here. I was going to wait until the party was over, but then you had to go rub against me like you wanted to be fucked in the middle of the dance floor. I damn near bent you over and pounded into you for everyone to see."

Placing a finger under her chin, he bent over with a mischievous grin while appreciating the sight of her needy body waiting for him. "And you would have let your Daddy do it, isn't that right, baby?"

Layne was getting antsy just thinking about it, shifting her position there on the floor. Her knees parted slightly as her hand began to slide up the inside of her thigh towards her center. "Yes. I need you, Gage. Please." Her eyes were saturated with the need for the pleasure she knew he could give her.

He squatted and grabbed both of her wrists, making sure she didn't have a chance to touch herself. Pulling her up onto her feet, he clicked his tongue at her in disappointment. "Baby, you know you aren't allowed to touch yourself without my permission. You weren't thinking about doing that, were you?"

She whimpered, and it was music to his ears to hear how much she craved him. Her hands were in small fists as he held them up in front of her.

Swallowing hard, trying to get past the neediness in her voice, she begged him again. The intensity for which she had to have him nearly made her voice waver. "I'm so wet, I want your cock so badly right now."

Chuckling, he leaned in and gave her a delicate kiss. "Baby, you're going to need to do better than that." He backed her up until they were at the cross. His hands turned her so she was facing it. With ease, he latched each wrist cuff onto her, leaving both hands raised above her head.

Gage left her ankles unrestrained for the time being. His hands dropped to the bottom of her dress and yanked it up so that it was bunched up around her waist, leaving her round and firm ass exposed to him. His fingers hooked onto the sides of her thong and slid it down her legs until it was removed entirely.

As he stood, he ran his large hands over the backs of her thighs. Layne shivered in anticipation as she pushed her hips back towards him.

Fully enjoying seeing her like this, Gage smiled before his palm smacked down hard on her ass. The contact left a red mark on her fair skin that had his cock twitching in excitement.

"Tell me what you want." He began to undo his pants, no longer able to stand the way his dick was struggling against the confines of his pants.

"I want to be fucked by my Daddy. I want your cock showing me that I'm all yours." She squirmed while standing there, unable to move her hands as she felt her arousal beginning to creep down from her core.

Gage pushed his boxers down on his hips so his decorated cock sprang out. Layne wasn't the only one who was leaking, a clear liquid dripped from the tip of his cock. "Mmm, that's what I like to hear."

He stepped up behind her, his hand burying itself in her hair as he tipped her head back so he could see her face.

"Baby, I'm going to make you feel so good tonight. I want the whole damn club to hear you."

Her lips parted slightly as she felt every part of her body yearning for him. Using just the rounded head of his cock, he rubbed it along her crease. With a tremble in her voice, she moaned out, only to have it devolve into a whimper again when he moved his dick away from her body.

"Fuck! Please!" She was pretty sure this was torture as she stood there being taunted and teased by him.

Letting go of her hair, he smiled and dropped onto a knee behind her. He finally locked her ankles into the soft cuffs attached to the bottom of the X.

"Be careful what you ask for, baby. Don't you dare come until my cock is in you, do you understand?"

Layne was quick to nod if it meant that she was going to finally be able to feel the pleasure he was withholding from her.

Another swat landed on her ass, echoing across the room. "You know the rules; I need to hear that you under-stand." His palm gently rubbed over the area he had just struck, easing away the sting across her ass cheek.

She winced lightly as the spank landed. "Yes, Sir."

"Good girl." His hand lightly patted her ass in approval.

Gage's hand dropped between her legs, his fingers stroking over her wet slit. Finding her clit, he massaged a few circles over it before running his fingers back to the entrance of her cunt.

Two fingers pushed into her nice and slow until the

silver rings on his fingers were just barely inside of her. He groaned, feeling how turned on she was for him.

"Fuck!" She moaned out, finally getting the first run of pleasure through her veins. Layne's head dipped back as she gave herself over to the feeling.

His fingers pulled out of her before sliding in just as slowly as they had before. This time, he leaned over and pressed his lips to the back of her bare shoulder. His breath was warm against her skin as he murmured to her. "Does your Daddy know how to take care of you?"

She moaned out again, this time trying to push her hips down onto his fingers. "You always know how to make me feel so damn good."

"Mmhmm. Would I ever let my cock near any other woman?" He lightly bit the top of her shoulder.

Layne shook her head. "No."

"That doesn't sound like you're very convinced, baby." He plunged his fingers into her again, still keeping things at a slow and drawn-out pace.

Each breath she took was getting a little heavier while his fingers stroked inside of her. Struggling to concentrate with his fingers working her, she responded through a moan, "No, you're all mine. You only want me, and there isn't any other woman who gets to wear your collar except me."

Gage brushed her hair away from the back of her neck and laid several kisses over her shamrock and luck tattoo. "That's right, baby. You're my Lucky Charm, and you'll always have me and my swords. I would suffer every horrible and unimaginable form of torture if it meant being with you."

Being satisfied with her response, he rewarded her with his fingers moving more quickly inside of her.

She moaned out, her tight walls wrapping around his digits. The sensations began to grow sharply with each movement he made. Feeling her release approaching, she tensed up, trying to keep it at bay. "You're getting me close." Layne squeezed her eyes tightly to aid her control over her body.

Deviously, he smirked and slid a third finger into her. "Better not come, or else you're not going to get this hard cock that is waiting for your hot little pussy." He rubbed his dick against the inside of her thigh just to see how tightly she could hold on.

Her body was beginning to shake as she pulled on the restraints, keeping her limbs still. She cried out her next moan in a mix of pleasure and frustration in trying not to let herself cave. "I want to come! Please!"

Just when she thought she wasn't going to be able to take much more, Gage pulled his fingers out of her. She let out a sigh of relief that she could catch her breath. Her body began to relax as the edge of her orgasm began to distance itself slowly.

Gage grasped her hips with his hands after lining up his cock at her entrance. He sank his length into her slowly, wanting to bask in the way her body tightened around him until he was up to the hilt inside her.

"Fuck, baby. Your cunt takes me so well every damn time." He groaned into her ear.

Layne nearly melted against the cross the second he pushed himself into her. Her moan was full of satisfaction as he stretched her walls to accommodate his size.

He drew his hips back and shoved his cock back into her again, this time a little more forcefully. "You did so fucking well following directions. My little brat is finally learning that she gets rewarded when she does what her Daddy says, huh?"

Each movement he made had her unraveling at the seams. Waves of pleasure began filling her body, all coming from the way his cock made itself fit inside her pussy. "God, yes!"

Finding himself struggling with his urges, he grinded up against her ass, burying his cock even further into her. He panted as he rocked his hips forward, fucking her a little faster and a little harder.

She began to gasp for air as each thrust into her body spurred a jolt of pleasure that was ready to overflow. Being locked between him and the frame, she found herself unable to escape the mounting tensions in her body. "Ah! I'm gonna come!"

Gage slammed his cock into her, groaning as he feverishly began to chase after both of their releases. "Fucking come for me. I want my cock soaked by all of you." He continued to hammer himself in a frantic rhythm into her.

Her body locked up around him as she screamed out, pulling hard at each of the cuffs around her wrists as she came. Layne could barely draw in any oxygen between each shout of ecstasy.

Feeling her pussy squeeze onto his dick like it was a goddamn boa constrictor, he growled out a moan. Gage continued to fuck her through her orgasm, making sure he kept her in an intense and hazy state of bliss.

"Mmm, this pussy of yours is gonna get loaded with my cum soon, baby. Are you ready for it?"

She wasn't even sure that she was in a full state of awareness as she gave a weak nod. Breathlessly, she answered, "I want to be filled with your cum. Fuck, please."

With a shudder, Gage drove his cock hard into her as he roared out like a feral beast. His release struck, his dick pulsing as his seed fired out of the tip and into her well-fucked cunt.

He collapsed against the back of her, trying to catch his breath while inhaling the sweet scent of her body. "Jesus-fucking-Christ…"

Layne moaned quietly in agreement.

After taking a moment to regain himself, Gage reached up and unlatched her wrists, freeing them from the top of the cross. Pulling out of her, he made sure to do the same with her ankles, always keeping a hand on her to keep her steady.

He glanced up at her body while freeing her legs from the restraints and smirked. The sight of his cum was already beginning to leak out of her swollen cunt. "Damn, I could stare at you like this all fucking day."

She looked behind her at him with a sated smile. "You'll never hear me complain."

Gage swiped a line of the white liquid off her thigh with his fingers, then shoved them both back in her pussy with a smile. "My cum needs to stay right where it belongs." He winked at her.

Chapter Twenty-Two

GHOSTED

Emerging from the private room, Layne's hand was wrapped around Gage's as she stuck close to his side. He had spent nearly twenty minutes giving her appropriate aftercare and ensuring they didn't leave that room until he was convinced she had recovered enough.

They both made their way back into the main area of the club, where everyone was still partying the night away. Gage led her to the bar, where he ordered them both drinks.

As the bartender began crafting the cocktails, Hunter approached Gage, leaning in and whispering something into his ear.

Shouting over the thudding bass of the music, Gage pulled back and yelled, "What?!" Struggling to hear what Hunter was trying to tell him.

When his buddy tried to shout into his ear again, it was to no avail. Gage shook his head and gave a tug on Layne's hand. He nodded his head in the direction of his office, where things would be a little quieter.

Stepping away from the bar, Layne began to follow but then stopped short. She lifted a finger for him to wait. His eyes stayed glued to her as she released his hand and squeezed back through a couple of people to grab the drinks, waiting for them unattended at the bar.

Once she had the two glasses, she came right back to Gage. They made it to his office, with Hunter joining them. Closing the door for additional buffering from the loud party music, Gage took one of the glasses from Layne.

"What were you saying out there, Hunter?" He remained standing by the door.

Layne leaned back against a wall and observed quietly as she sipped her beverage, licking her lips at the sweeter-than-expected taste.

Hunter looked at Layne and then at Gage, wondering what he should say since it had been made clear that they weren't supposed to let Layne know their purpose for being there tonight.

"I was just trying to update you. Jax said everything has been all clear on the inside, and Dev said the same for the outside. No signs of…anyone." He shoved his hands into his pockets.

Picking up that this wasn't just typical security measures, Layne furrowed her brows. As she typically did, she inserted herself into the conversation. "What's that supposed to mean?"

Her eyes shifted to look at Gage as she tilted her head questioningly as she stepped away from the wall.

He cleared his throat, avoiding looking at Layne. "Nothing. Just making sure tonight went smoothly."

"Bullshit." Layne was now changing her stare to direct it at Hunter.

It wasn't an easy feat for a woman to make Hunter feel uncomfortable, but the way Layne was looking at him, he got the sense he didn't want to fuck around and find out with this one.

Gage saved Hunter from trying to explain himself, "Layne. It's not a big deal. I just wanted to make sure tonight went off without any issues."

"And by issues, you mean Liam." She cut straight to the point.

He looked at Hunter and waved him off with his hand. The man walked by them both, slipping out the door without another word.

She sighed as she looked at Gage, clearly frustrated.

Putting his untouched drink down on his desk, he stepped up to Layne. Both of his hands landed on her upper arms as he looked into her eyes. "Baby, I needed to make sure we had people I could trust."

"I have a team for this sort of thing, I don't need you bringing in fucking SEAL Team Six." She rolled her eyes.

He grinned at the comparison. "It's just for tonight. Though, if you keep scowling at me like that, I may see if they can sign on full-time." His hands rubbed over her arms gently.

"I swear to God, Gage, if I see them hanging around after tonight, I will kick your ass." Her finger jabbed him in the chest to accentuate her threat.

"Noted," he chuckled. "Now, let's go back and enjoy the rest of the party, okay?" He walked over to the desk and grabbed his drink, taking a large sip.

He coughed and scrunched up his face. "Fuck, this is definitely your drink. You and the damn ass water you call whiskey." Gage's least favorite liquor was whiskey, that shit burned like a motherfucker on a good day. The brands Layne enjoyed were some high-octane blends that left him questioning if she had any taste buds at all.

Layne laughed as she continued drinking Gage's cocktail. "Well, you're stuck with it now. I'm really enjoying your Negroni." Playfully, she stuck her tongue out at him.

He shook his head and took another sip, trying to get past the harsh bite of the alcohol. Swatting her ass with his hand, he nudged her towards the door. "Damn brat. Get out there before I give you something else to do with that tongue."

With a giggle, she opened the door and went back out to the club. Once they were back on the dance floor, Layne leaned back against Gage's chest as she suggestively moved her body against him to the pulse of the music. Idly, she sipped on the drink in her hand.

Her mind wandered as to what delicious trouble they were both going to get to once they got back to his condo. Gage's hand roamed over her body, wondering how he got so damn lucky with a woman like Layne. This night was turning out to be everything he had hoped for and more.

While she was lost in her thoughts, her eyes caught a face in the crowd. It startled her so much that she dropped her drink. Her body immediately went stiff as a board.

The music began to fade, the volume becoming more tolerable as it transitioned to the next song.

Gage straightened as Layne's glass shattered against the floor and splashed the beverage around their feet. He came around to face her, his face filled with concern. "Baby, are you okay?"

Layne craned her neck to try and look around him to see if she could catch another glimpse of the face she saw. "I…" She looked all around them, and she wondered if she had seen anything at all. "Yeah, I'm fine. I just thought…"

"You're as pale as a ghost, Layne." He also took a look around at their surroundings. He didn't see any threats, but he did see Joey over by the bar and flagged him down.

God, was she losing her mind? Her heart felt like it was leaping over massive hurdles inside her chest. She looked at Gage and tried to force an at-ease smile on her lips. "I promise I'm good."

Gage chugged down the rest of his drink, not liking the way she looked so spooked.

Joey wasted no time in forcing his way through the crowd of people when he saw Gage's hand wave him over. "What's wrong?" He looked at Layne and immediately got on the defensive, seeing how shaken she looked, even if she was trying to conceal it.

"Nothing is up." Layne tried to calm them both down.

"She just clammed up and dropped her drink," Gage explained. "I'm going to take her home." He set his empty glass on the tray of a waitress as she walked by.

"I will go update Jax and the rest of the guys, then meet you back at your place." Joey patted the side of

Gage's arm. Then, he reached out and captured Layne's chin between his thumb and finger. "Seatbelt on," he demanded with a smile before he locked his mouth on hers firmly.

She happily accepted his kiss, returning it with one of her own. "It's a five-minute drive, and you both are over-reacting."

The look they both gave her after that said it all. They had every right to be on edge, given everything all of them had been through. Her face fell as she slumped her shoulders in defeat.

Satisfied that Layne wasn't going to put up any more of a fight, Joey left to go find his brother's backup crew. Gage wrapped an arm around her shoulder and guided her towards the door.

Once outside, Layne looked at the cars parked out front. She didn't see his busted-ass Jeep anywhere. "Where did you park?"

Gage pulled out Layne's car keys from his pocket and pressed the remote start on the key fob. "Ran into a bit of car trouble when I went to leave this morning, so I took yours."

She couldn't hide the fact she wasn't surprised. "The Jeep wouldn't start—again?"

Leading Layne towards the silver BMW, he kept his head on a swivel. "Look, she's an old gal. Some days, she needs a little extra love to get movin'."

"For fucks sake, Gage, that damn Jeep has been revived from the brink of death five too many times." Arriving at her car, Gage made sure she was strapped into the passenger seat per Joey's instructions, five-minute drive or not.

He came to the driver's side, sliding in behind the wheel with the intention to be her chauffeur back to Hudson Yards.

She looked over at his profile while he focused on the road. At this time of night, the roads were mostly empty, making the trip rather peaceful.

Layne wondered how it was that she had two handsome men willing to go above and beyond for her. As irritated as she got with their protective efforts, deep down, it made her feel more valued than her family ever did. That feeling of being worthy was something her brother was slowly trying to destroy.

A few beads of sweat started to appear on Gage's forehead. He blinked his eyes several times as the traffic lights and their surroundings began to gradually shift in his vision. His hand came to his eyes, trying to rub the focus back into his brown hues.

Layne noticed his drawn-out blinks and the way he wiped the sheen of sweat from his head with the back of his hand.

"Gage, are you okay?" She reached over, placing a hand on his bicep.

His foot pressed the brake to roll to a stop for a yellow light. Layne's voice sounded so far away, like he was in an underwater cave. His breathing grew shallow while attempting to swallow the pooling saliva in his mouth, willing himself to stay conscious as he struggled to maintain clear thoughts.

Gage's hand dropped to the shifter, attempting to push it into Park but missing the knob.

Noticing that his eyes were fluttering, she cursed and shook his arm harshly. "Hey! Stick with me!"

Somehow, she heard the impact a microsecond before she felt it. An unexpected force slammed into the back of her car, launching it across the intersection and only stopping when the front of her vehicle collided with a pole. Another impact hit the backend again, crushing the Beamer further against the pole.

The hit was strong enough that airbags popped off after the first hit, providing a little bit of buffer from the way they both were violently jerked around inside their seats. Fortunately, seat belts kept her and Gage from suffering worse injuries.

Moments after the wreck, Layne was slumped in her seat with a small line of blood trickling from a minor head wound a couple of inches above her eyebrow. It was unclear how long she had lost consciousness in the aftermath of the incident.

Trying to open her eyes, she squinted at an imposing light shining directly on her face. The door on her side of the car was wide open, a presence looming there over her. Her head was pounding, and for a brief moment, she couldn't even recall where she was or what had transpired.

"What…?" Layne groaned as she turned her face away from the bright light. She lifted her hand to try and shield her eyes.

A hand roughly grabbed her by the hair, turning her so

that the light continued to blind her vision. "Stupid little bitch," the faceless voice said with such an air of disdain.

The voice was rough like sandpaper, prompting all the hairs on the back of her neck to stand on end. It elicited fear to perk up from her gut, telling her to sound all her alarms. Yet, her body wouldn't coordinate the efforts on behalf of her head.

The flashlight came down harshly, striking her across the face. The hit knocked her back into her seat. Layne noticed Gage still in the driver's seat, slumped over the steering wheel, and passed out.

She winced, squeezing her eyes tightly with the pain radiating from the side of her face. The man who had been speaking to her cursed as he seemed to talk to himself, "Fucker and his timing." Something fell into her lap.

Turning her head back towards the man, Layne's eyes strained as they opened back up to see the outline of a man jogging back to a pickup truck waiting next to her car. Her body wanted to drag her into the dark of unconsciousness again, but she willed herself to try and see the person responsible before it did so.

Just when she thought she wouldn't be able to hold out any longer, the man turned and looked over his shoulder at her. A fucking evil smirk on his face. The same face she thought she had seen at the club.

No. Fucking. Way.

The man climbed into the heavy-duty pickup with front-end damage before it peeled off, the tires squealing against the pavement as it did so.

Her head was spinning through its haze as she tried to

distinguish what was truth and reality. Did she simply hit her head hard enough to land in some mental ward where nothing was real anymore? None of this made sense, and that made her head ache even more.

Rolling her head to look back over at Gage, her hand shakily reached out. Her fingertips barely rested against his side in an attempt to provide comfort via touch for them both.

Joey's voice sounded miles away as he shouted her name. Hearing him, she knew she was safe—they both were.

She surrendered, and her eyes fell shut.

Chapter Twenty-Three

GAME

"I'm getting really sick and fuckin' tired of doctors and hospitals," Layne griped as she sat in a chair next to Gage's gurney in the emergency room. She removed the ice pack from her forehead.

After she had raised all hell refusing medical treatment, they were now just waiting on Gage's discharge papers after being stuck there for several hours. Unfortunately, coming to the ER wasn't ideal, but the NYPD was a bit too quick to arrive on the scene shortly after Joey did. It seemed the new brass was making a stink about response times.

"Baby, I wish you would have let the doctors check you out." Gage sat on the edge of the makeshift bed, looking about as worse for wear as she did.

She looked down at the cold pack that was doing little to alleviate her headache. "It's just a bump. I'm not the one who got roofied."

Joey pulled the small bag out of her hand and gently

applied it to the side of her face where the flashlight had struck her. "But you were its intended victim," he countered.

As the stinging cold pressed to the tender spot on her face, she gave a light hiss of pain as she winced, trying to pull her face away. Joey's hand held onto the side of her head, preventing her from evading his efforts to alleviate the swelling.

"Since Gage doesn't remember shit, what do you remember?" Joey wanted to be pissed at his brother for getting behind the wheel and risking their girl's life, but there had been no way of knowing that the Rohypnol was in his system until he was already on the road. It wasn't until the doctors got Gage's blood work back that it was confirmed he had been inadvertently drugged when he consumed Layne's beverage.

Both sets of brown eyes were staring at her, begging her to recall even the slightest detail. She frowned, unsure that she had anything rattling around in her brain that was of any use. "I told you, I don't know what I saw. When we left Cassidy's, I had a pretty heavy buzz. The next thing I knew, all I felt was the car getting slammed into, followed by a bright ass fuckin' light in my face."

Gage held up a piece of paper that they all had read multiple times. "This note left behind in your lap doesn't even make sense. Are you sure it wasn't Liam?"

"I know my brother's voice; it wasn't his. Though I'm sure he had something to do with this." She leaned forward and took the piece of paper from Gage. Her eyes scanned over the words again.

Family First. Fucktoys Second.
Time to honor your commitments to this family.
430 at 830 on 227 for 611.

Frustration overcame her. None of this made sense. It looked like some cheat code for a game console. She was on the verge of crumpling up the note and tossing it in the trash when her phone began to ring in her pocket.

The familiar name on the screen popped up, prompting her to immediately answer. "Hey, what do you have for me?"

Cowboy, the technological genius, didn't sound like his typical giddy self on the other end of the line. "Hi there. Using the password you gave me for that contact of yours, I was able to coordinate a meeting for you."

Oh good, this was perfect timing to meet with a Russian who quite possibly was off his rocker. "Mmhmm. You don't sound like this is a good thing."

A slight pause before Brandon responded, "There's not much that creeps me out, but doing some digging on this guy… Well, just be careful, is all I'm saying. Does Joey know that you're meeting him?"

"No, and I expect it to stay that way for now." Her eyes glanced over at the man who had altered the course of her life forever. She wanted to tell Joey everything, especially given her shitty choices lately that had landed her in hot water with both of her guys. There's no way they would understand why she was doing this, though.

When her nerdy friend didn't respond, she prompted him, "You got it?"

"Yeah, yeah. I just," he sighed. "He'd want to know." He also didn't want to be on the receiving end of Joey's anger when he found out that he had helped Layne with this.

"There's a lot of things we all want, but that's not how life works. Anything else?"

Brandon was able to confirm that one of the men in the Chinese restaurant was indeed Nicholas Orellano, but all the scans of the second man in the ballcap were coming up with nothing at all: shit angles and no matches in public or private databases.

"Keep looking. Text me what I need to know, and I will take it from here." She ended the call with a tap of the screen and tucked her phone away.

Joey and Gage were both staring at her, expecting a recap of her conversation.

Gently, she eased the ice pack in Joey's hand away from her face. "Cowboy confirmed that Orellano was with Liam at the restaurant, but he said whoever else was with him is like trying to track down a damn ghost. He hasn't found anything so far."

"Our work is cut out for us then. We find Orellano and go from there." Joey was determined to make it as simple as that.

Seeing that Layne didn't readily agree, he rested a hand on her knee. "Layney, it's a step in the right direction," he tried to reassure her.

She frowned as she stared down at the note in her hand again. "It's always one step forward, two steps back, Joey. I feel like we keep showing up late to the party. We get a lead, and Liam is already three steps ahead of us."

Gage wrinkled his forehead in deep thought. "You need to stop trying to think like your brother and start thinking like Liam."

Layne lifted her eyes to look at Gage, overcome with confusion at his statement. Initially, she wondered if his brain was still half-drugged at the sense he wasn't making. "What?"

Lifting his brow, Joey also looked at Gage. "Yeah. What?"

Easing himself off the gurney, Gage came over to Layne, squatting in front of her chair. "If you stop approaching this like Liam is your family and start considering him like the violently unhinged asshole he is, the less predictable you'll be to him. I guaran-damn-tee you that he's been banking on the small part of you that remembers a time when he wasn't this warped."

It was hard for Gage to imagine that Liam wasn't ever this big of a psychopath, but Layne needed to see that any memories of Liam resembling a human being should remain in the past.

She sat there, letting his words sink in. The more she thought about it, the more she realized how much she was at fault for letting this situation get out of her control. If Liam wanted to go to war with his sister, he was going to be shit out of luck. Layne was going to bring the war to him as the judge, jury, and executioner of O'Reilly Enterprises.

Joey had driven them all back to O'Reilly Manor after escaping the slow as fuck discharge process, none of them wanted one another out of sight after everything that had transpired.

It had been late morning by the time they rolled in and crashed into bed together. Everybody got the hours of sleep that were much needed after being awake for nearly a day straight. Evening was rolling around, and that's when Gage turned over in bed, and his hand reached out to stroke over Layne's body. His fingers danced along a hard and abnormally large bicep rather than the slender one he had been expecting.

Lifting his head from his pillow, he opened his eyes to find Joey staring at him.

"Good morning, sunshine." Joey snorted.

Grumbling, Gage withdrew his hand quickly before stretching out his body. He felt like absolute garbage, despite all the fluids the hospital had given him trying to flush his system from the commonly used date rape drug. The car accident didn't do him any favors either.

"Where's Layne?" Gage groaned out his question past the unforgiving headache pulsing at his temples.

Tossing the sheets aside, Joey slid out of bed. "Probably downstairs, the way you were snoring like a broken chainsaw." He rubbed a hand over his face to try and erase the last remnants of sleep from his eyes.

Moments later, both guys came down to the first floor, each wearing just a pair of sweats. They followed the scent of freshly brewed caffeine coming from the kitchen despite the late time of day. Both of them came to a sudden halt as they saw Layne there, fully dressed and finishing off her cup of coffee. She looked ready to attack whatever was on her agenda. As far as they both knew, nothing should have been on her calendar for tonight.

She gently set her empty coffee mug into the sink before buzzing around the center island to snatch her phone off the charger on the counter.

"Layne? What are you doing?" Joey watched her with confusion splashed across his face.

When she didn't acknowledge either of them, Gage reached out and latched his hand onto her forearm to force her to take a moment and talk with them. "Baby, you look like you're ready to go somewhere."

Sighing like she had too much to do and not enough time, she stopped and looked at her two guys. "Yeah, I have a last-minute meeting I need to go to."

Joey's jaw immediately clenched as he suppressed his grumbling. "When were you going to tell us?"

She gently coaxed her arm from Gage's hand. "I know how this looks."

Gage lifted a brow at her. "Really? Because it looks like you were ready to bail without saying a damn thing."

Exhaling a short breath, she knew that this was going to be a hard pill to swallow for all of them, but better now than never. "Hear me out."

"Hear you out?" Joey grumpily replied. "We've been over this, Layne. Where you go, we go. End of story. Fuck, we can't even keep you safe when all three of us are together." Each word he spoke bearing more of his aggravation.

Layne stepped up to Joey and placed a hand on his bare

sides, hoping her touch would assist in getting him to listen to her. "I know, but this is different. I have a shot at hitting Liam where it hurts and getting one step ahead of him. This is one meeting I can't risk anyone knowing about, so I need you both to stay here."

Gage's hand slid up her arm onto her shoulder. "You can't seriously expect us to—"

She cut Gage off, "I can and I do. I love you both more than life itself, but I can't be the leader I need to be with my head tied up in my emotions. You're the one who told me to stop treating Liam like my brother, and that's why I'm doing this. Liam expects me to be with one of you at all times. For all I know, he's got people watching who comes and goes from here. He's not going to give a fuck if one of you leaves to go to Mickey D's for a late-night snack. But more than one person leaving this house?" She shook her head, imagining what lengths her brother was possibly going to in order to bring her down.

He hated to admit it, but he was starting to see her logic, and looking over at Joey's face, his brother also saw the point she was making.

Joey grabbed her face with both his hands. "I'm not budging on this, Layney." He was being a stubborn asshole, as usual.

As she went to look at Gage for support, Joey turned her face back at him. "Don't look at him, you're answering to me right now."

Her intoxicating green eyes were as calm as the sea before a storm. "You and I both know that I'm doing this with or without your permission. I promise you that I will take every precaution I can, but I need to take this chance. You wanted me to light my fire and let it burn, and I'm standing here telling you that I need a bit of oxygen to do that."

Staring silently into her eyes, Joey's conflict was clear.

Layne spoke in a whisper, "Please. I'm going to be late."

"Fuck," he cursed under his breath before pulling her face to his. Joey's lips locked onto hers as he hungrily kissed her.

When he pulled back, his hands were still tightly gripping her face. He forced his words out. "You fuckin' watch your ass. If the wind so much as blows the wrong damn way, you get the hell out of dodge. Do you fucking understand me, Layne?"

After she nodded, he dropped his hands from her face and wrapped his arms around her. Squeezing her tightly against him, Joey kissed the top of her head several times.

No sooner did Joey release her than Gage pulled her to him by the back of her neck. He pressed his forehead to hers. "Do you know what I'm going to tell you, Lucky Charm?"

She gave a slight smile. "To be careful?"

Gage grinned. "No, baby. I want you to go be a badass bitch, but when you get back here, your ass is ours." Using his mouth, he sealed that promise with a scorching kiss.

She let herself get lost in the way their lips wrangled with one another before easing away from him. Layne looked at both of them, knowing she had to do this for all of their futures if they were going to finally make progress.

Exchanging a round of 'I love you's,' she strode out of the kitchen. Her hand plucked Joey's motorcycle keys off the hook outside of the door that led into the garage.

Once inside the garage, she secured her designated helmet onto her head as she straddled the sports bike. Turning the key, she felt the purr of the motor between her thighs as the bike came to life.

Layne took one final look at her phone to confirm the details of her meeting. After she secured her phone in her jacket pocket, she pulled down the visor over her eyes.

Daniil Parshikov may be one unpredictable and possibly crazy Russian, but today, he was going to meet one bloodthirsty and pissed-off Irish Car Bomb. With any luck, they would both come out of this meeting as allies. If not, then she was prepared to burn this city to the ground to get what she wanted.

Both guys were left standing in the kitchen, looking at one another.

"So," Gage broke the silence, "are we just going to…?" He looked at Joey questioningly.

Joey stood there with a hand on his hip and the other on the edge of the counter, his jaw set in a hard line. He looked over at the time displayed above the stove. "I'm giving her a ten-minute head start."

Chapter Twenty-Four

SET

Zipping through traffic, Layne constantly kept an eye out all around her. It wasn't the concern of her guys following her but the paranoia that it was whoever else might have eyes on her back.

Constantly checking the mirrors, she twisted the throttle to speed up as the cold air whipped around her. Even with the black leather jacket zipped up over her upper body, the late autumn air cut into her. The dark blue jeans she wore did little to keep her legs warm as the temperature was rapidly tanking outside.

Layne's mind was racing just as fast as she was weaving through traffic and illegally splitting lanes. There were no guarantees in this business you could trust anybody. The only person she was going to be able to rely on today was herself.

Everything she had learned about this man, Daniil, was that he had grown up in this life much like she had. Rumors swirled about his family's involvement in some sort of mass casualty event, and that made Layne even more wary than she already was. It was one thing to take out people on the same level as you in this life and entirely another to be involved in wiping out civilians.

When she arrived at their designated meeting spot, she parked Joey's bike out front of the pretentious luxury hotel in the heart of Brooklyn. The building towered high, with the exterior appearing recently renovated. The valet stand was populated with clean-cut staff standing at full attention and ready to serve.

The doorman dressed in his blue and gold uniform gave a discreet nod of his head at one of the valet attendants. Eagerly, the young guy rushed over to Layne, trying to assist her off the sports bike decorated with various skull stickers.

Ignoring him, she swung a leg over the seat and stepped up onto the sidewalk. Removing her helmet, she smoothed her hand down over the french braid she had styled her hair. She hoped, with it being a short ride here, that she somehow escaped dreaded helmet hair.

Instead of passing over the key to the kid waiting to whisk her ride to a garage somewhere, she made sure the bike was locked. Joey would kill her if she allowed anyone else near it, let alone touch it.

Before the young kid could utter a word, Layne shoved a hundred-dollar bill into his palm. "Nobody touches the bike. Got it?"

Holding her helmet by the chin strap in her left hand, she glanced up at the name in golden script above the entrance: The Alderson Hotel. It may as well have just stated that this was a place to overpay for a subpar bed and ridiculous amenities that nobody actually used.

Walking past the doorman who held the door open for her with his mouth agape, she entered the grand lobby where the opulent decor continued to be constantly up in one's face. A few people dared to give her some dirty looks, and she couldn't blame them. Layne was sticking out like a sore thumb. Her face was sporting the car wreck's injuries, and she wasn't dressed for the goddamn Kentucky Derby like the rest of the rich assholes.

Crossing the floor to the elevators, she stood and waited for the next one to arrive to take her upstairs. As she stood there, a bellboy joined her at her side. He puckered his lips at her before grabbing the front of his pants suggestively.

Layne noticed the lewd gesture from the corner of her eyes and not-so-subtly shot him the bird, hoping he would get the hint. If she hadn't been worried about scaring the crap out of some little old lady, she would have been tempted to grab the bellboy by the front of his pants in an unpleasant fashion.

When the ding sounded and a set of doors opened, she boarded the elevator. The bellboy attempted to follow, but she extended her arm across the width of the opening. "Take the next one."

Layne would love to boast it was her charming personality that scared him off, but raising her arm lifted her jacket enough to reveal the high-voltage taser secured on her hip.

The taser wasn't the only weapon she brought with her. Various blades were concealed all over her body, her favorite Glock was tucked into the back of her jeans, and the high-impact helmet didn't hurt as an impromptu tool to inflict blunt force trauma if things went tits up.

After the elevator brought her to the sixteenth floor, she traveled down the hall and stopped at room 1621. Her knuckles rapped against the door demandingly, meetings like these didn't call for a delicate tap at the door.

While waiting for the door to swing open, she rested her hand on her pistol at the small of her back.

Each second that passed felt like years until, finally, the door swung open, and she saw a well-dressed man standing before her. The first thing she noticed was he wore his money well. While Layne may not have been your stereo-typical Uptown girl, most days, she didn't look like she was hurting for funds. The only thing about her today that looked like it was hurting was the bruising on her forehead and cheekbone from the car wreck yesterday.

She hadn't known what to expect, but she hadn't expected him to look anything less than disfigured and crazy-eyed from the little she had heard of his reputation. Instead, he had that rugged and dangerous type of charm cloaked around him. Layne guessed that not every rumor had merit after all.

Skipping the pleasantries in favor of wanting to get down to business, "You going to let me in, or are you waiting to see if I shoot you?" she asked. She typically did a good job masking her nerves with her attitude, but given the past few months, her anxiety was at its peak.

He widened the door enough for her to barely pass. "You're not what I expected."

"I'm not what I expected either," she snorted, dropping her hand from the weapon holstered at her back and stepping past him into the room drenched in luxury items.

She set her helmet down on a small table as her eyes scanned the room for any signs of a potential ambush. Nothing seemed out of place, at least for a place of this caliber.

The room was laid out in three sections. Upon entry, you were greeted with a living area straight ahead of you and a kitchenette to the right—as if the wealthy elites who frequented this type of place actually cooked for themselves. To the left of the sofa in the living space was a door to a separate room where she could just barely see the corner of a bed inside.

Layne turned to face Daniil after hearing the door shut. "I don't trust you," she spoke with honesty as she watched each move he made as he stepped further into the room.

He cocked his head slightly. "Then, why are you here?"

"As much as it pains me to say it, I need someone that can't be trusted." Keeping the status quo of how she operated her business was getting her nowhere except closer to the grave.

He made a sound somewhere between a grunt and a chuckle.

Layne explained, "My brother has decided to make it his life's mission to either destroy me or drive me to insanity. So far, he's making good progress on the latter."

"From the looks of things, he's not doing too bad on the former." He motioned at the cut above her eyebrow and the bruised cheekbone she was sporting. Daniil walked by her to the small wet bar, where he retrieved a previously poured glass of alcohol.

Her jaw tightened as she tried to prevent her irritation from reaching her voice. "He's getting help, and I need to know how the fuck he's always one step ahead of me."

"What do you want me to do?" He sipped from the glass in his hand.

She stomped over to him after pulling a piece of paper from her pocket and slammed it down on the wet bar. "Find this asshole. I want to know everything he knows. I want to know everything from the moment he met my brother to the last time he jerked off." Her eyes flared with her rising temper.

Seemingly unrattled by her minor outburst, Daniil picked up the paper, unfolding it to reveal the name— Nicholas Orellano. Committing the name to memory, he dropped it back down onto the counter.

"I've heard you have quite the *personal* security team." As Layne's expression slipped in surprise that he knew anything about Joey or Gage, he added, "Did you think I would agree to this without doing some research of my own?"

He set down the empty glass after consuming the remainder of the amber liquid. "Why not allow them to do their job and take care of you?"

She rolled her eyes at the concept she had grown tired of since the day she was born. "There are complications."

He smirked. "It is not a very complicated concept for a man, or men, to take care of a woman." The innuendo quite clearly rested on top of his words.

Her shining green eyes narrowed. "My needs are more than taken care of. What I don't need is to be treated like an object incapable of making my own choices. If I wanted that, my life would be a whole lot fuckin' easier."

She nodded to the ring she observed on his left hand. "Is that what your wife wants, to be just another possession you have ownership of?"

Judging from the way Daniil's eyes darkened, Layne's words struck a nerve as she brought up his wife. She didn't feel the least bit remorseful. If there was anything she had learned, it was that nothing was off-limits when it came to this lifestyle.

She shook her head, beginning to wonder if this jackass was as good as she was told. "They're too invested. They're too worried about me to worry about themselves."

"Ah, so this is the problem, isn't it? You can't trust them, or you can't trust yourself. So which is it?" He posed the psychoanalytic question to her, and the way her face scrunched up said she wasn't taking it well.

"I never said that," Layne was quick to spit out.

He shrugged. "You didn't have to."

Patience was sure as hell not her strong suit, and right now, it was wearing thinner than a split hair. "Look, can you help me or not? For someone who supposedly knows how to get shit done, all I hear is a lot of damn bull-shitting."

"How badly do you want the information from this man?" Daniil pulled his phone out, appearing to quickly fire off a message.

"I don't give a rat's ass if you want to pluck each hair

from his head one follicle at a time or you simply beat the crap out of him. Whatever makes you happy and gets what I want from him." If it were up to Layne, she'd just shoot first and ask questions later. However, in this situation, she needed answers before any killing happened.

He seemed pleased that the options were limitless in the way he extracted information for her. "I don't hand out favors for free," he noted.

"Good, 'cause I don't accept handouts. Name your price, and I will make sure you will get it." She crossed her arms in front of her stomach, waiting to see how much this was going to cost her.

"$100,000," he said without so much as an ounce of hesitation.

Without the blink of an eye, she responded, "Done. You'll have it by tomorrow morning." There was no price too high to keep Joey and Gage from stupidly getting caught in the crossfire on her behalf.

"One more thing," Layne stepped uncomfortably close to him with a murderous look in her eyes with her hand digging in her pocket. "Tell him he can choke on this on his way down to hell." She grabbed Daniil's hand and pressed a small metal object into it.

After she withdrew her hand, left in Daniil's open palm was the same casing that housed the bullet that penetrated Joey's chest on their wedding day. Orellano may not have pulled the trigger, but he sure as hell put the gun in Liam's hand.

Daniil grinned as he held up the shell between his thumb and forefinger, letting his imagination conjure up all the creative ways to inflict this small piece of metal into his assigned target.

"I will contact you when it's done." He pulled his phone out again and looked at an incoming message. He raised a brow and looked at Layne. "Looks like you have company waiting for you downstairs."

When Daniil rotated his phone so she could see, there on the screen was a photo taken from the lobby of both Joey and Gage at the front desk, appearing to be asking questions.

"Oh, for fucks sake." She should have known better.

Pocketing his phone, Daniil walked over to the door and opened it for her. "Take it from me, no matter what you do, men like that will pay any cost for the right woman."

She shook her head as she grumbled angrily at their inability to follow simple instructions. Layne snatched her helmet off the table on her way to the door. "I'm about to hand them the fucking bill for not listening to me."

Daniil walked out with her, catching a ride in the same elevator down to the lobby. She was fuming as they passed each floor. When the doors popped open, they both stepped out.

Approaching the line of elevators were Joey and Gage. Both of them stopped short when they saw her and Daniil exit the elevator. Various emotions flickered over their faces from relief, surprise, suspicion, and their possessive jealousy over her.

Leaning in close to her, with Daniil's large frame blocking the view of both De Luca men, he whispered into her ear, "Here's the key if you need it." His hand slid the keycard to the hotel room into her back pocket discreetly. He winked at her before stepping back and gesturing to a few of his men seated in the lobby to take their leave.

Layne gave a brief nod, still seeing red that the guys had so blatantly went against her wishes when she was doing her best to keep them out of trouble. Her eyes stared at both her men's faces, trying to find the restraint not to shout and cause a scene there in the lobby.

"In the damn elevator. *Now*." She ground out past her temper before turning and catching the elevator doors before they shut. Layne stepped inside and waited for Joey and Gage to join her, dead set on making them aware of how they fucked up.

Chapter Twenty-Five

MATCH

The entire ride back up to the sixteenth floor was in strained silence, with Layne's anger rolling off her like a summer storm. When the elevator doors slid open, she stalked down the hallway until she pulled out the keycard to open room 1621 and stepped inside. She didn't bother checking if the guys followed, she merely assumed that they would since that was what they were seemingly best at.

Once Joey and Gage were in the room with her, she slammed the door shut behind them.

"Who the fuck was that downstairs?" Joey turned to immediately jump onto the topic he was interested in most. Jealous? Joey? Never.

Layne stood there staring at both of them, her blood pressure spiking through the damn roof. She tossed the motorcycle helmet onto the table with such force it didn't bother staying and instead slid right off and fell onto the floor with a thunk until it rolled across the dark gray carpet. She didn't give a fuck about being gentle with much of anything right now.

Her hands jerked at the sleeves of her leather jacket, stripping it off and pitching it at a chair, revealing the white lace blouse underneath. With her temper being at an all-time high, coupled with her stress, the room felt sweltering.

Ignoring Joey's question, she tossed out her own, "How about we start with why the fuck you both are here? I told you both to stay back."

Gage crossed his arms in front of his chest, "We gave you enough space before we followed you here. Nobody trailed us."

"You don't know that!" she screamed at him, only imagining how all of this was going to blow up in her face if Liam got wind of what she was doing or who she was doing it with. "I told you both to leave me alone for a damn reason! What part of that did you not understand?!"

Barely clinging to any sense of calm, Joey shook his head. "You're overreacting."

That was probably the worst thing he could have said at that moment. "Do not talk to me about overreacting!" her voice remained elevated as she shouted at him.

Layne continued to lash into them, "You left me under the impression that you were going to do as I asked. I came here so that I could find a way to strike at one of Liam's top guys without him seeing it coming. I jumped through fifty goddamn hoops to set up this meeting, and you both were so willing to put it all in jeopardy!"

Leaning over to balance on one leg, she removed one shoe quickly, followed by the other. Both shoes were angrily discarded to the side, but not after contemplating throwing them at both of her guys like she was playing the milk can game at a carnival.

It was Gage who made the first step towards her. She glared at him with the weight of violence in her eyes, stopping him from approaching unless he wanted to feel her wrath next.

Gage raised his hands up innocently and retreated from the step he had taken towards her. "What about the risk you were taking? Did you consider that?" He offered an opposing viewpoint.

"I took this risk so you both didn't have to. The two of you have been so wrapped up in keeping me safe, and at what cost, hm?" She pointed at Joey. "You get fuckin' shot, and you," she pointed at Gage, "get drugged and into a car accident."

She knew neither of those things were their fault, but it had all been attacks on her that had caused them suffering.

Her chest was aching at the thought of how all these things could have ended poorly. The thought of losing either of them would wreck her soul, especially if it was because of their involvement in her life. Tears began to prick at her eyes.

Forcing her voice to remain steady, ignoring the emotions shining in her eyes like morning dew on a clover, "When does it fucking stop? When one or all of us is dead?" The words barely made it out of her mouth.

The air was thick with silence as she stared at both of them, her question going unanswered. Finally, Joey's shoulders relaxed, seeing past her anger and straight to the fear behind her rage. "Layney, I'm not going to apolo—"

"Shut up. Apologies aren't what I need." She plucked the taser from her hip and set it on the table before removing several knives that had been concealed underneath her clothes. The last item she drew was her firearm, the cool metal feeling comforting in her hand. Staring down at the semi-automatic, she shook her head, wondering how her life had spiraled so out of control. Layne needed to snatch some of that control back.

Her eyes lifted from the weapon in her hand to the two men in front of her. "On your knees, both of you." There was no uncertainty in her voice as she gave them both the order.

Slowly, Gage turned his head to Joey, looking for some indication that his brother had heard the same thing as him. The way Layne was holding onto the gun made him wonder if she was planning on fucking shooting them both.

Joey didn't take his eyes off Layne before he dropped down to his knees, his hands hanging down loosely between his thighs. He sat back on his feet, seeming all too willing to let Layne do as she wanted.

After seeing Joey lower himself, Gage mirrored the action and stared at Layne, trying to guess what was going on inside her head.

She walked around behind them and let them stew in

their thoughts for a few minutes. Both of these bad boys could think about what they had done.

Setting the gun down quietly on the sofa behind her, she leaned over between them. Her hands grabbed them both by their sandy blonde hair and pulled their heads back so they were staring up at her.

"Dicks out," she demanded.

Clear from the expression that washed over both their faces, it had been an unexpected turn of events. Being able to catch them both off guard by her request had Layne's excitement at her core growing warmer by the second.

Complying, each opened up their pants and shoved at the waist of their underwear until she was greeted by the sight of both their cocks. Each thick length was growing harder before her eyes.

"Good boys," she purred out in praise. Her hands shoved their heads forward roughly as she released her grip on them. "Now, I want you both to show me how you stroke your cocks when you're thinking about me."

She straightened and watched as Gage took his swords into his hand and began to work in long, slow movements. Her eyes glanced over at Joey, and he was eagerly gliding his hand over his swollen cock at a slightly faster pace.

Layne leaned over and whispered into Joey's ear, "You might want to slow down. If you come, you lose. And I plan for us to be here for a little while." She smirked as he gave a quiet groan in response and pulled back on the pace of his hand.

Her teeth gave a light tug at the curve of his ear before she stepped between them, turning to watch their efforts.

Layne's desires were rising within her, prompting her to give a hard swallow to maintain her composure. She could feel her thong quickly getting soaked with her arousal as they both submissively followed her orders. Having them jerk themselves off because she said so unlocked something in Layne that she wasn't even aware she enjoyed.

Gradually, her anger was melting now that she had them both finally listening to her. "Whose idea was it to follow me here?"

Joey piped up with a confession, "Mine."

That wasn't a huge surprise; her forever and always stalker. "Of course it was, you just can't help yourself. Can you, Joey?"

She stepped in front of Gage. Her fingers settled underneath his bearded chin, tipping his head back gently to look up at her. "Looks like you're up first."

Barely touching his skin, she trailed her fingers down the center of his throat slowly. Her slender fingers wrapped around his silver chain, peeking out of the collar of his tee, twisting it several times around two of her digits before tugging. "Up."

His hand fell away from his inked cock as he stood. Layne used his necklace like a leash, leading him to the armchair within Joey's sight. Turning Gage, she released his necklace and pushed him so he fell back into the chair.

Layne dropped down to her knees, shoving his muscled thighs apart so she could settle between them. Her fierce green eyes looked at Gage. "I want you to tell him how good I make you feel."

It took an act of God for Gage not to push his luck and

give Joey a cocky grin that he was going to get some action while his brother remained in the doghouse.

Layne took hold of his hard dick, her grasp at the base as she angled him toward her. Lowering her mouth over the rounded head of Gage's cock, she sucked on him aggressively, refusing to be gentle. After taking several inches of his swords deeper into her mouth, Gage rested his head back against the chair and groaned out in pleasure.

"Baby, your mouth around my cock feels so good." His hips pushed up towards her with increased need. His hand slid onto the side of her head as her lips sealed around his swollen length. Resisting the urge to grab her hair and force her head forward, he clutched tightly with his other hand on the arm of the chair he was in. "Fuck, I love what you can do with your mouth."

Watching as Layne began to blow, Gage had Joey's need for any part of her body skyrocketing. His hand started to move faster over his dick until he remembered Layne's warning, forcing him to painfully ease up. God, he knew just how good her throat felt, and he would have done anything if it meant she would stop what she was doing and come suck his dick.

She continued to lower her greedy mouth down onto Gage, her tongue taunting the underside like a velvety snake. With each bob of her head, his hips pushed up to get rewarded with the tightness of pushing beyond her gag reflex.

His hand began to clutch harder onto Layne's head. "Fuck, Layne, yes. Make me come, baby." The desire was dripping off of Gage's words as his pleasure began to shift into a frenzied need.

The feeling was taken away all too soon after he mentioned coming. Layne slid off him, her hand gliding up to the end of his cock that ached for release. Her thumb rubbed over the head, mixing her saliva with the precum leaking from his tip.

Gage whimpered, "Come on, don't leave me hanging."

Layne smirked as she removed her hand. "I'll let you come when I decide you've earned it. You're still in trouble for going along with Joey's idea." She pushed herself onto her feet, leaving him there, wanting the one thing she refused to give him. His balls ached as she brought him so close to satisfaction, only to rip it away at the last second.

For a split moment, Joey felt smug that he wasn't the only one being toyed with by their girl. When Layne turned and approached him, he was certain that it was his turn in her mouth. However, when he started to get off his knees, she pushed him right back down again.

Lightly, she scolded him, "I didn't tell you to get up. You have work to do." His chocolate eyes stared up at her, begging so loudly for her touch he didn't need to verbalize it.

Her hands tugged her shirt up over her head, dropping it at her feet. Next, she shimmied out of her jeans until all she was left standing in was a blush pink bra and panty set.

Without looking behind her, she gave Gage his next order. "Gage, back as you were on your knees for me with your hand back on your cock."

Following instructions, her Daddy was behaving so

nicely for her even though he was never the one in their relationship taking orders.

"Looks like someone is finally getting a taste of how it feels to be the sub," Joey smirked as he glanced over at Gage, who was no longer asserting himself as the Dom here.

Grabbing Joey's jaw, Layne turned his gaze back towards her. "And you're going to learn what happens when you run that bratty mouth of yours."

Taking two handfuls of Joey's hair to balance herself, she draped a leg over his shoulder while she balanced on the other. Layne gave a giddy grin. "My turn to feel good." She urged his face towards her waiting pussy.

More than happy to get a taste of her, Joey shifted the crotch of her thong to the side and dove into the sensual buffet that waited for his mouth. His tongue immediately lapped at her sweet arousal. If he ever ended up on death row, he'd want Layne to be his last meal.

She moaned out at the first contact, her hips grinding up against his lips. Each movement was a mix of sensations coming from the coarseness of his stubble, his punishing lips, and the firm flexing of his tongue. "Oh God, yes..." Her head tipped back as the sinful vibrations of pleasure coursed throughout her body.

Gage was left to watch and listen as Joey got to indulge in Layne's body, while he only imagined what it would be like to be balls deep in her while she made those delicious sounds. His hand squeezed his cock tighter at the thought.

Joey's hands came up to hold her steady, his fingers digging into her ass cheeks while he reveled in the taste of her cunt on his taste buds. Every moan she released drove him to taste even more of her.

The sensation of a groan of approval from Joey had her body beginning to shake as her release queued up. Gasping for air between her pants, she started to slip off that delicate edge. "Joey! Don't stop!" Her hands fisted his hair tightly to make sure he didn't draw back from her.

Taking advantage of her current state, Joey took it upon himself to inch one of his fingers into the tight hole of her ass, only far enough to send her careening into her orgasm.

She screamed out as she came, feeling her heated core bear down while her cum got devoured by Joey.

His scalp was nearly on fire the way Layne's hands were tugging on his hair, and it only fueled his need for her. She could ride his mouth like a fucking pony if it meant hearing her orgasm ricochet throughout her body like this.

Layne's breaths came out hard as she tried to reel herself back in from the ecstasy attempting to lull her into a sedative state. It was Gage's groans as his hand twisted along his cock that brought her mind back to dealing with these two. They both needed to learn their lesson of how to listen to her.

Her fists slowly unfurled to let go of Joey's locks of hair, pushing his hands away from her ass. Carefully, she removed her thigh from his shoulder and stepped back from him on shaky legs.

With the satisfaction still saturating her eyes, she looked down at him and tried to bite back her smile. "I didn't give you permission to touch my ass like that."

"It was worth it," he responded with a sly grin before he

sucked off the taste of her from the finger he had used on her back door.

"We'll see if you still feel that way in a few minutes. Both of you, strip and get on the bed." No sooner had she said it than they were both rushing to shed all their clothes and wait for her in the bedroom.

Ditching her bra and panties so she was equally as naked, she followed them to the edge of the mattress and took a moment to enjoy the sight laid out before her. Both men were lying there, ready for her, with their cocks harder than steel in anticipation. All of their tattooed images on display across their flesh for her to admire.

She crawled onto the bed between them with a mischievous sparkle in her green hues. "For both of you not listening to me earlier tonight, neither of you will get to come. Joey, since you couldn't be a good boy, you get to watch me fuck Gage since he knows how to keep his hands to himself."

Before Gage could settle in and gloat, she issued her warning to him. "I'm fucking you for me, not for you. I'm the one in charge tonight. Do you understand?"

He still couldn't help but grin like a fool as he cheekily replied, "Yes, Mistress."

Layne straddled Gage's hips and roughly grabbed his arms, shoving them above his head. She looked over at Joey, "Make sure his hands stay right where they are."

Joey should have been a lot grumpier that he wasn't the one getting fucked, but at least he got a front-row seat to watching Layne take Gage's cock without the intention of giving him a happy ending. Seated near the headboard above his brother's head, he grabbed Gage's wrists and tightly restrained them.

"Damn, ease up asshole, you don't need to hold them that tightly," Gage complained as Joey intentionally went above and beyond the call of duty.

Before Gage could continue to bitch, Layne guided his thick tattooed cock into her tight pussy. He gave a husky groan as he felt himself disappearing into her.

She echoed the same level of pleasure, her face shifting as she felt the fullness deep within her. Rocking her hips, she began to ride him, beginning the chase for her own climax.

"That's it, baby. Show me how you can tame my cock," Gage moaned out.

With one hand planted on his firm chest, she clamped the other down over his mouth. "Mmm, Gage, I don't want to hear your filthy mouth right now."

Gage's restraint was slowly crumbling as he pushed his hips up to get his cock further up into her. His hot and heavy breaths got trapped under Layne's palm.

Wrapped up in her cloud nine of pleasure, Layne missed the exchange of looks between the guys. Just as she was finding her rhythm, the dynamics shifted hard and fast.

Joey released Gage's wrists, allowing him to roll over and use his weight to pin Layne underneath his body. She shrieked out in surprise at the sudden change of position. Taking advantage of her surprise, Joey captured her wrists, holding them in his firm grip as he kept his front-row seat at the head of the bed.

Not waiting for her to begin to yell at either of them,

Gage began bucking his hips, ramming his cock into her. Each hard thrust jostled her body against the mattress as she moaned out, her full tits bouncing on her chest wildly.

"Did you really think I was going to let you dictate when I get to come, baby?" Gage huffed out between each of his movements as his dick slammed its full length into her repeatedly.

Her loud moans were strung together as she writhed and squirmed, her narrow wrists engulfed in Joey's hold that prevented her from gaining any leverage after this sudden mutiny.

Layne shook her head at Gage, "No."

With his Dom voice dropping a register, Gage dragged his lips over hers. "No, what?"

"No, Daddy!" she cried out as her orgasm was preparing to violently erupt inside of her.

"You better sing my favorite fuckin' song while you soak my dick with your cum, Layne." Gage firmly ordered her as he pounded into her body, their flesh smacking together. The tip of his cock was relentless as it jabbed at the especially sensitive spot inside of her.

The closer she got, the more she fought and trembled against Joey's restraint. Her toes curled as her legs began to kick at the mounting pressure that she was unable to escape.

Gage's hands clamped down onto her thighs. He had her legs pinned wide open as he watched his cock shine with the wetness from her body every time he withdrew it before shoving it back inside of her.

It only took a few more strokes of his dick before her

cunt spasmed around him, and she ferally screamed out. Her release took her hard. It was taking everything Gage had not to unload into her right then and there.

"Fuck! Layne!" He groaned, continuing to try to hold his shit together, his own body on the verge of shaking. As Layne rode her burst of pleasure, her walls continued squeezing onto Gage's cock. Grinding himself into her depths, he tensed up as he yelled out as his seed flooded into her.

Panting heavily, Gage eased out of her and collapsed down onto his back at her side. Layne lay there blissfully like a well-used ragdoll. It made it easy for the guys to shift her so her back was on Gage's chest with his half-hard cock nestled against her ass.

Joey took up the space between her legs, draping them over the crooks of his arms. He had enough of the taunting and teasing she had done earlier; it was his turn to get his fix of her. The sight of his brother's cum slowly leaking from her pussy had his cock twitching as it felt like it was growing beyond the hardest he had ever felt it.

Breathlessly, she lay there with heavy eyes from the residual high her body had just surrendered to. "Both of you are shitty subs," she teased while lazily smiling.

Smirking, Joey used the round head of his cock to collect some of the escaped white fluid from her pussy and push it back into her entrance. "Layney, don't act like you don't fuckin' love it when we take any part of you the way we want."

Feeling him barely inside of her, she whimpered.

Gage's hands ran over her body, one traveling south to

her clit and the other up over her stomach until he roughly grabbed her breast. He whispered into her ear from behind, "You've been a naughty fuckin' girl, baby. The second I'm fully hard again, you better prepare your tight little ass." His fingers pinched at her stiff nipple, causing her to let out a small yelp.

Seeing Gage's fingers begin to circle Layne's sensitive bundle of nerves, Joey slowly sank into her. Fuck, he loved how wet she was right now, and he wanted nothing more than to add his own cum to the mix. "I'm going to fuck the good girl back into you even if it takes me all goddamn night, Layne."

Between the two of them, Layne's antsy movements got her nowhere as they both focused on different parts of her body. Her body felt on fire from the overload of sexual stimulation she was receiving.

The way Joey pulled his cock back out so incredibly and intentionally slow had Layne whimpering at the loss of being full.

"What was that, Layney?" He smiled as he held his hips still, letting her yearn for him a little longer.

Gage's hand moved across to her other breast, twisting the nipple between his fingers. Everything they did to her body left her barely able to find words.

"I need your cock," she finally managed to let out in a heated whisper.

"You didn't want it earlier," he grinned as he gave her the shallowest little fuck as his hips made tiny thrusts at her opening.

She groaned desperately. Each tease of her body left her

nearly in tears at the intense ache at her core. "Damn it, Joey, please!"

There was a rumble coming from Gage's chest against her back as he quietly chuckled at how much she wanted things her way.

Joey leaned over and locked his lips against her mouth, kissing her roughly. Her moans soaked into his mouth as she still wiggled between the two guys.

Barely separating their lips, Joey gazed down into Layne's eyes as a smile tugged at the corners of his mouth. "Layney, when are you ever going to learn? I'm always going to come for you. There is nothing you can do to stop me from making sure you always stay ours."

With that declaration, he drilled his cock into her, groaning out at how readily her body drew him in.

As Joey filled her greedy pussy and began to fuck some sense into her, Gage's dick was rapidly getting harder, being pressed against the warmth of her ass. It had his cock quickly recovering at the way she moved with each of Joey's pushes into her body.

Gage growled from behind her, "How's it feel when your bad boys take care of you, baby?" His fingers continued their massage of her clit. He whispered into her ear, "You'll always be ours, Layne."

Layne's body was trembling as she watched Joey's body take control of her own. No one could give her pleasure the way both of them did, whether they fucked her separately or together. As pissed as she had been that they could have fucked everything up today, a part of her, deep down, was glad they had.

She was theirs in every possible way. Now, her job was to make sure it stayed that way. Up 'til this point, Layne had been doing things all wrong. Instead of worrying about pushing them away to keep them safe, she needed to keep them closer than ever.

The three of them were the perfect match, and together, they would watch Liam's world burn.

Chapter Twenty-Six

UNIT 33

Waiting to hear back from Daniil on whether or not he was successful in his endeavors to track down and get information out of Orellano had been brutal. Each phone call, every knock at the door, any carrier pigeon, was a reason for Layne to perk up in her seat.

After her personal revelation at The Alderson Hotel, while she got her insides rearranged by the two men who had promised to be her everything, she had looped Joey and Gage in on how she had come across Daniil.

Expectedly, Joey had been pissed that Brandon had kept his mouth shut. Fortunately, Layne was able to soothe his anger down a few notches with a few sweet nothings and strokes of her hand before he marched downtown to scare the poor kid senseless.

Currently snuggled between her two large De Luca men on the sofa, she tugged the blanket over her lap as they watched the hockey game together.

"You've got to be kidding me! Where's the slashing call?!" Gage yelled at the television, raising his hands in the air.

Layne snagged another chocolate-covered rice cereal treat out of the bowl Joey was hoarding. The powdered sugar coating left a dusting on her fingertips after she popped the square into her mouth. Listening to Gage get all worked up like the referees on the ice could hear him through the television screen made her giggle.

"Makes up for the tripping call they missed earlier," Joey argued before he snatched up Layne's hand and sucked the white confectionary coating from her fingers.

Watching the guys bicker when their favorite teams played each other by far was one of Layne's favorite things to keep her mind preoccupied when they all weren't naked.

Her phone began to ring and vibrate against the coffee table. Not wasting any time, she leaned over to scoop it up into her hand without any hesitation in answering the blocked number.

"Hello?" There was a pause as she listened, sitting still as a statue. The way she tensed up prompted Gage to mute the game and Joey to put the snack bowl on the side table.

Her jaw tensed as she ground her teeth together when the caller laid the news on her. She squeezed the phone tighter in her hand, "I appreciate it, Daniil. Thanks."

Hanging up the phone, she shook her head. "Motherfucker."

Gage's hand squeezed her thigh. "What is it?"

Both of them were now staring at her with concerned eyes.

"I need to meet with Ethan, Jonathan, and Sammy. We've got a fucking problem." She tossed the blanket off her legs. It looked like this wouldn't be a night off from work after all.

***

After the wedding, Layne had paid some of her grunt workers to go to Liam's place, change the locks, and throw all his shit into a storage unit. Layne had been intending to go through her brother's belongings to see if there was anything of value but hadn't yet had the opportunity. The whole shitshow of her husband getting shot, getting stabbed herself, her Daddy getting drugged, her car getting wrecked, and trying to keep her illegal business ventures afloat was a major time suck.

She called up her top associates and had them meet her, Joey, and Gage there at Southside Storage for an urgent debrief. Joey lifted the storage unit's metal door; a single light bulb provided enough light to reveal the half-filled rental resting on a concrete pad.

"You think there's something in here that's useful?" Sammy asked as he walked into space with Jonathan and Ethan trailing close behind.

"I know there is," Layne said as she waited for all six of them to be inside before pulling the garage-style door closed.

Jonathan picked up a dusty bobblehead figurine before tossing it back into a box. "Looks like a bunch of crap to me."

Ethan sighed, imagining that this was going to be a long night of digging. "Do you have any idea of what we're looking for?"

Joey and Gage grabbed a chair, centering it in the open space.

Layne nodded. "I do, and it's right here." Her eyes scanned the interior of the unit before she looked at Jonathan. "Take a seat."

"What?" He blinked a few times as he pointed at his chest. "Me? Why?"

Joey grabbed Jonathan's shoulder and shoved him into the chair. "She said sit."

Her associate stumbled into the chair; the confusion was as clear as day creasing over his face. Both Ethan and Sammy looked at one another, mirroring the same cluelessness.

"I want to make something very clear." Layne pulled out her gun, tugging the slide back to load a bullet into the chamber. "I made it known when I took over the business that I would be setting some incredibly high standards. When those standards aren't met, it does not make me very happy."

She walked over to Jonathan and straddled his lap, putting the deadly end of the pistol right against his dick. Looking at her negotiator in the eyes. "Is there something you want to tell me?"

Ethan and Sammy took a few steps back, the look in Layne's eyes gave them enough warning not to interfere. Their boss may have looked like an otherwise sweet girl you'd meet on a night out, but she sure as hell had her father's commanding presence when it came to business matters.

Jonathan struggled to find his words, ultimately stuttering out, "N-no. No, of course not!" His eyes pleadingly looked to everyone else in the room there with them. "What the fuck is going on?" Looking for answers from anyone who would take pity. No one did.

Her hand grabbed his face with her other hand, squeezing it tightly so she could look at him. "I'm teaching a lesson in loyalty." She jabbed the gun harder against his junk.

"Layne! Jesus! Stop!" Jonathan's words mushed together by her fingers painfully digging into his cheeks. He began to push up from the chair, but Joey's hands shoved down onto his shoulders from behind.

Layne calmly gave her order to the other two associates, "Sam, Ethan, please make sure Jonathan stays put while we have this conversation."

Without hesitation, both guys came over and took Joey's place. She wanted them to see what happened when she was disappointed.

"Jon, you're a hell of a negotiator. You've helped close a lot of deals for me and smoothed over a lot of relations with other factions on my behalf. So, I want you to negotiate. Show me how good you are." Her hand released his face, but she kept her weapon right where it was. The urge to prematurely fire it off right then and there was incredibly tempting, given her newfound knowledge.

"You're fucking crazy! Negotiate what?" He had the nerve to look ignorant.

Her words were void of any emotions as she gave a nonchalant shrug, "Your life. Why I shouldn't blow your dick to pieces. I mean, I think it's pretty damn obvious."

Gage and Joey hung back, watching as Layne rightfully tormented the guy.

"Uh," was Jonathan's first word as he sat there with Layne sitting on his legs. "I love my dick. Like really love it. I don't want it shot to shit. Layne, I don't know what has set you off, but I swear I will do anything to help you out and make it right."

Was he kidding her right now? Layne rested a hand on the back of Jonathan's neck as she laughed darkly. "Holy shit, do you hear yourself right now?"

Nervously, Jonathan tried to read her laughter and gave a half-chuckle, trying to find humor in the situation to placate her.

"You should see your face right now." Layne smiled as she gave a softer laugh this time.

"Hah, yeah…" The bead of sweat on his forehead began its slow descent towards his brow.

Shifting back a few inches on his lap, Layne pulled the trigger. The bullet easily tore past the thick denim of Jonathan's jeans and straight into his cock.

Her other two associates simultaneously flinched and cringed; you could notice their legs flexing as they had fear struck into their own dicks.

Jonathan immediately jolted and howled out in agony.

Layne's grip on his neck rotated to squeeze his throat, minimizing the sound of his yells.

"You are a fucking liar, Jon!" She yelled at him to be heard over his pain as the blood began soaking his pants, spreading outward over the crotch area. "You've been working for Liam this entire goddamn time! How are you going to make that right?!"

She moved the Glock, so it was now pressed against Jonathan's shoulder as he jerked and writhed, tears streaming down his face. "No, no, no, no!" His denial was on repeat, or perhaps he was in disbelief she had just put a bullet through his penis.

Glancing up to see the shock on the other two's faces, she began laying out everything she knew.

"No? No, you weren't helping Liam? You're telling me that you didn't tell him when I was at the hospital with Joey? You didn't feed him information about my every move? You sure that you didn't give him the heads up where I was having dinner down in Times Square?" Each recounting of all the puzzle pieces clicking into place made her anger tick up another notch.

Her face came up to his so close their noses were touching, and she didn't care how much spit came out with her words. "What about all my discussions with other factions that you were handling? Huh?! Did you fuck those up for me, too?! Is that why no one seemed willing to help me!?"

Jonathan cried out again, reeling from injury, filling his body with unimaginable pain. "Gah!! Pleeeeease!"

Layne pulled her face back to give a little more space.

"I hate to tell you, Jonathan, but Nicholas isn't as tight-lipped as you thought. A friend of mine had him spilling everything he knew. Imagine my goddamn surprise when he told me one of my own fucking men was betraying me!" Layne was beyond pissed, and every word she spat out was laced with her dangerous venom.

When Daniil had called her to alert her he had tracked down Orellano, he informed her of everything that spilled out of the man's mouth. It had taken some extremely aggressive forms of persuasion, which the Russian had been all too happy to resort to. Nicholas had dropped Jonathan's name like a two-ton weight. He mentioned another man, but when questioned further, it was determined he knew nothing about Liam's other partner.

"What is Liam's plan, Jonathan? Hm? You better tell me something, or else I will make the pain you're feeling now seem like a mild headache." She dug the muzzle of the pistol harder into the front of his shoulder.

When it was clear he was too distracted to answer her question, she crashed the side of the gun across his face. "What's his plan?!" Her voice echoed against the walls of the small space of the storage unit.

She saw the defeat and surrender begin to peek through Jonathan's tough front as he sobbed. He choked on his words, "He…H-he wants you to," he gasped for some air between his fits of pain. "Meet at Eric's old place. It's on the note." He took several large breaths, trying to get through the intensity of the wound between his legs.

Layne thought back to the note left for her after the accident. *430 at 830 on 227 for 611.* The first number was the house number of Eric's old residence. The second must have been the time, followed by the date. However, her mind was drawing a blank on what the fourth number represented.

"What's 611?" she asked after being unable to figure it out on her own.

Jonathan shook his head. "I don't know." When she went to lift her pistol again, he screamed out, "I don't know! I swear! I just gave him info; I didn't ask questions!"

Well, that was fucking useless.

"Layne, I'm sorry." Oh boy, here came the apologies that she hated so much.

She got off his lap, pacing a few feet in front of him. "Who is helping him?"

"I told you, I don't know!" He brayed like a wounded jackass.

Bang!

Another bullet ripped through Jonathan, this time, it was the top of his foot. Layne looked up to see Ethan holding his gun out. "You piece of shit! If you don't start giving her answers, I will personally shove this gun up your ass and pull the trigger."

Color Layne impressed that Ethan was harboring the same amount of anger and resentment that she was. He was going to need a damn promotion.

Jonathan was now hysterically screaming, the words coming out of his mouth were a combination of nonsense and curses.

Layne's fingers rubbed across her forehead, trying to

gather her thoughts past the incessant whines and whimpers as Jonathan's body became crippled from the attacks.

She tapped the side of her pistol against her thigh to help her think. Deciding that Jonathan was no longer of any use to her, she lifted the gun to aim it at his chest.

His eyes went wide, seeing that another shot was about to be fired. "Some old fuck! Real twisted!"

"Thanks. Your services are no longer required." Layne pulled the trigger, and the bullet found its home, lodged into Jonathan's heart, obliterating the critical muscle.

Sammy shook his head in disgust that out of the three of them, it was Jonathan who was working with Liam this entire time. "Layne, I had no idea…"

Sighing heavily, she nodded. "I know, nobody seemed to."

"Dickhead," Ethan said under his breath.

Layne returned her Glock to the holster in the back of her pants and pulled out her phone.

Gage raised a brow and came up behind her. "Who are you calling?"

"Liam," his name rolled off her tongue, drenched in disgust.

"Layney," Joey said with a warning tone.

"Don't worry, I'm making this short and sweet," she reassured both of them.

Putting the call on speaker, the other end of the line rang a few times before her brother answered.

"This is a pleasant surprise." Liam sounded far too excited to hear from her.

"Southside Storage, unit thirty-three. Come pick up

your shit, motherfucker." Her finger tapped the end call button. A moment later, she sent a picture of Jonathan's hunched-over corpse to Liam.

The time of playing by her brother's rules was over. Now, she was playing by her own.

Chapter Twenty-Seven

ALWAYS & FOREVER

There wasn't a price Layne wouldn't have paid to see Liam's face when he received the picture of Jonthan's dead body. She hoped he shit his pants and was prepared for her to begin executing anyone else that got in her way.

Thanks to finding an unexpected ally in one particular Russian, her brother had to know about good ol' Nick's demise by now. May that fucker be suffering in hell alongside Jonathan.

With two birds down, she couldn't afford not to press forward, full steam ahead. Liam needed to feel the pressure to a point where he would royally fuck up. If he didn't make a mistake, she sure as hell wasn't going to stop until he did.

As for the note that her former associate had partially deciphered, it seemed they had less than a week before Liam expected her to roll up to the old Ellis residence and wave a white flag.

Good thing she didn't plan to surrender if things didn't go as planned. No, she would march over there beating her war drums for all of New York to hear if it came down to it.

Layne came downstairs wearing nothing but a black silk kimono robe overtop a silk lingerie set. O'Reilly Manor was expectedly quiet at eleven at night. With Gage meeting up with his friends to set up a plan to keep tabs on the perimeter of their home there on the Upper East Side, it was just her and Joey holding down the fort.

Joey had been stuck in the garage working on his car since dinner. It had been his way of busying his mind before he made the next strike in the early hours of the morning.

She quietly opened up the interior door that led into the garage and leaned against the frame as she watched him.

He was leaning over the side of the black Challenger, working on something under the hood of the vehicle. From this vantage point, she was happy to be standing there, appreciating the view of his jean-clad ass.

Joey's tee was draped over the seat of his motorcycle parked next to the car, leaving him shirtless and enhancing the already delicious sight. Each muscle in his back flexed as he worked.

Without turning to look at her, he spoke, "Eye-fucking me again, Layney?" Smirking to himself, he gave another twist of the socket wrench. Layne wasn't nearly as stealthy as she thought she was.

After being called out, she convinced herself that if she had been trying to be sneaky, he wouldn't have known she was there. Stepping onto the cool concrete of the garage floor, she was careful to watch where she walked to avoid tripping on any scattered tools.

"Was just seeing when you were planning on heading out." Layne stopped at the front bumper as she looked at him with gentle green hues.

He sighed and rested his forearms on the edge of the car, and looked over at her. She may have tried to silently admire him moments ago, but Joey made no such effort to conceal the way his eyes appreciated the woman standing there in the garage with him.

The silk robe was tied around her slender waist and draped over the rest of her petite figure. Its length fell to just above midthigh, making it unlikely she was wearing much of anything underneath. If he was lucky, she was wearing nothing at all.

Joey straightened up and tossed the wrench into the open toolbox next to the front tire. "I'm almost done here." He wiped his hands on the thighs of his stained pants, though it did little to remove the black smudges on his hands.

Crossing her arms in front of her stomach, her hands lightly grasped onto her elbows. "Everything all set for Liam?" The plan they had conjured seemed karmic, considering the last time an O'Reilly was executed. However, just thinking about some of the ways it could go wrong had Layne feeling incredibly uneasy.

Picking up on her restlessness and the concern settled in her stance, Joey stepped up to her. "It's going to be okay. You forget how long I've been doing this, Layne. I will head over to Eric's old place, install the explosives on the truck that Ethan says matches the description of the one that was involved in your accident, and hightail it the fuck out of there. With any luck, Liam will get what's been coming to him. If not, it will take out whoever is helping him."

"I know." The tension in her body didn't let up.

Sullied hands or not, he decided he couldn't hold back from using his touch to reassure her. Joey lightly wrapped his hands on either side of her neck just under her jaw, his thumbs caressing the lower lines of her face.

Cocoa brown eyes stared at her as he searched for what was weighing on her mind. "What are you really worried about?" he asked.

Trying to beat down her heart's emotions, she blinked back a few tears. War came with unexpected casualties, ones that you didn't get to pick or choose.

"Don't make me ask twice." He gave a small smile at her that didn't quite reach his eyes.

Filling her lungs with a heaping amount of air, she tried to steady her voice. "There's been a lot going on. When are we all just going to get a break and have a shot at normalcy again?"

His hands fell from her so he could draw her up against his bare chest, wrapping his arms around her upper body into a tight embrace. "We'll get our chance, I promise." If his new deal with Commissioner Saito held up, their opportunity would get here sooner rather than later. "Did you make the call we talked about?"

"Yeah…" The tone of her voice carried a mixture of regret and hesitation. Layne wrapped her arms around his waist as she rested her face against the warmth of his skin. Her cheek pressed against the scarred shamrock tattoo over his heart, the disrupted inkwork around the scar was a souvenir of him saving her life.

Joey's fingers smoothed back a few stray locks of hair away from her face. He hesitated as his words began to stick to the back of his throat, refusing to come out easily. Briefly, he shut his eyes tightly and kissed the top of her head, finding the strength to open up the last piece of him to her.

With eyes back open, he eased her face away from him so he could look at the woman who had changed him before he had even met her. "Layne, there's something I need to tell you."

Scrunching her eyebrows together, she wasn't sure what emotion she should prepare for. "About what?"

Immediately, his heart felt a pang of guilt, seeing that she was already hesitantly putting up her defenses. His large hands grabbed her face so he could make sure she saw the honesty in what he had to say.

"Layne, you are both my biggest regret and my greatest salvation. I never want to know life without you in it." In a rare moment, his eyes glistened as his sight remained locked on her. "There isn't a day where I don't regret all the negative impacts I've had on your life, but you saved me before you ever knew me."

As she began to part her lips to ask questions, his thumb sealed her lips shut. "Let me finish telling you what you deserved to hear long before now."

She stood there with her eyes filling with the heaviness of emotion as he began his final confession.

Joey's thumb rubbed across the perfect shade of pink of her lips. "You were never meant to be mine. Hell, you were never meant to become the woman you are now. I..." He braced himself for the moment he wished he could erase from his history. "You were supposed to be in the car with your mom."

Layne felt a whirlwind of confusion as she tried to wrap her brain around his words. "W-what?"

He frowned. "The contract was for both of you. I did months of surveillance, watching and waiting for the right time. The day I set the device on your mom's car, I realized I could never come back from taking your life before it even began. So, I made an anonymous call to your dad, threatening your life, knowing he would react by becoming even more overprotective."

Her eyes searched his face, noticing all the years of guilt coming to the surface. She struggled with the new revelation that her life could have been cut short at Joey's hands not once but twice. On the day she lost her mother, she couldn't understand why her parents wouldn't let her go out, and now it was all becoming clear.

Joey dropped his head down shamefully. "Layney, I'm so sorry I didn't tell you before now. It never felt like the right time."

Seeing a fresh line of moisture trail down his cheeks, she frowned.

"Hey," Layne said with gentle reassurance. "Look at

me." Her fingertips came up underneath his scruffy chin to tilt his gaze back up to her.

His eyes met hers, expecting the worst of words to be spoken.

"I have learned to open myself up and lower the walls I have spent years building up because you make me feel safe. I have chosen to love you even knowing your past. You have always protected me, even when I didn't know I needed you to. That's not something I can be angry at you for." God knew she hadn't made his life any easier some days, but Layne wouldn't change their pasts no matter what she was offered in exchange.

No matter how you looked at it, Joey had spared her twice in her lifetime when he could have snuffed out her flame.

Her hands cupped his cheeks, her fingertips swiping away the pain expelled from his eyes.

Layne brought her mouth to his, kissing away all the doubts and regrets he had about his past. Lovingly, her lips pressed to his to do her best to put his conscience and soul at peace.

After feeling his body soften into her affections, she eased out of the kiss with a sweet smile.

Gradually, relief filled him, and Joey leaned in to steal another quick kiss from her. "You'll never know how much I love you, Layne."

Her hands slowly trailed down the front of the hard muscles of his stomach. When she spoke, her words were just one notch above a whisper. "Try showing me."

She didn't need to ask him twice. Joey's fingers

purposely unknotted the sash around her waist as he began backing her up to the workbench at the far wall of the garage.

His hand slid up the back of her neck with a gentleness as his tattooed fingers embedded themselves into the depths of her silky chestnut hair.

As the sash came undone, the kimono fell open to reveal the forest-green lingerie underneath. Joey's desire for her still had a fiery edge to it despite the way his touch had become gentle.

Quickly, he cleared just enough space on the workbench for her ass before he lifted her and set her down on it. With his hands on her waist, he stood between her thighs as he took his time kissing her. First, it was reveling in the taste of her mouth; then, it was exploring across her jaw and down along her throat.

Layne dropped her shoulders so the silk material of the robe slid off her upper body, pooling around her as she let him spoil her with his affections. Quietly, she moaned as his tongue flicked out across the sensitive spot where her neck met her shoulder.

Her body was already reacting to their deep emotional and physical connection, her core growing damp with arousal. The tips of Layne's fingers hooked onto the front of his jeans, tugging him closer to her center.

When he pressed himself against her core, her breathing hitched at the sensation of his hard cock struggling against his jeans.

"Joey," she said, his name already sounding breathless. "I need you to fuck me."

His palms ran over the front of her bra, taking in the feel of her breasts held captive in the cups. He shook his head at her request. "I'm not going to fuck you; I'm going to do better than that. You're going to feel how deep my feelings run for you, Layne."

After his hands drifted behind her, he popped the clasp on her bra to free her rounded breasts and hardened nipples from the fabric prison. The stubble on his face brushed against her fair skin as his mouth continued its mission to love every part of her. From her collarbone, down over her chest where her heart was beating excitedly, each curve and peak of her breasts, and down the center of her stomach.

Layne's hands held onto his shoulders as he lowered himself down her body, continuing to slowly drag his lips across her flesh. Eventually, his fingers shimmied the thin straps of her thong away from her hips until it popped free and easily slid down her legs onto the floor.

For all the attention he was giving her, he passed by where she hoped his mouth would end up. Instead, he worked his kisses down one leg and then up the other. When he was finished, he straightened up and lifted her from the workbench, wrapping her legs around his hips.

Joey pecked her lips and smiled. "Don't give me that look."

Her arms wrapped around his neck to keep herself close to him, and she rolled those lively green eyes of hers. "What look?"

"The look where you get impatient and want my cock bad enough you don't realize you're pouting." He chuckled and walked with her out of the garage, carrying her through the house until they came to the living room, currently cast in darkness.

Carefully traversing his way through the room, he made it to the gas fireplace. Using one arm to support her against him, his hand reached out to flip a switch on the wall so that the soft glow of flames illuminated the room.

Arguing, Layne responded, "I don't pout." She pouted stubbornly.

He lowered them both down to the floor, setting Layne on her back. Joey kicked off his shoes to the side before he stripped himself out of his jeans and boxer briefs. The amber lighting from the fire at their side danced across his body, revealing the long length of his dick.

Kneeling between her legs, his hands ran up along her inner thighs. "Don't lie to me, Layney," he playfully teased her with a grin. His tongue ran over his lips as he looked down at her pussy. There was just enough light that he could see the gleam of her excitement across those pretty lips.

Whimpering quietly, she shifted her hips, her body ready to feel the pleasure of his touch.

Leaning down, his fingers spread her folds to expose her even further to him. Joey's tongue ran from her, opening up to her clit in a languid stroke.

It triggered a delightful shiver from Layne as she gasped out.

He continued to taste her arousal, his tongue progressively teasing her sensitive nub. Every contact made with her body was purposeful toward incrementally getting her closer to the cusp of an orgasm.

Nearing her release, Layne's hips rode against his mouth to seek out the key to her ecstasy. One hand grasped onto the top of his head while the other clawed at the soft area rug underneath her.

She was getting so damn close, and Joey knew it would only take one more graze of his teeth across her clit before she would be swept away in her release.

Opting to pull back, he shifted himself over top of her. Passionately, he kissed her, letting her taste the flavor of her own body on his tongue.

Positioning the tip of his cock at the opening of her cunt, he spoke against her mouth. "I'm yours, always and forever, Layne."

He took his time as he slid himself into her, basking in the feel of the slow stretch of her walls around his thick cock.

Layne moaned out at the gradual entry into her body, the pleasurable sensation being drawn out. Her hands ran over his shoulders onto his upper back as she held him close.

"Mmm, yes, Joey," her sweet sounds were made on the cusp of each of her breaths.

Continuing at the same pace, he pulled back out so the rounded head of his cock nearly popped free from her entrance. Then, he sank himself back into her.

Meanwhile, his face pressed against the side of her neck, inhaling the scent of rain-kissed daisies on her skin. He needed to be as physically close to her as possible while cherishing all of her body. Her breasts were pressed up against his chest, allowing him to feel the rise and fall of her lungs, seeking out oxygen while her heart pounded just beneath the surface.

Each movement of his hips built a slow burn of sensations inside her body. Layne's hips matched his movements, ensuring he was buried far into her at the base of every thrust.

Hooking her ankles behind him, she began to lose control of the sounds she was making. Each push of his cock into her had a deep spark growing with intensity inside her lower stomach that threatened to burn her alive.

Looking up into his eyes, she gasped for air after a long moan. "I love you. So much. Always and forever will never be enough time with you, Joey." Her hands never wanted to let him go.

He groaned, feeling the tight space of her pussy begin to bear down around him. "Layney…I'll always need to feel this way with you." Joey's words were rushed out at the end as his hips began to falter in their relaxed rhythm. His dick now rocked into her quicker and with more force.

Her fingernails dug into his back as she shuddered, and it felt like an eternity left on the cliff of her release. Then, there was nothing but a flood of warmth and a spike of sudden ecstasy as she cried out. Layne came hard, her body latching onto him as she surrendered to the carnally induced high.

Despite the way her cunt squeezed him tightly, refusing to let go, Joey kept rolling his hips into her, fighting the resistance. With an eager growl and several more thrusts, he felt the electricity ricocheting down his spine. Every inch of him pulsed as his cum was unleashed deep inside her, all too quickly filling up the home his cock had made for itself.

He continued to love all of her for several more rounds until Joey had Layne passed out contently in his arms as he lay there with her on the floor of the living room. Both of them were covered in each other's sweat and bodily fluids, and most importantly, their love for one another stained their souls.

Joey eventually carried Layne upstairs to their bedroom, tenderly tucking her into their bed. Making her understand the depth of his love had been his top priority. Now, it was onto the next—blowing her fuckin' asshole brother to kingdom come.

Chapter Twenty-Eight

BURN

"Layne," Gage shook her shoulder.

She mumbled something incoherent as she began to rouse from her slumber.

"Baby, wake up," his voice sounded urgent.

Layne finally rolled onto her back in bed, her body getting even more tangled in the sheets. "What is it?"

Gage hated that he was going to have to wake her for this, but he had waited long enough that his gut was at the bottom of the pit of despair somewhere.

He laid it on her, "Joey isn't back home yet."

Without coffee having her running on all cylinders, there was a little bit of lag as her brain began to process his words. She turned her head to the side to see the clock on the nightstand, showing it was shortly after ten in the morning.

The instant everything came together, she pushed herself up onto her elbows. "What?"

Fighting with the sheets tangled around her, she scrambled over to the side of the bed where her phone rested on its charger, pulling it from the cradle to scroll through any and all messages. Nothing from Joey.

Trying to grasp the seriousness of the situation, she asked Gage, "He hasn't called you?" Layne glanced over at him as she tried to avoid jumping to any conclusions. Internally, she was panicking like fuck.

He just shook his head as he looked at her apologetically, wishing he had a better response for her. There wasn't anything he hadn't already tried to eliminate as a reason for his brother having not made it back home after leaving to go set Liam's potential demise.

"Fuck." Layne scooted out of bed and grabbed one of the guys' spare shirts, yanking it down over her head. These days, it was difficult to tell which tee belonged to which of her men, not unless they had worn it and it held either the scent of toasted vanilla of Gage or the musky leather and sage of Joey.

She dialed Joey's number as she stepped over to the window, peering outside as she waited for him to answer. Her fingernail lightly tapped against the pane as her nerves began to fray.

Ring. Ring. Ring. 'The number you are trying to reach is currently unavailable; please leave a message after the tone.'

Layne hung up and redialed his number. Her eyes scanned the snowy landscape of a frigid February day just outside. Perhaps his car got stuck? The Challenger was shit in the snow. A million thoughts filled her mind as she hardly paid attention to the unanswered rings in her ear.

"Goddamnit, pick up," she whispered to herself.

Finally hearing the generic voicemail switch on again, she hung up and turned to face Gage and shook her head grimly. "Nothing."

Her stomach felt sick; this wasn't like him. "Fuck, fuck, fuck. Fuck!" She brought a hand to her forehead as worst-case scenarios began to bounce around inside of her head.

Gage came up and grabbed her shoulders; he kissed her softly. "Breathe. Let's just try to stay level-headed. There are still some good reasons why he may not be back yet." Internally, he was feeling anything but calm. He knew as much as she did that something had to have gone wrong, and the likelihood of his brother forgetting to check in was next to zero.

She stared into Gage's eyes that attempted to mask his concerns, but she saw right through it. Layne's lower lip quivered. "We almost lost him once, I can't even—"

"Sshh," Gage stopped her from going down that negative path. "There are a thousand explanations."

"All of which leads to Liam." She pressed her lips firmly together as she tried to see past her own spiraling emotions.

His hands grabbed her face firmly as he leaned in so their foreheads were touching. "Don't think like that," he sternly demanded of her. Both of them couldn't afford to be lost to their fears.

Layne's phone began buzzing in her palm. She glanced down and saw Liam's name appear–so much for avoiding their worst nightmares. Turning the screen to Gage, she said, "This can't be a coincidence."

Without waiting for Gage to provide alternative reasoning, Layne put the call on speaker. Putting on her best front, she steadied her voice, "What do you want, Li?"

Her brother darkly sniggered. "What do I want? More importantly, what—well…who do you want?"

She bit into her lower lip so harshly, trying to contain the rage that wanted to lash out at him that she swore she was going to break the skin. Unclear of how much silence had passed between them, she finally began assembling her strength to ask the question she needed an answer to. "Is he alive?"

Dramatically, Liam sighed. "Always with the dumb questions, Layne. If he wasn't, it wouldn't do me any good to try and get you down here, now would it?"

"Yes or no, Liam." The bile was rising quickly in her throat as she waited for a straightforward response.

Liam paused before replying to her, "Yes. For now."

The sick feeling temporarily waned as she at least had something to put her at ease, a sliver of hope. There was no telling if Liam was lying or not, but any hope was better than none.

Her brother continued, "You want him? You know where to come find him. Don't wait too long, though. When I get bored, bad things happen, sis."

She snapped, "Don't fucking threaten me, Liam." A heated and violent sensation was now flowing through her veins. "You want the O'Reilly empire to yourself? I will be fucking hand-delivering it to you." Her thumb smashed the red button on the screen to disconnect the call.

Gage opened his mouth to say something, but before he

had the chance, she screamed and threw her phone across the room. It collided with her dresser, shattering the glass screen and falling to the floor. "Motherfucking piece of shit!"

Her chest rose and fell with the sheer amount of fury boiling up inside her. It wasn't until Gage grabbed her shoulders tightly and turned her to face him that she saw something other than blinding red.

"Look at me!" His grip on her continued to remain as firm as his voice. "I need you to keep your shit together, Layne. He knows that you're ready to run over there with guns out."

"Damn straight I am! He has six fucking holes in his body, and I'm going to put a bullet in every one of them!" Layne was prepared to go on a murder spree and take out anyone who got in her path. "This is it, Gage. I refuse to let him or anyone else fuck with our lives anymore. I'm *done*."

Nodding, Gage was on the same page with her but had to be the sanity check to make sure she didn't do something that got herself killed. While he was willing to spend an eternity in the afterlife with her and Joey, it wasn't something he wanted to start today. "Go hop in the shower; I will make a few calls and start packing."

Despite being amped up and anxious to get out the door, Layne showered and let her vivid imagination come up with every potential way of killing her brother. If Joey was anything less than unscathed, she would make her pain felt by all of the criminal factions in New York if she had to.

Getting ready to bring a war to your psychopathic brother's turf wasn't as quick of a process as she wished. Gage had been right in trying to get her to slow down and think things through. If he had let her leave right after that phone call, she would have left most of her arsenal at home so she could choke the shit out of Liam with her bare hands.

Instead, dusk was cloaking the city on a below-freezing winter's night. The snow on the roads and sidewalks helped cut through the darkness of the day's end.

Gage parked his Jeep in the church parking lot across the street from Eric Ellis's former residence. "This is it?" He stared at the massive corner property in disbelief. Valuing his life, he decided against asking Layne if Eric had been making up for lack of size in other areas.

"Yeah, Eric was a bougie asshole when he made the move here." Layne unbuckled her seat belt and swung open her door, hopping out onto the cracked pavement of the parking lot.

He hadn't been willing to say it, but fuck, Gage would have purchased the home in a heartbeat if it hadn't been for the bad blood associated with it. Now, he just wanted to see this gorgeous piece of architecture burn to the ground.

Layne had her hair pulled back into a simple ponytail and dressed in black from head to toe. Stretching her skull mask with the green and orange ribbons across her face, she looked over at Gage as he also got out of the Wrangler.

"Jax and his guys in position?" Layne questioned as she double-checked the weaponry hidden all over her body.

Gage nodded. "They're all set, just waiting on you, Lucky Charm." Whatever waited for them inside, he hoped that they had brought enough bodies to overcome it. There were eight of them, nine if Joey was in any type of fighting form. Truth be told, unless his brother was dead, he'd be prepared to inflict pain on anyone who stood in his way. Included in their headcount were Layne's top guys, Sammy and Ethan. Hunter had been sure to pick them up on his way here.

Her eyes looked across the street at the imposing home that stretched up three floors, four if you included the rooftop. Never did she want to step foot in this house again, but if it meant there was a shot of getting Joey back in one piece, there was nothing that would keep her out.

Before she could leave Gage to take the first steps on her own, he came up to her and adjusted her jacket over her body, making sure it fit snugly around her. "Baby, I love you. You are more than my stars and moon; you are my universe. Just remember what I said, okay?" He leaned in, tugging her mask down enough to fiercely kiss her, spreading his love for her into her soul through their mouths.

She nodded and echoed back to him what he had told her on the way here. "Headshots are permanent, everywhere else is an excuse to haunt your demons."

Trying to give her a proud smile, he coupled it with another tender kiss on her forehead. "That's my girl. We'll be in your shadow, okay?" His fingers adjusted her mask back into place.

It was now or never that she put an end to this feud with

Liam. Taking one more deep breath, she blew it out harshly. "I'm good, promise. Liam will be finding his way to the grave tonight." Even if she had to go with him.

Gage's hand lightly patted her on the side of her face. He hated that he had to abandon her side, but there was no way that it was going to do any good to walk up to the front door with her. There was no question that there were bigger battles to fight on the other entrances around the property.

"Go ahead and make that asshole pay his debts." It took everything in him not to cling to her. If he knew he could whisk her away elsewhere, perhaps kidnap her to some-place safe, he would have done it. Joey would have wanted him to do it, but he couldn't justify abandoning such a major pillar in their lives. Layne would never survive it, and neither would he.

Layne tried to keep her voice void of any emotions that would make him feel uneasy, "I love you; I promise I won't stop fighting for all of us. Don't ever give up on me." If she was going to keep her head in the game, she needed to quickly eliminate all the mushy feelings. Yet, there was still the softness in her eyes as she looked at Gage one last time before jogging across the street toward the house that would be the end for at least one person tonight.

Her boots gave the softest crunch against the compacted snow as she approached the front door of the house she had sold only months ago. This place must have been home to some satanic rituals at some point, given the people it attracted. Not only was it associated with her ex-husband, but now Liam as well, so much for family bonds being the strongest.

Layne knew that Liam was expecting her, so there was no use in sneaking around. Hell, he was probably anticipating some of her crew to be in the area. The element of surprise may have been gone, but that allowed her insight into what he did or possibly didn't know. He knew she'd be coming, and she could rely on that information to drive her actions.

Her finger reached out and pressed the small gold button next to the door. A series of chimes sounded off deep into the house, being easily heard from right outside the door.

Scanning the exterior, everything inside the home looked dark and ominous. It was confirmed when the front door swung open, and she found herself peering into nothing but shadows.

Here went nothing. With a hand resting on the butt of her gun on her hip, she took the first step inside. Swallowing hard as her eyes fought the darkness, Layne glanced around with each advance into the main hall.

The last remaining clip of light from outside dissipated when the front door slammed shut. A voice bounded against the walls and echoed up into the height of the arched ceiling. It wasn't the words spoken that spooked her, but who was saying them that drove terror straight down her spine. All the hairs on the back of her neck were on end, and her skin became littered with goosebumps.

"So glad you could join us, Layne. It's been too long since we've had a family reunion." The male voice matched the one the night of the car wreck. With a clear head, she recognized it now. It didn't make any sense, but everything she thought she knew was wrong.

"How?" was all she asked into the darkness that surrounded her.

There was no response, only maniacal laughter.

Spinning around, she strained to hear any threatening movement that may have been approaching her.

A light flickered on, and she came face to face with a ghost. Layne gasped as her eyes widened at the familiar face. It was no longer her mind playing tricks on her; he was actually standing there before her. This motherfucker came back from the grave.

Her body went rigid before she said his name out loud, "Uncle Mick."

Chapter Twenty-Nine

GREATEST ACT OF LOVE

I t sounded insane, even to her, to say the name of a dead man out loud. Every plan that she had plotted inside her head hadn't accounted for his presence.

With a cocky smile, he took a step closer to her. "Speechless? I guess death isn't the end after all." Each word he spoke sent a chill through her body like pointed icicles stabbing the strength of her resolve.

Layne pushed past all the questions clouding her brain and lunged at Mick, barreling her shoulder into his chest to knock him off balance. Despite the minimal light, she was able to grab hold of his shirt with one hand while her other drew her firearm.

Mick's bear paw of a hand was soon wrapped around her wrist as she struggled to aim the gun at the fucker who should have been buried six feet under. So much for head-shots being permanent. Questions could be asked later.

As his upper body strength quickly overtook her, she thrust her heel up into his gut. Her wrist broke free from his grasp as they both stumbled back from one another. Aiming the weapon in his direction, she pulled the trigger to fire off the first shot.

With her finger squeezing the trigger, a force slammed into her head from behind. The bullet from her gun shot up into the darkness, missing its intended target. Her Glock clattered against the floor and slid several feet from her. Immediately, she dropped to the ground harder than a bag of cement. Trying to maintain her wits, she winced at the pain blossoming across the back of her skull.

Layne had been so distracted by Mick's resurrection that she hadn't realized there was another goon waiting to strike.

Weakly, she attempted to scramble onto all fours, only to have the rubber sole of a boot force her back down onto her stomach. Mick had a satisfied smirk stretched across his weathered face as he walked toward her.

"As I've always said, you're a stupid little bitch," Mick spoke with such disdain that she was certain that she'd be seeing either brimstone and hellfire or pearly gates soon enough.

Despite the sweet allure of unconsciousness wanting to drag her under, she stubbornly willed herself to keep her eyes mostly open. However, it was questionable how much she succeeded in those efforts as her recollection of the trip up to the former ballroom one floor above was spotty after she had been yanked to her feet.

When the double doors swung open to the expansive room, the lights from the chandeliers were blinding in comparison to the rest of the lack of lighting throughout the house. With one hand of the miscreant latched on the back of her neck and the other squeezing her upper arm painfully, she had nowhere to go.

Layne was still feeling wobbly on her feet, and as she looked at the occupants of the sweeping expanse of the ballroom, her remaining strength was ready to check-the-fuck-out.

There were hired hands all around the room, more than she wanted to give her brother credit for. At the center of it all, Liam was standing there with a stupid fucking glass of whiskey in his hand like he suddenly was the epitome of sophistication amongst douchebags. To his right, tied to an ornate gilded chair, was Joey.

Controlling her facial expressions was never a strong suit, and seeing half of her heart strapped down to the chair with obvious wounds to his face and bloodied clothes made it nearly impossible. There was no telling just how much of Liam or Mick's hatred he had endured in her absence. With the skull mask covering the lower half of her face, she considered it a blessing in this instance.

"Sis!" Liam exclaimed, like he was seeing her for the first time in years. "I am so happy you made it! Fuck, you certainly took your time, didn't you?"

Mick walked past her to join Liam at his side, wrapping an arm around his shoulders like a proud papa. "I told you, Liam. It just requires a little bit of patience."

Still being detained by the asshole at her back, she began quickly assessing the already dire situation. Her emerald eyes kept glancing over at Joey. His eyes were shut, and all she could do was pray to see them open one more time. Duct tape was not only covering his mouth but bound his hands behind his back and adhered his ankles to the legs of the chair.

"You got me here, Li. Congrats," she spoke up without looking at her brother. Layne took notice of several other men standing along the far walls. Even with her anticipated support on its way, they were still outnumbered.

She continued, "I guess this means you win." Her words lacked any level of sincerity.

The sound of her voice prompted Joey to open his eyes wearily. He was alive, and that in and of itself was motivation to keep fighting. If she had walked in here only to find him dead, she would have gone blind, unleashing the wrath of all hell's inner circles.

Sipping from his glass, Liam was all too happy as he smiled. "Oh, I've always been the winner, Layne. I've just been waiting to see how long you were willing to keep pathetically playing along."

Her eyes met Joey's, trying to convey reassurance to him with looks alone. It was interrupted when Mick stepped between them, breaking her line of sight.

Layne ground her teeth together as she glared at Mick. "How the hell are you even here?"

The man, who she could have sworn had been killed in the dining room of O'Reilly Manor, seemingly had an aversion to death.

Mick grinned at her before turning and walking to Joey's side, gripping his shoulder firmly. "Well, it seems your fucktoy here isn't as great of a shot as he thinks he is. You should have seen his face when I caught him trying to set an explosive on my truck last night." He gave a laugh reminiscent of a clown on crack.

He lifted two fingers to a spot just behind his ear, tapping a scar at the base of his skull by his hairline. "Call it a blessing from God, maybe even a damn miracle, but the bullet entered behind my ear here and came out just above my occipital bone. Head wounds bleed like a fucker, though, don't they?"

"And your funeral?" Layne inquired.

"A setup," Mick responded with a shrug like he was discussing the weather. "I had a real come-to-Jesus moment after that night. I realized with your dad withering away and Liam having no one to guide him; there was a real opportunity to see to it that the business remained in good hands. He's been so kind to make sure I've had adequate accommodations." Mick gestured at the room they were all in.

Liam added his side of the story, "You look as shocked as I was, Layne. When Uncle Mick showed up at my door, I couldn't believe it. He explained what really happened that night and how he wanted nothing but to see the family business thrive in the hands of its rightful owner. The only problem is you kept doing what you fucking do. You kept ignoring your place."

Taking another sip of the whiskey, Liam went to the other side of Joey and spat at the side of his face. "Then, you invite this asshole to live permanently between your legs and reap the benefits of a business that isn't his."

Joey grunted and pulled against his restraints in the chair. Layne's body tensed, waiting on edge for Liam to be stupid enough to do something that would force her to try to take on every fucking soul in this room by herself.

Chuckling, Liam looked at his sister. "To add insult to injury, you had to drag his brother into it. Speaking of which, I'm sure he's not too far. The great thing about Eric was he knew how to make a home a fortress, so my men will find him before he gets too far."

Liam looked at Mick like he was some savior. "Nevertheless, Mick has been guiding me and teaching me how to take back control of what is rightfully mine. If it wasn't for him, I may have eaten a bullet after Dad died."

If only.

Her brother continued to reminisce, "I was in a dark place, Layne. But once Mick helped me see my true potential, he made sure that my failed assassination attempt on your life became my advantage. He has been by my side nearly every day, ensuring that I never fail again."

Jesus Christ, Layne would have thought that Liam was ready to drop to his knees and start sucking Mick's cock the way he was placing the man on a pedestal.

The man she used to call her uncle had the largest shit-eating grin on his poorly aged face. "Layne, I'm rather hurt. It took until tonight to recognize me after all the chances I gave you. My years may not have been kind, but just because I was sporting a beard and a baseball cap, you still should have seen it. I expected better from you, sweetheart. Your dad would have been so disappointed."

Racking her brain for what she missed, she cursed as she realized that he had hidden in plain sight, starting with the day at the Chinese restaurant.

She looked over at her idiotic sibling, who didn't deny any of Mick's account of events. "Liam, you stupid fuck." She shook her head in disbelief. "Do you think he gives a shit about you? He betrayed our family. Once you're no longer of value, he will betray you, too."

Barking back at her loudly, Liam's face turned bright red, "Betrayed?! Let's talk about betrayal, Layne! How about not just you fucking the psycho who killed Mom but marrying him, huh?! How about your betrayal in trying to take over what belongs to me? FUCK YOU!"

Her brother's insults fell flat against her defenses. If he wanted to pitch stones in an attempt to hurt her feelings, he would need to try harder.

"I told you," Mick spoke knowingly as he walked to Liam, "She doesn't think she's done anything wrong. Typical woman, all wrapped up in her feelings. That's why women don't deserve to be in our position of power."

Glaring at Mick as he added his damn two cents, Layne was determined to make sure the next time he was shot, he wouldn't be able to come back from the dead.

"Oh, there are plenty of things I've done wrong. Starting with letting Liam get away with all his shit for this long," she confessed.

Gulping down the rest of the drink in his hand, Liam lazily tossed the glass to the side, where it shattered upon impact with the floor. He snapped his fingers at the nearest man willing to follow his unspoken orders. His lackey brought him a heavy length of chain.

The odds weren't in her favor, and she was beginning to think that maybe Gage and the rest of the crew ran into trouble down on the sublevel. Shitty odds never stopped her before, though.

Liam swung the end of the chain in his hand threateningly as he stalked towards her. "Time to pay the piper, Layne." Arriving in front of her, he wound up and whipped the chain at her. Instinctively, she raised her free arm to block the lash of metal.

As the links made contact with her left wrist, she embraced the pain and rotated her hand to wrap the chain into her grasp so he couldn't pull it back.

Simultaneously, the fucking cavalry finally burst through the doors, and Gage poured in with Jax, Devon, Isaiah, Hunter, Ethan, and Sammy.

The intrusion set chaos into motion, and unlike the rest of these assholes, she had learned to embrace chaos a long time ago. Layne jerked on the chain, circling her wrist, causing Liam to stumble off balance towards her, where her foot kicked harshly into his chest, sending him right back again.

The goon at her back had been distracted by her backup charging in, so when she bent over, she propelled him over her right shoulder onto the ground. She swung the weight of the chain, and it crashed right into his temple, knocking him out.

Gunfire erupted around her as her small army began picking off targets.

Layne immediately ran towards Joey, dropping to her knees and sliding a few inches towards his feet. She shook the chain from her wrist and withdrew the pocketknife Liam had gifted her with. It took nearly no time to slice through the silver tape and free Joey's hands and ankles, freeing him to rip the tape from his mouth himself.

Shoving the knife back into her pocket, she exchanged it for her gun, which she thrust into Joey's palm. No matter what Mick said, she trusted Joey's aim any day of the week.

"You okay?" There wasn't much time to have a long-winded conversation as she snatched up the heavy-duty chain from the ground.

Joey nodded. "You're late." He raised the gun and fired a couple of shots at the nearest threats.

She lightly scoffed, "It's your job to be on time, not mine." Layne grinned behind her mask as her eyes darted around the room, looking for Liam and Mick. Landing eyes on her brother first, he was ducking behind a column and returning gunfire as he began making his way gradually toward the curved staircase that led to the next floor up.

Before she could visually track down Mick, a few of Liam's hired hands ran at her and Joey. Despite the rough shape Joey appeared to be in, you'd never know it by the way he fought off the first attacker that made it to them.

Layne wielded the chain to smack it against the arm of a man who came at her. However, she fell forward as another one pummeled into her from behind. "Oof!" She hit the ground hard.

No sooner than she met the floor, the weight on her back was lifted. Gage easily jerked the man off her and shoved him toward Joey, who dropped him like a fly with one shot between the eyes.

Both De Lucas grabbed one end of the metal chain

wrapped around her left hand and assisted in pulling her up to her feet as it felt like shell casings were raining down all around them.

Joey and Gage glanced down at the links in her grasp, the irony not lost on them that what should have been an item used to keep a person bound, their feisty shamrock repurposed it as a weapon.

With the others managing to hold their own, she searched for any sign of Mick. "Where did Mick go?"

Taking a quick glance around, Gage responded, "He's got to be here somewhere. We'll find him."

At that time, another wave of Liam's supporters swarmed into the room. *Fucking hell.*

The three of them immediately got put on the defensive, as everyone began utilizing whatever they had to survive. Joey emptied the remainder of the bullets in the gun Layne had given him before he began physically assaulting anyone who looked like a threat.

Wrapping the metal chain around some asshole's neck, Layne left it pinched around his throat, letting him choke to death before she moved on to the next person looking to die.

Layne caught sight of Liam as he cowardly made a run for it up the stairs several feet from where she was. There was no way he was escaping so easily. "No, you don't, little fucker," she murmured.

Using her small figure, she managed to push through a couple of guys as she ran for the stairs after her brother.

Joey tossed one of Liam's goons off him, slamming a fist into his cheek and knocking him to the ground. He looked up as Layne ran up the stairs two at a time after Liam. "Layne!!"

The shouting of her name prompted Gage to thrust a knee into the scrappy asshole he was dealing with before directing his attention to the same sight that had Joey barking out their girl's name.

"Devon!" Gage shouted, glancing over his shoulder at his friend nearest to him. "Need your help over here!" If they were going to chase after Layne, they needed to get past the group of men blocking their path.

Layne made it halfway up the stairs before she turned to look at both men. It was a split second or less, but her face softened with a silent apology clouding her green eyes. She tore her skull mask from her face, dropping it to the ground at her feet. Her perfect lips mouthed her love for them with those three little words before she continued her ascent up the steps, following Liam behind the door at the top.

Just like that, she was gone.

Chapter Thirty

DEATH IS NOT THE END

She chased Liam through the door at the top of the stairs. It led into the hallway on the third floor.

"Li! Get the fuck back here!" she shouted while watching him blatantly ignore her.

Her brother rounded a corner, and she heard a door slam shut. Quick to make the turn, she noticed a door that looked different from all the others. Panting from the pursuit, she pushed through it and saw a steep set of stairs that led to a single metal door that was just drifting closed.

Layne steeled herself as she followed, prepared for whatever showdown was going to happen with her brother. When she made it out the door, she got blasted with a gust of freezing air that whipped her ponytail around erratically. He had led her up to the roof.

The visibility of the night air was shitty, thanks to all the fat snowflakes that kept swirling around as they descended from above. Each flake that fell stuck to her chestnut hair and contrasted against the black of her clothes.

He couldn't have gone too far, and the moment she thought as much, he crashed into her side, knocking her to the snow-covered ground.

Without hesitation, she rolled and began swinging her fists at his face. Scrambling, she fought for the upper hand as they exchanged hits. Eventually, she was able to use leverage from her foot to create enough space between them so she could push herself onto her feet.

Liam got to his feet and stared at her with intense hatred. "You fucked up this family, Layne!"

Each of them was panting from the scuffle, their warm breaths visible when meeting the extremely cold winter air.

"Get the fuck over it," Layne shook her head, and with every step closer he took, she took two away from him. "You have always been the one with the problem!"

Trying to keep tabs on each movement her brother made down to the flexing of the muscles in his arms, she reminded herself to also be aware of her surroundings. Her eyes stole quick looks at what was there on the top of the roof. Other than weathered patio furniture and HVAC systems, she had little to work with in the open space.

Liam angrily roared at her, "You've always tried to hold me down! Dad spoiled you and made you the fuckin' favorite when it should have been me! You don't deserve shit!" His hands wildly flailed as he shouted.

"You're a goddamn spoiled brat, Li! You could have had everything! I overlooked so many of your faults in hopes that sometime you'd grow the fuck up!" She had always been willing to maintain what should have been a steadfast alliance with him, but his destructive behaviors ultimately obliterated any chance of that ever happening.

He charged at her, and when she turned to get out of his way, her foot caught on an old broom left buried under the snow. The trip sent her down onto her hands and knees, giving Liam just enough opportunity to grab her by the back of her jacket and yank her back onto her feet.

Forcefully, he shoved her forward into a large condenser unit. Layne yelped out as she felt the unyielding impact of the metal casing against the front of her body.

When he pulled her back to slam her back against it one more time, she extended her foot in front of her to prevent another collision. She pushed back with just enough oomph that she could duck and turn under his arm, forcing his grasp on her jacket to break. Her elbow jabbed into his side, eliciting a grunt from him as he stumbled.

Layne and Liam continued wrangling with one another, both their feet occasionally sliding against the slippery snow underneath their shoes. The ledge of the roof was getting closer, and Liam's hand had found its way to her throat, latching onto it like the jaw of a rabid dog.

Fighting against the slowing oxygen and blood flow to her brain, her spine was suddenly bent backward over the partially raised wall that separated them both from a four-story free fall. Snowflakes fell into her eyes as she clawed at Liam's hand on her neck.

"Go burn in hell, sis! Don't worry, your shithead manwhores will be joining you shortly!" Liam's other hand was gripping the front of her jacket, and despite her struggles, her lighter body weight was getting eased off her feet as he began shoving her over the wall.

If she was going down, she was going to try and drag Liam with her. No longer fighting his chokehold on her, her hand fumbled until it found the pocketknife she had used to free Joey earlier. Without a second thought, she flipped open the blade and jammed it home into Liam's chest. It would have been sweet justice if she had struck his heart, but with her vision struggling under his choking grasp, she didn't get that lucky.

As the blade drove into her brother, his hands released her before she hit the point of no return over that wall. Layne gasped and coughed for air as her feet hit the ground on the side of the wall she was grateful to be on.

Drawing the short blade out of him, she angrily punched him across the face while he was still stunned. Her eyes stared at her ultimate betrayer as he slipped and fell to his knees with a hand grabbing at the wound in his chest.

Layne walked behind him, grabbing a fistful of his auburn hair. She jerked his head back so he was looking up at her. "I should thank you for hating me so much. You've made this so much easier." In a smooth motion, she slashed the edge of the blade across his throat, blood flooding from the critical arteries that she just severed.

There were some gurgling sounds before enough of Liam's blood stained the snow around him, and he fell into permanent unconsciousness. Seeing that he was well on his way to hell, she released her grasp on his hair and watched his lifeless body fall forward onto the ground.

She let out a relieved breath that it was over. Part of her

mourned that it had to come down to this, something that could have been unavoidable if Liam had chosen a much different path in life. The other part of her was just happy to live another day without his constant attacks on her happiness.

Getting pulled from her thoughts, she heard the roof access door open up as Joey and Gage pushed through. Her gaze softened as she looked at them both, seeing the relief evident on their faces, seeing she was ok.

"It's over." She sighed and gave a small smile.

The familiar sound of a gun popping off echoed throughout the air. One, two, three quick shots went off in succession.

Joey went from a moment of intense happiness that Layne had finally ended Liam's pathetic existence to one of seeing his worst nightmare.

Layne's body jerked as all three shots landed on her chest, tearing holes in her jacket. The force knocked her down, her body hitting the ground hard.

While Joey's only instinct was to get to Layne, Gage's eyes followed the trajectory of where the gunshots came from. Standing across the way was Mick, smirking at the successful strike against the last of the O'Reillys.

Feeling the phantom pain of what it was like to have a single bullet enter his chest, it ached more painfully as three hit Layne's. With pain riddling his voice, he yelled out her name, "LAYNE!" Joey didn't give a fuck if he took a hundred more bullets, he only cared about the woman he loved that had just been gunned down in front of him.

Needing to eliminate the active threat, Gage retrieved

his gun from his thigh holster and began firing at Mick, quickly working on emptying his last damn clip as he ran towards his target. "You motherfucker!!"

At least one of the bullets found its way into Mick's stomach, causing him to stagger. It gave Gage enough time to tackle him to the ground, using the butt of his gun to repeatedly smash into his face. This old shitbag deserved to feel his wrath before he died.

Making sure Mick stayed dead this time, Gage used the last bullet in the chamber at point-blank range between the man's eyes. That was a moment he wished he could relive over and over again. Instead, just the memory of it would have to suffice for Gage.

Arriving at Layne's body lying on its side, only a few feet from her brother's, Joey dropped to his knees next to her. She lay there still, nearly looking like an angel as the snowflakes clung to her dark eyelashes.

Horrified, Joey stared down at her, paralyzed by his fears becoming reality. Hidden behind her closed eyelids were the sparkling emerald hues he had fallen so desperately in love with. The pink, pouty lips he had kissed countless times were partially swollen and bruised from her altercation with Liam.

"Fuck, fuck, fuck. Layney!" Joey's hands grabbed her, trying to rouse her awake. His teardrops felt frozen against his cheeks as his panic set in. His hands began to tug at the busted zipper on her jacket from one of the bullet holes.

After the ringing in Gage's ears stopped from firing that bullet into Mick's shitty face, he could hear Joey behind him shouting at Layne. He got up and ran over to the two of them, kneeling on Layne's other side, across from Joey.

Losing Rosie had broken both Joey and Gage, and Layne had mended that wound; losing Layne would destroy them both beyond repair. Already, Joey was beginning to lose his shit as he fought with the zipper with trembling hands. Joey's voice cracked under the emotionally charged whisper, "Layney, you can't…*please.*"

Gage swallowed against the lump forming in his throat, preventing him from getting any words out. Layne had to be okay, she was meant for so much more than this. Yet, he was terrified to see anything that said otherwise.

Pushing past his fear, Gage finally shoved Joey's hands away from Layne's jacket zipper and forcefully tore it open.

Joey straightened as he saw what lay underneath, sitting back on his heels. "What the…"

"Thank fuck…" Gage leaned over and laid his head on Layne's stomach as he blew out the breath he had been holding.

Underneath the jacket was a slim bulletproof vest that had a cluster of the three bullets lodged into it.

Sitting back up to look at her, Gage was grateful he had managed to convince Layne's stubborn ass to wear the vest tonight. Otherwise, he would have never forgiven himself.

Layne's eyes slowly opened as she stirred with a groan, "Fuuuck." She winced at the burning sensation against her chest. Despite the vest doing its job, it sure as hell did little to ease the sting of the impact that had stolen her breath away. She had a feeling the bruising was going to be quite the collage of colors.

Before Layne could make the effort to sit up, Joey pulled her upright and locked his arms around her. "Layney, you fuckin' scared the shit out of me." There wasn't much that frightened him, but losing her was a fate worse than death.

Her muffled voice spoke into Joey's chest, "If you keep squeezing me so tight, I'm going to die of suffocation." She groaned again as the aches and pains were screaming throughout all of her body.

Gage's arms joined Joey's as they both embraced her with the unspoken promise of their everlasting protection. "We aren't ever going to let you go, Lucky Charm."

Kissing the top of her head, Joey lovingly smiled. "You're ours, always and forever."

———

The priest stood between the two headstones as he spoke loud enough for all to hear, "Two young lives, lost all too soon. Liam and Layne O'Reilly, two vibrant souls who have gone home to be with the Lord."

Gage and Joey stood there next to each other in their black suits, gathering amongst the others who had come to pay their respects to the O'Reilly siblings.

Joey leaned over and whispered to Gage, "This is weird, right?"

Gage lifted a brow and whispered back, "Which part? The part where both of these coffins are empty? Or the part where the woman over there," he pointed at the dark-haired woman who had introduced herself as Nicole, "has been ready to jump your bones now that you're technically widowed?"

Layne had been extraordinarily clear that there was no way in hell Liam's corpse was being buried next to her unoccupied grave, and neither of them could argue with her. She had chosen to have his remains cremated and then dumped into a randomly chosen porta potty. Joey chose to pay his respects to Liam in the most appropriate fashion afterward. A little harsh? None of them thought so.

She sat in the back of Joey's Challenger and waited patiently as she observed the funeral services from behind the dark-tinted windows. Trying to pass the time, her hands fidgeted with the hem of the black dress she had chosen to mourn her life as the head of O'Reilly Enterprises.

Layne recounted the events that transpired the night she killed Liam. After both her men smothered her with their happiness to see she had survived Mick's final effort to destroy her, they continued their extraction plans. The intention wasn't just to get the hell out of that house of horrors but to remove them all from the insanity of her days of leading a criminal organization.

Instead, the business was left in Sammy and Ethan's capable hands. If everyone thought she had gone down in a blaze of glory, it gave the three of them a chance at something they never really had. It gave them a chance to enjoy time together without new and constant threats looming over them.

The most heartbreaking decision to make was deciding

to keep as few people in the know about her survival, which included Layne's bestie. Joey had been tasked with making the call to Rebecca to gently break the unfortunate news to her. However, things didn't pan out as expected when she called bullshit on him.

One would have thought Rebecca was in denial, but the reasoning for her disbelief was pretty sound. Rebecca argued that Joey would have been in prison on numerous murder charges if Layne was truly dead–she wasn't wrong. In fear for his own safety at Rebecca's hands, Joey caved and added her to the short list of people who knew of Layne's true fate.

Ultimately, Rebecca decided to stay down in Baltimore, having found her own happily ever after.

There were still a few matters to wrap up before they could ditch the city life, but things were well on the way to finding new adventures to get lost in.

When the graveside service wrapped up, Joey and Gage both returned to the car, taking up the two front seats.

"Was it a nice service?" she asked, hoping that her funeral was exactly how she pictured it.

Gage smirked as he turned to look back at her, "Baby, if you're asking if shots of whiskey were passed around and everybody raised them in a toast to you…"

"Oh, come on! It's part of my final wishes, and nobody had the balls to at least honor that small request?" She crossed her arms in front of her chest, clearly disappointed.

Joey looked into the rearview mirror at her and smiled. "Layney, are you seriously going to be upset that your fake funeral didn't live up to your expectations?"

She rolled her eyes at the stupid question. "How else am I going to make sure that I get the funeral I deserve when I *actually* die?"

"Are you rolling your eyes at me?" Joey smirked and started up the engine.

Gage looked at his brother with a devious grin. "I think she is." He turned back around in his seat so he was facing forward. "We'll have to do something about that when we get back home. I have a new toy with my Lucky Charm's name on it."

They all headed back to Gage's condo in Hudson Yards. With Layne supposedly six feet under, the last thing they needed was anyone to spot her coming and going from O'Reilly Manor. It was a temporary living space, and as long as she had both De Luca brothers there with her, she didn't care where she was holed up.

Stepping inside the front door, Gage shed his suit jacket, draping it over the back of one of the kitchen stools. Joey unbuttoned his jacket as he went to the fridge, pulling out three bottles of beer.

Layne leaned back against the edge of the kitchen's center island and smirked as she looked at them both. "I have some news."

Both guys looked at her curiously; there wasn't usually anything that came as a surprise to either of them.

Joey popped the caps off of all three bottles before setting them on the counter next to Layne. "About what?"

With ease, Gage grabbed her waist and sat her down on top of the counter. His hands trailed over her hips down to the hem of her dress. Sliding his hands under the skirt of her dress along her bare thighs, he gave his boyish grin. "It better have to do with your lack of panties," he ran his tongue over his bottom lip, thinking about all the ways he could have her in the kitchen right then and there.

She smiled and shook her head. "Not quite." Layne pulled a small envelope out of her purse that was on the counter next to her. "It was bothering me that Liam's creepy and cryptic note never really made complete sense. He wanted something to do with 611, and it was driving me insane that I couldn't figure it out."

Taking a swig of his beer, Joey looked at the envelope in her hand. "I assumed he was just clinically insane and making shit up."

She began to explain about the day before they all had ended up going down to the former Ellis residence and how she had made her routine bank run. "While I was at the bank, the teller reminded me that there was a safety deposit box my dad set up in my name. It just so happens the number of the box is 611."

Taking the envelope out of her hands, Gage took a peek inside. "And this was inside?"

Layne nodded, unable to contain her infectious smile.

Reviewing the contents, Gage got excited as he saw the small object tucked inside, along with a sticky note. He handed the envelope to Joey, who also took a look, and his face lit up.

"Fuck, yes." He leaned in and lovingly kissed her. Things were looking up for the future.

Gage greedily pulled Layne's face away from Joey so his lips could seize her attention.

"It's going to be a hell of a Christmas this year," Joey set the envelope down as his mind began to pour over all the possibilities that awaited.

Layne giggled as Gage began to get carried away with his kisses that were now being showered over the side of her neck. Her eyes shone with true happiness as she had everything in life to look forward to. It was a happiness that she had never known before she gave her heart over to these two great men.

Despite everything they all had endured, finally, all three of them were going to get their happy ending. There was nothing more Layne could have asked for than to have her heart bursting with everlasting love and to forever share her life with Joey and Gage De Luca.

As it turned out, she really did have all the luck.

Layne POV

"So, that's my story. That's everything I have to tell." I look at the two agents seated across from me. Both of them have their jaws halfway to the floor. Perhaps I should have spared them a few of the more colorful descriptions. What could I say? Life is too short to spare the details of great sex.

One of the men straightens his already straight tie as a means to regain his composure. Clearing his throat, he stumbles over his first few words. "Ms. De Luca…"

"Mrs.," I correct him.

He tries again. "Mrs. De Luca, that… That was a very thorough recounting of events."

I smile sweetly at him, reveling in the fact he is so damn uncomfortable right now.

His partner begins pouring himself what must be the fifth cup of water he's chugged in the last hour.

"You asked me to give my version of events and spare

no detail. Didn't you?" I smirk, knowing I damn well went above and beyond what the Unwind and Unorganize Program was looking for.

On the day I called Detective Adams to inform him of my potential interest in the initiative, I was surprised to discover the commissioner himself had told him to not only expect my call but prioritize it. The detective swiftly put me in touch with his federal liaisons.

Several discussions on the terms of my cooperation occurred before we ultimately reached an agreement. Now, here I was, giving these fuckers enough information to hit several criminal faction kingpins where it hurt the most.

Sure, I may have left out some details for those who were friends in the loosest definition of the word—allies, if you will. I'm not stupid enough to burn *all* my bridges. I don't have a crystal ball telling me if and when I will ever return to this line of work. The one thing I do know? This is it for me—for us—for now.

Mr. Tie-Straightener shuffles through a folder over-flowing with multiple forms. "There is, um, just a few more pieces of paperwork to sign, and then you can be on your way."

Finally, his well-hydrated partner is put together enough to try and make light conversation. "How far along are you?" He nods at the large belly in front of me.

The asshole is brave enough to assume a woman is pregnant? I'm even more tempted to fuck with him. I barely resist the urge and give a glowing smile instead as I rest my hand on my bump. "Just entered my third trimester.

It's twins, so each week from here on out is considered a win."

The man nods and seems to try and focus on the mundane details. "Any names picked out?"

I nod while rubbing my hand over the roundness idly. "Joseph Elliot, after the father, and we are naming our daughter Shannon Marie after my mother."

After pulling another form out of the folder, the man leading the discussion hands several pages over to me with a pen. "These all lay out the terms of your immunity and confirm you have fulfilled your end of the bargain by providing relevant information on the organized crime units here in Manhattan."

I read over each word, scrutinizing the way everything is phrased to ensure that the government doesn't end up fucking me over due to a typo.

Once I'm satisfied, I scribble my name at the bottom of each page before laying the pen on top of the stack.

"Is that all? It's been a long couple of days on my back." My wince as I shift in my seat supports my complaint. This entire process had been in play since the moment we realized the threats would never stop coming, not if my lifestyle didn't change. If I ever had a shot at living a normal life, I needed to take steps to create it for myself.

Both agents nod and stand from their seats. The one asking about my pregnancy is quick to help me onto my feet. Graciously, I accept.

"You have the utmost appreciation of the Federal

Bureau of Investigation, Mrs. De Luca. Per the terms of your immunity agreement, a contact from our witness protection program will be in touch with you," he says as he walks me to the door.

"I look forward to it." With that, they make sure I find my way out of the federal building located not too far from the World Trade Center.

Right out front, waiting for me, is my ride. Gage smirks as he leans back against the side of the same shitty Jeep that just won't have the sense to finally up and die. I guess, in a way, I can relate as I continue to live my life, refusing to lie down and succumb to death.

He approaches me, reaching out for my belly. "Have I told you how hot as fuck you look? My cock is telling me that this needs to be an ongoing condition for you." Gage's hands cradle my stomach before he lays a kiss on it.

I roll my eyes at whatever breeding kink he has driving his dick wild right now. "Don't get your hopes up."

He follows up with a kiss to my mouth. "We'll see."

I climb into the Wrangler, struggling to get the momentum to put my ass in the seat, but with a little nudge from Gage, I am finally in and settled. My seat belt stretches across me to make sure all things precious to both of my guys are secure.

Gage jogs around to the driver's seat and gets in. "He's waiting for us."

Smiling, I can't wait to finally see his face. The Feds had been far too interested in Joey's criminal history and all the contracts he had taken from the moment he stepped foot in my life. To spare us both the risk of pissing off

Uncle Sam, he has been keeping his distance and lying low.

It was a brief drive across the bridge into Brooklyn. I was all too ready to hop out of my seat the second Gage parked by the quiet little beach Joey and I had dubbed as our spot. His beloved Challenger was parked right beside us, and he stood on the beach watching the sun reflect off the calm water lapping at the shoreline.

To say I was running for him was the biggest overstatement of my life. This massive weight I carried on the front of me slowed me down tremendously. How did women do this more than once? I will never know.

Joey turned as I approached, and his face lit up. "Layney." His lovely brown eyes soaked in the sight of me. "Fuck, I didn't expect you to look this goddamn gorgeous." Clearly, he is pleasantly surprised at how well I wear the extra curves. I'd know that heated gaze anywhere.

My steps come to a halt in front of him. "Don't get any ideas." I grin and finally begin shifting things underneath my shirt while wrinkling my face up at the intense effort of it all.

His hand reaches out and takes hold of my chin. "We'll see." Those chocolate hues holding a promise within them.

These damn De Lucas and their hard-headedness when they get an idea in their heads…or cocks.

I welcome Joey's slow and intense kiss as he takes claim over my mouth, savoring each part of my lips before his tongue dives into my mouth. The kiss distracts the efforts of my hands underneath my shirt until, finally, I feel a sudden release.

Breaking away from his mouth, I let out a massive sigh of relief as the prosthetic belly falls to the ground with a ceremonious thunk. "Jesus, you have no idea how heavy and hot as balls that shit is." Makes me glad that I have no intentions of thrusting my lifestyle onto any innocent souls in the near future. No child needs to grow up in a life riddled with danger the way I did.

Gage catches up to us both and smiles. He leans over and picks up the rounded stomach from the ground. His hand dives into a small slit in the side, digging around for what is just underneath the surface.

When Gage's hand pulls back from the silicone, he holds a small electronic chip between his fingers. "How long do you think it will take before the Feds realize that the entire recording of your interview is useless?" He flashed an amused grin.

Thanks to Cowboy, he made sure that what I confessed to could never be used against any of us. His new girl-friend, Amanda, works in the costume design department for some theater production company on Broadway. She was kind enough to hook me up with the prosthetic to house the interference device. Who was going to question a pregnant lady?

The FBI may now know the names of major players and know who to focus on first, but without solid proof, nothing I said could ever come back to haunt me.

I shrug innocently. "Hours, maybe days." Either way, I expected all of us to be long gone before then.

Joey pulls out his car keys and dangles them in front of

my face. "You're in charge of taking us where we're going now, Layne."

I reach out and take the keys into my hand, looking them over.

Smiling to myself, I can say that my decision has come easily. "I think it's time I leave this city behind. My time here is done, and I'm overdue for a nice, long vacation. How does someplace warm and sunny with plenty of booze sound?"

Joey smiles as he pulls my face to his with his hands. "I don't care where we go, as long as we're all going together." His lips caress over mine once more in a reassuring and loving gesture.

When I slowly pull away from the kiss and look over to Gage to gather his opinion, he responds by hooking his finger under the thin chain around my neck to tug me closer. The charming grin on his face says it all; he wants this change as much as the rest of us.

"You better believe that no matter where we go, I'm going to be there to correct your bratty behavior," Gage's tone makes it clear that his words are a lifelong promise. One that he seals with a playful kiss to my mouth.

After we all make it back to where both cars are parked, I turn and look at the Manhattan skyline. My eyes grow wet at the memories of the place I had grown up calling home. Letting go was proving to be more difficult than I anticipated, but I knew it was the right thing to do for all of us.

It's going to be a long drive down to the Florida Keys, but maybe I could learn to call the ocean waves and sandy beaches my new home. They say home is where the heart is, right? I am lucky enough to have the hearts of two De Lucas following me no matter where I go. And for that, I am so grateful.

My dad had left a key and address of a house located in Key West in my safety deposit box. I don't believe in fate, but I do consider it a sign that this is ultimately what he always wanted for me. Closing this chapter of our lives means we have all the unwritten possibilities ahead of us.

I will never stay in my lane, even now that I have found closure. Now, as my life shifts, I know that Chaos and Wrath will always and forever be on either side of Luck.

THREE MONTHS LATER

The oscillating fan in the small grocery store continues on its back-and-forth pattern of distributing airflow. I take a deep breath as I continue to stare at the line of products in front of me. Joey and Gage are probably wondering what the hell is taking me so long; I only came in here for one thing.

A woman stops at my side, nearly passing me before she backs up a few steps. When I glance over at her, she's seemingly smiling to herself as she looks at me with a glistening of tears in her eyes.

"Can I help you?" Not that I work here, but what else do you ask when someone stops to stare at you?

She shakes her head apologetically. "Sorry, you just remind me of someone who was a part of my life for a very long time. Someone who I had to recently say goodbye to."

My face softens, my heart reaching out to this woman

who may have been a stranger but had an unexplainable sense of familiarity about her. Trying to put her mind at ease, I offer up some kind words, "Goodbyes are hard, but they provide the promise that something new is just beginning."

I reach out and give her hand a reassuring squeeze; it seems to provide her some solace as she gives me another sweet smile. "Thank you for everything," she says softly, returning the squeeze to my hand.

After she takes her leave, I'm left with my own words about beginnings as I'm once again looking at the shelf in front of me. I hastily grab a box at random and make my way to the checkout counter.

When I leave the store with my purchase in tow, Florida's humidity greets me. The island breeze is the only real thing, making it tolerable.

Crossing the parking lot, I climb into the front seat of Gage's Wrangler. After one too many tropical beverages on the boat this morning, Gage is squeezed into the backseat while Joey is behind the wheel.

"Get everything you need?" Joey looks at me curiously.

I nod and raise the bag in front of his view.

Gage leans forward between us with a giddy smile. "I'm feeling lucky."

I roll my eyes, of course, he is.

As Joey is pulling out of the parking space, another Jeep passes by us. Driving it is the same woman I had made a connection with inside the grocery store. She pops up two fingers on her steering wheel, giving Joey the signature Jeep Wave.

I watch as he gives her a smile with a hint of something grateful behind it as he returns the wave to her.

On the way home, I find myself lost in my thoughts as I look into the bag I'm holding in my lap.

There's only one question left.

Is the test going to be positive?

The End…?

ACKNOWLEDGMENTS

Nikki, my skittle wrangler: I know I came in a hot mess (and let's face it, I still am), but thanks to you my gremlin tendencies are reined in. I am so thankful to not only have an amazing PA but a great friend as well.

Maree Rose: You have brought these covers to life with your incredible talent. Thanks to you, these covers have really brought these stories to life.

Monique Shepherd: Thank you boo for being the inspiration to start this journey. If it weren't for you starting down the path of making your writing career a reality, I'm not sure I would have ever taken the plunge. Also, thank you for letting me borrow Daniil for a little while. I can't wait to see his own story come to life.

(READERS: You can more of Daniil in Monique's Rebirth & Ressurection series and in his upcoming story, Deadly Bonds.)

K.D. Smalls: Girl, I can't even begin to tell you all the things. Thank you for feeding my crazy, for being my soundboard, for stirring up trouble with me, and for being such an awesome friend. I'm so thankful our paths have crossed! I'm so proud of you my Cliffy Princess.

My team of Alpha readers (my ride-or-die crew): Amanda, Nicole, and Melissa you guys tell me all the things I need to hear. You call me out, lift me up, and have been my biggest cheerleaders. It's crazy how lucky I got with such perfect alpha readers who have become tried-and-true friends.

My husband: Oh, hon, I did it. I did the thing and I'm still doing it. Thank you for putting up with all my crazy late nights and supporting me regardless of the insanity. I love you so much and couldn't ask for a better partner to spend my life with.

My editor, Jessica: You know how I feel about comma trauma. Thank you for loving my characters as much as I do! Without your guidance, my manuscripts would be riddled with all my mindless typing filled with unorganized craziness.

All the readers and hard-core fans: Without each and every one of you, I would not be where I am right now, living my dream and sharing the stories in my head. Thank you for believing in me and trusting the stories I write. (I'm still not apologizing for the end of Incoming Layne Shift though.)

ABOUT THE AUTHOR

Sadie Winchester is a romance author residing in the Pine Barrens of New Jersey with her husband, her son, and their two cats (Thor & Loki). She began her love for writing in high school, drafting stories on a popular internet platform.

The dream of writing and publishing a full-length novel first manifested a couple of years after she married the love of her life. However, it took a back burner as she focused on other adventures and goals. Finally, after becoming a mother and finding a way to rediscover herself, she was inspired by another new author to commit to this long-term dream.

When Sadie is not writing up her stories or getting lost in books, she is spending time with her family. She enjoys working out, cooking, visiting microbreweries, and binge-watching *Supernatural*.

You can connect with Sadie in the following ways:
SadieWinchester.com or Linktr.ee/SadieWinchester

amazon.com/author/sadiewinchester

facebook.com/sadiewinchesterauthor

goodreads.com/sadiewinchester

instagram.com/sadiewinchesterauthor

tiktok.com/@sadiewinchesterofficial

bookbub.com/profile/sadie-winchester

ALSO BY SADIE WINCHESTER

<u>Broken Alliances Series:</u>

Stay In Your Layne

Layne Closure Ahead

Incoming Layne Shift

Chaos Luck Wrath

<u>Upcoming! Feathers of Darkness Duet:</u>

Sleeping Redemption

Redemption's Awakening